ROBERT B. PARKER'S
THE HANGMAN'S SONNET

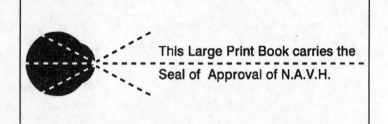

This Large Print Book carries the
Seal of Approval of N.A.V.H.

A JESSE STONE NOVEL

ROBERT B. PARKER'S
THE HANGMAN'S
SONNET

REED FARREL COLEMAN

THORNDIKE PRESS
A part of Gale, a Cengage Company

Farmington Hills, Mich • San Francisco • New York • Waterville, Maine
Meriden, Conn • Mason, Ohio • Chicago

LIBRARY OF CONGRESS CIP DATA ON FILE.
CATALOGUING IN PUBLICATION FOR THIS BOOK
IS AVAILABLE FROM THE LIBRARY OF CONGRESS.

ISBN-13: 978-1-4328-4314-4 (hardcover)
ISBN-10: 1-4328-4314-1 (hardcover)

Published in 2017 by arrangement with G. P. Putnam's Sons, an imprint of Penguin Publishing, a division of Penguin Random House LLC

Printed in the United States of America
1 2 3 4 5 6 7 21 20 19 18 17

For Chris Pepe

In death's black-lined womb I seek her grace.

The mirror has revealed my hangman's face.

— FROM *THE HANGMAN'S SONNET*

1

Fully sober for the first time in weeks, Jesse Stone was pounding the ball into the worn pocket of his old glove. As he slammed the ball into the glove over and over again, he stared out his office window at Stiles Island and the morning sunlight reflecting off the dark blue waters surrounding it. He was trying to steady his hands and empty his mind.

Some men prayed the rosary. Some meditated. He wasn't one to overthink things. At least he hadn't been until Mr. Peepers had shot Suit. Jesse could trace his self-doubt and second-guessing back to that bloody day. How many times in the last few months had he traced a jagged red line from the day Suit was wounded to the day Diana was killed? How many times had he rehashed the events between those two incidents, questioning his decisions? And today those questions rang in Jesse's ears as loudly as they ever had.

"Jesse," Alisha said, sticking her head through his office door. "I didn't expect you in today, with Suit's wedding and all."

He didn't turn around but stopped pounding the ball. "Just making sure things are in place, with most of us scheduled to be at the wedding."

The truth was that he hadn't slept more than a few hours last night, nor did he want to be alone in his house with his memories and doubts.

"We'll be fine. Nice tux," she said, noting Jesse's outfit hanging from his coatrack.

"Thanks." He turned slightly, smiled. "What did you come in here for, anyway?"

"Since you're in, there are some people here to see you. Should I send them in?"

He cursed under his breath. He was desperate for a drink but was duty-bound to stay straight for the rest of the day.

"Who?"

"Roger Bascom."

"Send him in."

"He's not alone. He's got two other people with him."

"What two other people?" he asked, his voice edgy, impatient.

Alisha shrugged. "Bascom didn't bother introducing them, but one of them is stunning. She's dressed in a few thousand bucks'

10

worth of clothes and jewelry. Her Christian Louboutin shoes and her makeup alone cost more than I make every two weeks. Believe me, Jesse, she'd get your attention if she was dressed in a potato sack."

"The third member of the party?"

"An older man. Well dressed, but he reminds me of a used-car salesman."

"Send them in," Jesse said, placing his ball and glove on his desk.

Roger Bascom was the head of private security for Stiles Island. Stiles, largely a playground for the wealthy, was under Jesse's jurisdiction. Most of the time there was little reason for his cops to venture over there to do anything but routine patrols. Early in Jesse's tenure, there had been a failed assault on the island by a gang of thieves, during which the bridge to the mainland was blown up and several cops, guards, and criminals had been killed. Since that day, the islanders had seen fit to get more serious about protecting themselves and their assets. Over the years there had been a gradual upgrading of security, in terms of both personnel and equipment.

Jesse didn't have much use for Bascom, a lean man with a military brush cut and a chilly demeanor. He took himself a little too seriously for Jesse's taste. Dealing with him was like dealing with a household appliance, only less enjoyable, but Jesse wasn't paying much attention to Bascom when the trio walked into the office.

Alisha's assessment of the woman with Bascom was spot-on. She wasn't yet thirty, drop-dead gorgeous, with hair that shone in the light like a blackbird's feathers in the sun. She had intense green eyes flecked with gold. Beautiful eyes, but intelligent and assessing. She had goddess cheekbones and a thin sculpted body that was only enhanced by the cut of her suit, the height of her heels, and her taste in jewelry. Alisha had gotten it right about the third member of the party as well. In his seventies, too tanned, with a head of wispy Einstein hair, he wore a light brown suede jacket over a white silk shirt, the open collar of which exposed a tangle of furry white chest hair. He also had on expensively ripped jeans and running shoes.

Jesse stood and got a third chair to add to the two that permanently faced his desk. He asked all three to sit and then went back behind his desk. He sat, too, keeping his shaky hands out of sight.

He nodded. "Roger, what's going on?"

"Chief Jesse Stone, meet Bella Lawton and Stan White. The chief prefers to be called Jesse." Bascom made a disapproving face.

Jesse ignored that and nodded to them. He saw that Bella Lawton's eyes focused on his baseball glove. Bascom noticed her notice.

"Chief Stone was a professional baseball player. In the Dodgers' system, I believe."

"Uh-huh. Now that we all know one another's names and you know I played ball, what can I do for you?"

Jesse saw Bella's eyes shifting from his glove to his tuxedo.

"One of my officers is getting married later this morning, so if you don't mind, can we get to the point?"

The three visitors looked at one another as if silently arguing about who would answer the question. Finally, Stan White spoke up.

"Terry Jester," he said, as if those four syllables were self-explanatory.

Jesse nodded, thinking that maybe they were.

2

Stan White stared at him impatiently, mistaking Jesse's silence for ignorance. That was usually a grave mistake. Jesse didn't mind. He knew that in most situations it was better to be underestimated, and cops were always being underestimated. Still, Jesse kept quiet. Silence could be a cop's best friend. He enjoyed watching White squirm. As he did, he took sideways glances at Bascom and Bella. Bascom was his usual unreactive Frigidaire self. Bella was trying unsuccessfully not to smile, and her smile did nothing to damage Jesse's opinion of her looks.

White had had enough of Jesse's silence and repeated himself, only louder. "Terry Jester! You've heard of Terry Jester, haven't you?"

"Who?"

White thought that if he kept repeating Jester's name over and over, it might get through to Jesse. He stood up, wagging his finger at Jesse. "Terry Jester. *The* Terry Jester."

Jesse shrugged and tilted his head like a confused puppy. "Sorry. I got nothing."

White turned to Bascom. "Is this guy for real?"

"Relax, Stan," Bascom said, shaping his mouth into something that passed for a smile.

Bella said, "I think Chief Stone — Jesse is . . . I believe the technical term would be *busting your balls.* Is that right?"

If she was trying to make a good impression, she was doing a hell of a job.

Jesse laughed his first meaningful laugh in months. "I'm sorry, Mr. White. I know who Terry Jester is. I played ball. I didn't live in a cave. Folks around here call him the Boston Bob Dylan."

But instead of calming down, White was apoplectic.

"Bob Dylan isn't fit to kiss Terry's tuchus. Until Terry went into semiretirement, their record sales were about the same. And as a poet, Dylan couldn't hold a candle to Terry. Dylan the genius . . . get outta here. You wanna see where 'Mr. Tambourine Man' comes from and all those swirling, rapid-fire words from Zimmerman, go get yourself

15

a copy of *Mexico City Blues,* for chrissakes! Terry Jester never had to rip off Jack Kerouac."

"Take it easy, Stan," Bella said, grabbing his forearm and urging him back into his seat. She turned to Jesse. "You'll have to forgive Stan. He's been Terry's manager for — how long has it been?"

"Fifty-three years." White puffed out his chest, a wistful look in his eyes. "We were just two kids, Terry and me, bumming around Greenwich Village then, not even eighteen. We didn't have two nickels to rub together, but we did gigs, had fun. I could sing a little, write a little, but Terry, Terry . . . He had the magic. He had the gift, the looks. Me . . . I had business sense and some family connections. One thing led to another and . . ."

Jesse said, "All very fascinating, Mr. White, but —"

"Stan, please." His agitation was suddenly replaced by a winning smile and polite charm. "Please forgive my outburst. Old men get impatient."

"No need to apologize, Stan, but what has all this to do with the Paradise Police Department?"

White said, "It'll be all over the local media soon about Terry and the album, so we thought we should give you a heads-up is all." White had leaned forward and whispered the words *the album* like he was giving Jesse top-secret information.

That got Jesse's attention. "The album?"

White raised his palms, winked at Jesse, and said, "You'll see. Terry might even sing a few songs from the album. That would be a once-in-a-lifetime thing."

Before Jesse could ask anything else, Bascom spoke up, "A month from tomorrow, Mr. White will be throwing a gala seventy-fifth birthday party for Mr. Jester at the Wickham estate on Stiles Island. There will be several celebrity guests in attendance. Some will be arriving by chartered yacht from New York City, but most will be coming by car through town. You will no doubt want to have your entire department on duty that weekend and alert your auxiliary as well. Mayor Walker has given Mr. White and Ms. Lawton her assurance that you will give us your full cooperation."

Jesse bristled at that. Not only was Bascom condescending to dictate how Jesse should deploy his department, but they'd gone over his head, directly to the mayor. Beyond that, the last thing Jesse wanted to deal with in high summer in a seaside town like Paradise was a celebrity invasion. As an L.A. cop, he'd seen what nightmares star-studded events created even in a town that lived for them and was equipped to handle them. Jesse kept his cool, ignoring Bascom and talking directly to Bella Lawton.

"That makes you PR," he said, nodding at Bella.

She smiled her electric-white smile. "Very good, Jesse. Yes, I'll be handling all the traditional, digital, and social media for the gala. And with all due respect to Roger's understated assessment of the attendees, we anticipate several megastars from across the artistic spectrum to be there. We're still waiting on Jay Z and Beyoncé, Clooney, and Jagger's people to give us a firm yes. But those are only some of the A-listers we're looking at."

Had he not been so desperately craving a drink at that moment, Jesse might have chided Bella for giving herself away. He had always been good at seeing the truth beneath the bullshit. It was one of the qualities that made him a great cop. What Bella had really said was that the response to the invitations wasn't what they had hoped for and they were going to put on a full-court press. *Press* being the operative word.

"Okay, thank you for notifying me," Jesse said. "I'll be in touch. If you don't mind,

I've got to get ready for this wedding."

Bascom just stood and left. White, confused by Jesse's terse dismissal, hesitated for a beat or two, then followed Bascom toward the office door. Only Bella lingered.

White called to her, "Bella, are you coming?"

"Go on, Stan. I'll be out in a second." She waited for White to leave before turning back to Jesse. "I guess I overplayed my hand there with the A-list-megastar routine. How did you know?"

"I worked LAPD for a long time and my ex-wife was an actress. Not many PR ploys I haven't seen."

"Sorry, Jesse, I meant no disrespect."

"I can take it."

She leaned across his desk. "I just bet you can."

A loud few seconds of silence followed as they both let Bella's comment hang there between them. She placed a business card on the desk, took a pen out of her bag, and wrote something on the back of the card.

"Listen, Jesse, I might have oversold it, but we really are expecting a crowd and there will be some marquee names among them. So please don't totally discount what we've said. That's my cell number on the back of the card. Call me . . . anytime."

19

When she left, Jesse picked up the card, but he was too preoccupied to care. Instead, he pulled out his side drawer and looked for the bottle he knew wasn't there. It was only another few hours, he told himself, and then went back to pounding the ball into his glove.

3

He'd already pulled the dresser drawers out one at a time, running his latex-gloved hands through the old lady's clothes. He'd turned the drawers over, searching for a hidden key, a note with instructions, or an envelope. Something. Anything. Now he moved on to her bedroom closet, gagging at the lavender, lilac, orange peel, and clove stench of the big potpourri sachet on the shelf. It wasn't just the potpourri getting to him. It was the way the mildew and camphor mixed and clashed with each other. Maybe it wasn't that at all. Since coming into her bedroom, he hadn't been able to escape the memories of his own grandma. Memories of how she used to powder herself up and pile on the clownish face paint over her sagging chicken skin, how she sprayed on sickly-sweet old-lady perfume to cover up the telltale scent of her own decay. He couldn't escape the feeling that she was watching him, judging him, especially when he touched the old lady's underthings. That really gave him the creeps.

After patting down her dresses, her coats, and inspecting each of her shoes, he grabbed a chair. He stood on it and began to remove things from the shelf: hat boxes, cardboard boxes, photo albums, letters bound together with faded red ribbon. This was more like it. He tossed each item onto the bed, gladly leaving the white satin sachet bag behind. As he stepped off the chair, there was a knock at the bedroom door. Heart thumping, he froze, one foot still on the chair seat, the other on the floor. He laughed at himself for reacting. The cops wouldn't have knocked, and unless the old biddy had Houdini skills, she was still tied up in the basement.

"What is it, Hump?"

A linebacker-sized man in his forties with a face pitted like a bad country road stepped into the bedroom. Six-foot-three and two-forty, going soft around the middle, he looked like he'd forgotten to take his shoulder pads off after practice.

"King," he said. "Why are you dumping out the old girl's panties and stuff on the bed?"

King shook his head at his ex-cellmate. There was a reason everyone who knew him called him Hump. Hump was a good guy and somebody you wanted on your side in a prison fight, but he wasn't the brightest gem in the jewelry box.

"Yeah, Hump. The thing we're looking for can be hidden anywhere. Don't pass nothing up. Look under lamps, ashtrays, under the phone. Come on, we went over all this already, right? It's worth ten grand to us."

"But why are you dumping —"

"Because I'm looking for a key, a safe combination, a note with numbers on it . . . like that. The man didn't say we would definitely find it here, only that it might be here."

"Okay, King. I got it."

"Hump, I'm glad I cleared that up for you, but why'd you come up here in the first place?"

"The old gal."

"What about her?"

"I don't think she's doing too good."

King raced right past Hump, taking the steps two at a time, and barreled into the spindly-legged table at the base of the stairs. The collision knocked a white-and-blue-speckled ewer and basin off the table. The antique porcelain smashed onto the wide plank flooring and cracked into a hundred nasty-looking shards. He didn't stop to check out the mess he'd made, hoping the job wouldn't end up the same way. He turned down the hallway and headed for the rickety basement stairs. They creaked and moaned under his weight.

"Hey, lady! Lady, you all right?" he called out to her even before he reached the basement slab.

She didn't answer. They'd been pretty gentle with her, up to a point. Sure, they'd made a show of their handguns, threatening to use them on her if she didn't behave. Maybe Hump had tugged her white hair a little too hard and King had had to slap her when she started squawking. The blow split her lip and she bled a lot more than he expected a dried-up old prune like her to bleed. Her skin was so brittle, so papery and white, she didn't even look like she had any blood in her. But they'd been gentler with her after that, careful not to break her birdlike bones when they tied her to a lally column. They'd used duct tape to bind her hands behind her and to wrap her ankles to the base of the pole, making sure not to cut off her circulation. When she started squawking again, Hump had shoved a balled-up sock in her yap and covered it

24

with a strip of tape.

King called to her again. "Lady!"

But when his eyes adjusted to the dim light and he saw her head slumped, body sagging, he knew it was a waste of breath. The only voice she would hear now was St. Peter's. King felt her neck for a pulse even though he knew he wouldn't find one. When he pulled the tape away from her mouth, King was sickened by the stink of vomit. The old lady had puked into her gag and choked to death, or maybe it had been a combination of things. Maybe it had just been her time. What the hell did he know about it?

There was a loud pounding as Hump came down the stairs.

"She okay?" he asked.

"Dead."

He crossed himself. "Oh, jeez, King. We killed the old lady. You said this wasn't that kinda job."

"Well, pal, she's dead, and unless you know how to unscramble eggs or raise the dead, we better find what we came to find."

"What should we do with the old lady?"

"We'll figure that out later. For now, leave her. She's not going anywhere."

Hump shrugged, turned, and went back upstairs.

When Hump was gone, King prayed. Not for the old lady, but for himself.

4

There were probably places Jesse wanted to be even less than here, but he just couldn't think of any at the moment. When he pulled his new Ford Explorer into the church parking lot and took his hands off the wheel, he noticed they were shaking worse than they had been when Bascom, White, and Bella were in his office, or earlier when he'd been standing before his steam-clouded bathroom mirror. Then he'd been studying the three-day growth of salt-and-pepper stubble along his angular jawline and square chin and the taut skin of his still-handsome face. He ran his fingers through his thick hair, found the gray creeping in there, too. He'd looked everywhere in the mirror except directly into his own eyes, because all he saw there was condemnation.

Stepping out of the black SUV, Jesse ignored the brilliant sun in the flawless, achingly blue skies above Paradise. Somewhere, a part of him recognized it was a perfect day for a wedding, but it was a muted, distant part of him, a part that ached nearly as much as the skies. He shoved his hands into his tuxedo pants pockets as he walked, not because he didn't want to see them shaking, but because he didn't want anyone else to see. He had the rings in his right jacket pocket. He'd checked before leaving the station house. Twice since. Jesse Stone had rarely dropped ground balls hit at him a hundred miles an hour on iffy minor-league infields, so he knew he could handle giving the preacher two wedding bands without making an error.

As skilled as Jesse had been at narrowing his focus to a laser point, at shutting out crowd noise or chatter from the opposing catcher, at ignoring competing theories about a crime, he had taken it to a whole new level. For the past several months, since witnessing the love of his life murdered right in front of him, Jesse had pared his existence down to three stark essentials: grief, regret, and Johnnie Walker Black. They had become like a noose around his neck to the exclusion of everything else, including his job as police chief.

He had done this dance once before, in L.A., after Jenn had cheated on him. It had cost him old friendships and the trust and respect of his peers, and, in the end, it cost him his detective's shield. That inaugural dance with scotch and regret was what landed him in Paradise to begin with. So far, mostly due to goodwill, sympathy, and a fair stretch of crimelessness in town, Jesse had avoided paying a price heavier than a hangover for his behavior. Molly, Suit, Peter, Gabe, Alisha, and just about everyone connected to the PPD had done their fair share of ass-covering for Jesse since Diana's murder. Yet his recent lack of diligence hadn't gone unnoticed by the Board of Selectmen or Mayor Walker. He had been warned in no uncertain terms to either clean up his act or be put on forced sick leave.

But it wasn't the warnings from the selectmen or the mayor that had temporarily shut the Johnnie Walker spigot on him. It was Molly Crane who'd done that. On Thursday night she'd locked Jesse's office door behind her.

"What is it, Molly?" he'd asked.

Though he didn't look up at her when she entered his office, Molly knew Jesse was annoyed at her. After more than a decade together, she had learned to read the subtleties in his voice and his body language.

29

She'd had to learn. Jesse wasn't a man to give much away, not about what he was thinking. Certainly not about what he was feeling. Just lately, though, there wasn't much mystery to what he was thinking or feeling. And the open bottle of Black Label on Jesse's desk cleared up any questions anyone might've had about his state of mind.

"Look at me, Jesse Stone."

He didn't, repeating the question. "What is it, Molly?"

"It's about Saturday."

Jesse finally looked up from his glass. "What about Saturday?"

"Listen to me, Jesse. Saturday will be the most important day in Suit's life and you're the most important man in his life. Don't you dare show up at the church drunk and don't you dare disappoint Suit."

"Who the hell do you think you're talking to?"

"That's a good question. Who *am* I talking to? It's hard to know these days."

He seemed about ready to explode, but said nothing. Molly walked over by his desk, grabbed the smooth rectangular bottle, capped it, and moved back toward the office door.

"Give the wallowing a rest for a few days,"

she said. "You owe Suit that much. You want to drink yourself to death or lose your job, fine, but on Saturday you need to act the part of the best man."

And that was that. Self-control wasn't usually an issue for Jesse, not even when it came to alcohol. He could go months without it. Had gone months without it. But as Dix had said to him, it was no more than a game he played with himself. It was like holding his breath. No matter how long he held it, he was bound to breathe again. And what did holding your breath ever prove? Problem was, Jesse didn't care about proving anything to anyone, not anymore. Still, Molly was right, he owed Suit a lot, and Jesse Stone paid his debts.

He walked around to the front of the old white church, its clapboards and pews said to have been cut from the same trees that went into the keels and strapping of the whaling vessels built in New Bedford, Mass. Jesse had always been skeptical of the claims linking Paradise to a whaling past, but he wasn't thinking about that now. What he was thinking about was a dive into the deep end of a scotch-filled pool. He patted his jacket pocket once again and, feeling the rings, pulled back one of the church doors.

5

Tamara Elkin was pacing just inside the church doors. The medical examiner, usually given to loose-fitting sweaters, tight jeans, and pointy-toed cowboy boots, was decked out in a deep burgundy cocktail dress that clung to her athletic body and showed a fair bit of her long, muscular legs. She'd been an Olympic-class distance runner in college until a slip during a steeplechase took her off the track team and put her on track for medical school. The black stilettos emphasized the sculpted beauty of her legs.

She lit up at the sight of Jesse, as she always did. Then she tempered her excitement, knowing that he was probably drunk and grieving. Those were pretty much givens these days. But she owed a lot to Jesse. He was the first person in the area to befriend her when she took the job as ME, and there was nothing she wouldn't do for him. She'd always wanted more than friend-ship from him, but less than commitment. Like Jesse, Tamara was divorced, and as she said, she was nobody's Miss Right. For more than a year now, she had pressed Jesse to let her become more than a friend. She'd been careful to back off the pressure since Diana's murder. If and when Jesse decided to let her in, Tamara didn't want it to come with excuses. She didn't want to hear that he had been too out of it to know what he was doing or that she was just a temporary salve for his pain. A friend with perks was one thing. A Band-Aid was something else.

Still, she worried that even after he got over his grief, there would always be one thing standing in her way. Tamara wondered if Jesse would ever be able to get past the image of her doing Diana's autopsy. She had tried to recuse herself from it, begged Jesse to let her find someone else for the job, but he was adamant that Tamara should do it.

"She's a person to you, not just another body," he'd said. "Please, I don't want a stranger to touch her."

Now he brightened at the sight of Tamara, smiling a half-smile.

"Hey, you," he said, kissing her on the cheek. "You look stunning."

"Hey yourself, Jesse Stone. You don't look too shabby your own self in that tux."

Tamara hugged him, and when she did she sniffed for hints of alcohol. She could feel her own smile when she detected none. She pushed back, looking into his eyes. She was tall to begin with, and in heels her eyes met his. And with her impossible mane of brown curls piled atop her head, she was taller than him.

"What are you smiling at, Doc?"

"You, Jesse. Your eyes."

"No red, huh?"

"No red. That because you used a whole bottle of Visine or —"

"Haven't had a drop of alcohol. Look," he said, showing her his still-shaky hands.

"That'll recede in time."

He didn't say anything to that. Not because he didn't believe her, but because he didn't intend to give the shakes a chance to recede. As Molly had said, he owed Suit to be all in today, to be present. Come tomorrow, all bets were off. If he felt like drinking, he would. And if he chose to, it would be a small gathering: Johnnie Walker, himself, and his poster of Ozzie Smith. What he enjoyed about Johnnie and Ozzie was that they didn't do any talking, though Jesse did sometimes feel judged by Ozzie's silence.

"You better get inside," he said. "Have you seen the bride?"

"Elena looks gorgeous, but you shouldn't worry about her. You better go find Suit. Last time I saw him, he was pacing a rut into the floor downstairs."

Jesse found Suit in a bare room with an empty coatrack, pacing as Tamara had described. For one of the few times since they had met, Luther "Suitcase" Simpson looked the part of a full-grown man. Suit, a former high-school football star, was always boyish in his looks and in his demeanor. All men, Jesse supposed, seemed to lose those last vestiges of boyishness when they were about to exchange vows. Jesse laughed to himself at the sight of Suit in a tuxedo. Though it was well tailored to his big body, poor Suit looked out of place in it. Unlike Jesse, Luther Simpson was not a man born to carry off a tuxedo.

Suit looked up and caught his boss and best man smiling at him. "Jesse!"

They took hold of each other's biceps, Suit beaming at the sight of his boss. Then, just as with Tamara, some of the sparkle went out of his joy. Only Suit wasn't quite as skilled as the ME at checking Jesse out for signs of cracks in his armor without being detected.

"Relax, Suit, I'm fine."

"You know, Jesse, I wouldn't blame you if you weren't. I mean, this could've been your wedding day, too."

"I'm fine."

It was a lie, of course. Things might not have been so intense for Jesse had it been anyone else's wedding. Diana had been killed saving Elena.

"You got the rings, Jesse?"

"Uh-huh," he said, pointing at his jacket pocket. "Right here, Luther."

"Okay, boss, you can call me that today, but when I get back from my honeymoon —"

He smiled. "I'll think about it, Officer Simpson."

"Thanks, Jesse. You don't know how much you being my best man means to me and Elena."

"C'mon, let's get this show on the road. I hear there's a gorgeous woman waiting to be your bride."

After he said it, Jesse noticed he wasn't the only man in the room with shaky hands.

6

They had pretty much taken the house apart and had run out of places to look. Neither King nor Hump would ever be mistaken for the next Einstein, but they had been thorough. They had run their hands along the exposed beams and joists in the attic and the basement, moved the furniture away from every wall, inspecting the plaster to make sure there were no hidden alcoves or secret little doors. They'd checked all the floorboards, pulled up the loose ones to see if there were any hidden compartments. They'd looked inside every jar, poured out every kitchen tin and poured the contents back in, and checked the toilet tanks.

"I don't got any idea of where to look no more," Hump said, sweat dripping from his forehead.

"Me neither, Hump. Me neither."

"But you said your guy was sure it was here somewheres."

"I know what I said and I know what he said."

"We been neat about our business till now, King, but should we start breaking things up? I'm good at that, breaking shit up."

"You are, I know it. I guess we got no choice, huh? I thought we would've found something by now. If we were gonna break stuff up or if I knew the old lady was gonna crap out on us, I wouldn't've wasted our time putting stuff back in place. But first things first, let's cut the old lady down and put her in her bed."

Hump liked that. He felt bad about the old woman dying on them. He felt bad about leaving her there the way they had, propped up against the metal pole in the basement while they looked at her old love letters, touched her underthings, and emptied out her medicines. It wasn't right to do that stuff, but they had money coming, at least five grand each, maybe a lot more.

"You think we're gonna get all the money if we don't find what we're looking for?" Hump asked as he followed King down the basement steps.

"We're gonna find it. We're gonna find it!"

King used his pocket knife to cut through the duct tape and the old woman fell into Hump's arms.

"She's as light as a feather."

"Come on, let's get her upstairs and get back to work."

They had her halfway up the steps when the doorbell rang, followed by insistent knocking at the front door.

"Holy crap, King. What are we gonna do?"

"You're gonna stay here and keep the old girl company and I'm gonna see if I can tell who's at the door. That's what," he said, reaching around under his jacket and grabbing the nine-millimeter he had wedged in his waistband.

At the top of the basement stairs, King hesitated, hoping whoever was at the door would just split when no one answered. He might as well have hoped to sprout wings and fly away. The bell rang again and the knocking continued. King slipped out of his shoes, put his back to the wall, and moved silently toward the vestibule.

"Mrs. Cain. Mrs. Cain, I've got a package for you. Mrs. Cain."

The bell rang a third time, followed by rapping on the front window. King didn't quite panic, but he realized that if the guy got a good look inside, they were screwed. The furniture in the parlor, like in all the rest of the rooms, had been moved, the rugs rolled back. And now with the old lady dead and without having found what they'd come for, there was no turning back if things went wrong. It wasn't until King got to the edge of the stairs to the second floor that things really went ass end up.

"Fuck!" he screamed as he stepped on one of the porcelain shards in his stocking feet. He could feel his sock soaking through with blood.

"Mrs. Cain, are you all right? Are you all right? Should I call the police?" The delivery man's voice was frenzied.

King, dragging his sliced foot behind him, limped quickly to the inside door, opened it, hobbled through the vestibule, undid the lock to the front door, and pulled it open just enough to get the delivery man's attention. Then King limped quickly back and waited behind the lace-curtained vestibule door. He pulled his T-shirt up to cover his nose and mouth in case he had to confront the guy. He heard the front door open, the thud of the delivery man's boots on the vestibule floor.

"Mrs. Cain. Mrs. — oh my God!" He'd seen the blood on the floor. "You hold on, ma'am, I'm calling —"

"Put the phone down, hero," King said, stepping out from behind the door.

But the man in the red, white, and blue

coveralls, stunned at the sight of blood on the floor and the situation, didn't react fast enough to suit King. For the sin of slow reflexes he got the handle of the nine-millimeter to his nose, the cartilage cracking with a sickening snap. The delivery man dropped the package and his cell phone to the floor. He crashed down himself shortly thereafter. King whacked the guy in the back of the head a few times until he was sure the man was unconscious. Then King grabbed him by the back of his collar and dragged him into the house, he relocked the front door, and called to his partner.

"Hump. Leave the old lady and get up here. We got more trouble."

"Oh, shit, King!" he said when he saw the mess in the vestibule and front hall.

"You don't usually have a way with words, Hump, but this time you said it all."

7

Jesse kept his promise to Molly, getting through the ceremony with a lot less trouble than Suit had. It was Suit who'd dropped the ring when he tried slipping it onto Elena's finger and Suit who was so nervous when it came time to say "I do" that Jesse had to give him a little poke in the ribs to prompt him. Other than Suit's endearing missteps, the ceremony had gone smoothly. And Jesse found he was so caught up in the joy of it that he felt lighter somehow. The burden of the recent past weighed heavily on him until Reverend Ross Weber had pronounced Suit and Elena husband and wife.

"I'm proud of you, Luther," Jesse said, slapping Suit on the shoulder.

The reception was in the back room at the Gray Gull and it seemed like half the population of Paradise was in attendance and happy to be there. But that was the effect Suit had on people. He was the guy everybody liked, the guy you could have a friendly drink with or tell your woes to. Everyone who knew Suit even a little bit called him a friend. It was one of the things Elena, who was by nature much more reserved, loved about her new husband. That was one of the things Jesse admired about Suit.

Jesse didn't make friends easily. Other than Suit, Healy, Molly, and Tamara, all of whom were connected to his work, Jesse could use one hand to count the friends he'd made since arriving in Paradise. Some of them had faded away. Others were dead. It had been the same back in L.A. Even when he played pro ball, he didn't have many buddies on his teams. His lack of friends wasn't because he was hard — though he could be if circumstance demanded it — or nasty — which he rarely was — or obnoxious. He was never obnoxious. It was that he kept to himself. Molly called him self-contained. And Tamara had pegged him early on, calling him the perfect embodiment of the cowboy myth: "The man who needs nothing more than his horse and what he came into the world with. Maybe he's nursing a broken heart or he's out there searching for the right gal."

Jesse had grown up in Tucson and loved Westerns. They were the only movies he enjoyed. So he'd always gotten a real kick out of Tamara's comparing him to a cowboy. He liked it right up until the moment Diana was killed. Because unlike the mythical cowboy, he'd found his right gal, but she was gone forever. The cowboy handbook didn't come with instructions on grieving. Although he'd been in therapy with Dix for years, he still wasn't a man to cry it out or let go. He knew better than to think grief was a sign of weakness.

The most surprising guest at the reception was Mayor Constance Walker, an old high-school friend of Elena's. She'd even been a good sport about dancing a slow dance with Daisy, Paradise's favorite lesbian restaurateur, and went with it when Daisy dipped her at the end of the song. If the reaction of the guests was any indication, the mayor had done herself more good than if she had kissed a thousand babies. Everyone was still applauding when Mayor Walker asked Jesse for the next dance.

He had little choice but to accept. Their dance drew less interest from the crowd than the dance with Daisy had. Molly, Healy, Tamara, and the groom watched nervously from the sidelines.

Waiting until they were a few steps into their dance, she asked, "How are you feeling today, Jesse?"

"Not drinking, Your Honor, if that's what you're asking."

As was often the case between a mayor and a police chief, the relationship between Walker and Jesse was fraught with all sorts of problems, many of them a function of their jobs. But the relationship between Constance Walker and Jesse Stone had always been a particularly chilly one. Some people just don't take to each other.

"Not drinking! Thank heavens for small miracles. Nice of you to show some respect for the bride and groom."

"Uh-huh."

There were actually two dances going on and Jesse knew it. The mayor enjoyed goading him, especially now that she knew he was vulnerable. But Jesse never took the bait.

"I see you're with Dr. Elkin. Dating again, Jesse? So soon?"

"Jealous?"

"I'm a married woman. Don't be silly."

"I've been called a lot of things, Your Honor. Silly was never one of them."

When the song ended, they made nice for everyone watching, applauding and bowing their heads to each other. But before they totally separated, they each got in a parting shot.

"Remember, Chief Stone, one more screwup."

"Your Honor forgets, I used to play hardball for a living."

"I hear slow-pitch softball is about your speed these days." She smiled an icy smile at him before walking away.

Molly waited until the mayor had gone to the bar before approaching Jesse.

"What was that about?"

"Nothing good, Molly."

Before the conversation could continue, the DJ announced that it was time for the toast and asked Jesse to come up and do the honors. When the maître d' shoved a glass of champagne in Jesse's hand, it was the first loose thread of his unraveling. He drank it down without thinking after he'd raised the glass and said, "To Luther and Elena, with our love and hope that all the best things come to you in your years together. Congratulations." The very slight buzz of the champagne pulled hard on that loose thread, but it wasn't until much later in the afternoon that it all went to hell.

Jesse was dancing another slow dance with Tamara and the rest of the wedding party just before the happy couple were about to leave for the airport. That was when Suit cut in and danced with Tamara. Elena and Jesse were left to dance with each other and it would have been impossible to tell which one of them was more ill at ease. It wasn't that they didn't like each other. They did, very much, but Diana had been killed in Elena's house while helping to save her. She couldn't look Jesse in the eye, and the stark reality of his dancing with Elena on her wedding day while his fiancée moldered in her grave did not escape Jesse. But they got through the dance somehow, Jesse hugging Elena, kissing her on the cheek when the music stopped.

"Thank you, Jesse. You being here for us . . . It means a lot. You know how terrible I feel about —"

He put his right index finger across her lips. "Shhhhh."

He held it together until the rice was thrown and the cans tied to the back of Suit's car rattled down the street. He held it together until the mayor was long gone. But after a pretty waitress with the same shade of blond hair as Diana's approached him to ask if he'd like something to drink, he'd had all he could take. Four Johnnie Walker doubles later, Tamara and Molly, propping

him up between them, walked him out of
the Gull to Tamara's car.

8

Tamara Elkin opened her eyes, her phone chirping madly. And when she did, she realized several things all at once: She was in Jesse Stone's bed, she was hungover, it wasn't only her cell phone chirping, and the sun through the bedroom window was making it nearly impossible for her to keep her eyes open. She'd made it no secret that she had longed to wake up in Jesse's bed, but not like this. Not when he had been plastered and desperate and sad. She didn't want him that much. No woman with any pride wants to be a man's fallback position.

She reached for the other side of the bed, touched the cool, smooth sheets, and breathed a heavy sigh of relief and disappointment when she understood that Jesse wasn't there and that he hadn't been there all night. With that, the memory of the evening flooded back in. She had driven Jesse home after he'd started falling apart at the Gull. She'd gotten him to slow up on his drinking by drinking with him, making him drink at her pace. It wasn't like Tamara Elkin couldn't drink. It was one of the things they had bonded over, and she could normally keep pace with him. These days, though, she didn't think there was anything except a sink drain that could keep pace with how much Jesse poured down his throat.

The other thing she realized was that when her cell phone rang and Jesse's phone rang simultaneously, it was never a good thing. It usually meant there was somebody dead within the confines of Paradise, and that death, to whomever it had come, hadn't come easy. It usually came with bullets or blood or broken bones. The morning after the very first time she had spent a night like this, a night of drinking with Jesse in his house, their phones had both started singing in discordant unison. On that occasion, death had come to Maxie Connolly, a woman who'd returned to Paradise to bury her murdered daughter. She'd been found dead on the rocks at the base of the Bluffs, her neck broken, her body battered.

"Tamara Elkin," she said, her voice a raspy whisper.

"Hey, Doc. It's Molly Crane."

"What time is it?"

"Ten twenty-three."

"That late!"

Her throat was cotton and she was thirsty for a few gallons of water. The second gallon to wash down the bottle of pills she wanted to swallow to ease the pain from the sword that was stuck between her eyeballs.

"You okay, Doc?"

"Not nearly. What's going on?"

"We got a body we need you to come take a look at."

She was impatient. "Homicide, suicide, what?"

"Looks like a definite homicide."

"Text me the particulars and I'll be there as soon as I can."

The sound of Jesse's landline ringing in the background hadn't escaped Molly's notice.

"Doc, I can trust you, right?"

"Sure, Molly."

"And we both really care about Jesse."

"Look, Molly, I assume Jesse's still out cold downstairs. I slept in his bed last night, but he wasn't in it. So just say what you've got to say."

"Okay, then. Do you think you can get Jesse to the crime scene with you? Alisha can't get in touch with him and you know

51

the mayor is looking for any excuse to —"

"I'll handle it."

"I can send someone over to help if you need it, Doc."

"I'll handle it!"

Jesse's landline immediately stopped ringing.

When she stood up, she thought her head might split in two. Although Jesse's house was pretty isolated, she threw on her dress from last night and went out to her car to retrieve the extra set of clothes she carried with her just in case. On her way out she checked to see where Jesse was and to make a preliminary attempt at rousing him. But when she saw him, spread out on his leather sofa, she skipped the wake-up attempt. Only after she came back in did she shake Jesse. It took a minute or two to get him to open his eyes. She handed him a full glass of water and two tablets.

"Take these," she said.

"Aspirin? I'll need more than two —"

"Fiorinal with codeine. They'll help with your hangover. I'm going to put up some coffee and then I'm going to shower in the guest bathroom. You better get your ass in gear, right now."

"Hold on a second," he said, his voice thick. "It's Sunday. I'm off work today."

"Didn't you hear the phones?"

"What phones? I didn't hear anything."

"I'm not surprised, given how much you had to drink," she said, picking up the near-empty bottle and shaking it at him. "This has got to stop, Jesse, or you've got to cut back."

He tried unsuccessfully to smile. "As I recall, you were doing pretty well yourself."

"Stupid me, I was trying to slow you down and now I'm suffering for it. Now please get showered and dressed."

"Why?"

"When our phones ring at the same time, what does it usually mean?"

"Trouble."

"Give the police chief a cigar."

"Details?"

"Molly said she thinks it's a homicide. All I've got is an address."

He didn't exactly spring to his feet.

"You need help, Jesse?"

He laughed. It cost him to laugh. He winced in pain.

"I'm not going to lecture you, because I'm no one to talk and because I don't know what it feels like to lose someone that close. It's your life to piss away if that's what you want, but I think you should give it a rest for a few days. End of speech. I'm going to

53

put up that coffee now."

Jesse popped the two tablets into his mouth, drank the water, and headed slowly up the stairs. As he did, he thought about what Tamara had said to him. Problem was he felt so vacant inside that he didn't know what to fill the emptiness with. At least he understood what was at stake, empty or not. He'd landed in Paradise after screwing up in L.A., but where does a man land after he screws up in Paradise?

9

Jesse climbed into his Explorer, which was still parked in the Gray Gull's lot, and waited for Tamara to drive away before checking himself out in his visor mirror. He supposed he looked about as good as anyone who felt like he did was going to look. He remembered what Tamara had said to him yesterday about his eyes. Only today it really was the Visine that had cleared the red out. He'd given his face a quick shave after his shower and splashed on some extra Paco Rabanne in the hope it might cover the stink of scotch in his sweat or at least distract people who got close to him. The coffee and Fiorinal had helped more than he expected they would, but not so much that he felt like doing anything more than sleeping for a week. Still he wasn't going to get any sleep, not for a while, anyway. He started up the SUV and turned out of the lot.

The address was on Berkshire Street in

the oldest part of Paradise, where the wealthier folks in town had lived before moving their fortunes and their families up to the big manor houses on the Bluffs. The homes in this part of town weren't very big by today's standards, certainly not as grand as the Victorian behemoths on the Bluffs, but many of them had water views and were within walking distance of the quaint small shops in town. You were also close enough to the bridge to Stiles Island that you could jog over and back, if running was your thing. Lately, Bostonians and New Yorkers armed with hedge-fund money and fantasies of a more rustic life had begun buying up the houses along Berkshire, Marblehead, Salem, and Salter Streets, a few of them converting the houses into B&Bs.

Twenty-one Berkshire faced Pilgrim Cove and had so far escaped the clutches of city transplants but wouldn't much longer, given the FOR SALE sign out front. Nor had it escaped the ravages of time and the weather. The old two-story's gray clapboards were in poor shape, chipped and flaking, some almost completely bare of paint and exposed to the elements. The steps up to the front door sagged in the middle. The windows were all single-pane affairs that probably rattled like mad in anything more than a stiff breeze.

Jesse wasn't thinking about stiff breezes or real estate values when he turned off Marblehead onto Berkshire. Although he didn't yet know who the victim was or the nature of the homicide, he was already at work on the case, running through scenarios, asking himself questions. *Which other houses on the street had the best views of 21? If there was gunfire, would anyone else on the street have heard it? If the crime occurred during daylight, how might the killer or killers have exited the house without being seen? If the killer or killers had a vehicle, in which direction would they have fled?* Like that. But when he approached the house, he stopped all the speculation and prepared himself to deal with what the crime scene presented. Experience had taught him that making prejudgments before getting to the scene could blind you to the evidence, and he couldn't afford any more distractions than he was already dealing with.

There were three Paradise PD cruisers parked out front: Molly's, because she was the responding officer; Peter Perkins's, because he was the only cop on the Paradise PD with forensics training; and Alisha's, because she was there to handle whatever task Molly gave her. Tamara's Wrangler Sahara was out front, as well as the medical examiner's vehicle, waiting for the body. What confused Jesse was the fire department ambulance pulling away from the address, siren blaring. There wasn't usually much need for an ambulance at a homicide. Because it was Sunday morning and people were either still at church or at brunch after church, there wasn't much of a crowd. The siren would change that. Alisha, the newest addition to the force, was walking the tape and handling the few onlookers. She lifted the tape as Jesse approached.

"Morning, Jesse."

"What's the story with the ambulance?"

"A MassExpress delivery guy was found tied up and semiconscious in the basement. That's why we got the call. He never showed back at his depot last night. Staties found his truck abandoned in Salem."

Jesse nodded. "They retraced his route to see what packages got delivered, which ones didn't, and tracked him back here. I'll have to talk to him. What about the rest of it?"

"Weird."

"Weird how?"

"Old woman in her bed, but she didn't die there. The house is a mess, but not much if anything seems to be missing.

58

Molly and Peter are inside. They'll fill you in."

Jesse was proud of Alisha, only the second woman to join the Paradise PD. So far, so good. The mayor and the Board of Selectmen had been less than thrilled at her hire, preferring someone with experience who was relocating or a retired big-city cop who brought his pension and benefits with him. Jesse could see their point of view, except he knew their real objection was to something they would never admit. Alisha was African American, and Paradise was overwhelmingly white. He didn't think much of Mayor Walker and her minions, but he didn't think they were racists. They were small-town politicos reflexively averse to anything that might upset their constituents. In the end, the mayor backed him up. Good thing Jesse didn't have to worry about pleasing voters.

There was something else he liked about Alisha. She never asked him about his drinking or made a fuss about Diana's death. She seemed to intuit that those were subjects Jesse would just as soon not discuss, especially with a rookie.

"All right, I'm going in. There's bound to be more of a crowd as folks get back from church and after Robbie's guy used his siren. You need help, call Gabe. You don't have to clear it with me."

"Watch your step when you go in. There's a blood trail in the vestibule. I'll be okay out here."

He was sure she would be. He was far less sure about himself.

10

When he got to the front door, he could feel the adrenaline kicking in. Even though he would pay a big price for it later, he was glad for the rush. It helped with the hangover. The only other thing that got his juices flowing like this was playing baseball on a big stage, and that part of his life had ended many years ago on a crappy infield in Pueblo, Colorado. Still, as much as he was energized, he never lost sight of the fact that someone had to die, often violently, for him to get this rush. He would have gladly traded in this feeling for there to never be another homicide within the confines of Paradise, but the universe didn't work that way. There was no one out there to bargain with, except maybe the devil. And Jesse knew how those deals usually turned out.

The front door was ajar and Jesse was careful not to use his hand to push it open or to grab the knob, though it looked like it had already been dusted. He nudged it open with his elbow and saw Molly standing in the hallway, scribbling notes on the pad she carried with her. He also saw the trail of dried blood Alisha had warned him about leading from the vestibule, down the hallway, and around the corner to where, he guessed, the stairs to the basement were located. There were smudged footprints and two different shoeprints in the blood, partials, but enough to make out size and manufacturer. Jesse didn't assume that the two shoeprints were from two suspects. For all he knew, one of the prints came from the MassExpress guy. It would be foolish to draw any conclusions.

"What do we have?" Jesse asked, getting Molly's attention.

"Peter's already taken samples, photos, and done the preliminaries upstairs and on this level. He's in the basement now, but Lundquist and the state forensics team will be here soon enough."

Jesse felt the heat rising under his skin. It was his call whether or not to bring in the staties. Ever since Healy had retired, he was less apt to rush to ask for help from the state police. He liked Lundquist, Healy's acting replacement, well enough. Healy had given Lundquist his full backing. It was just that

Jesse was slow to give his trust. He'd found that trust given slowly was like a smart investment. It paid dividends over a long period and when it went wrong, the damages were minimized.

"Who told you to call in the staties?"

"C'mon, Jesse," she said. "Do you have any idea of how out of it you were yesterday after Suit and Elena left the reception? I'm surprised you can even stand up. And for goodness' sakes, we tried calling you for a long time there. What would you have done? I was covering for you in case the mayor got wind of it. This way I could tell her you instructed me to get the state cops right on it."

He knew she was right, that he owed her his thanks, not his anger, which should have been reserved for himself. Molly had covered for him over the years on the few occasions he had lost control of his drinking. Beyond that, she had made the right call. If the rest of the crime scene looked anything like the hallway, Peter Perkins would be overwhelmed.

"Where's the body?"

"Upstairs." Molly pointed with her pen. "The ME is still up there with her."

"ID?"

"Maude Cain, ninety-one. She's lived here

her whole life."

Jesse put up his palm. "Wait. Cain . . . Cain. Cain as in Zachariah Cain?"

"That's right. Cain as in the man the library is named for. They go back to before Paradise was Paradise."

Jesse knew some of the local history, but not as much as lifetime residents like Molly. Sometimes, as he had learned when the bodies of Ginny Connolly and Mary Kate O'Hara were found in a collapsed building on Trench Alley, small towns hid their pasts from outsiders. That's why Molly, besides being the best cop he had, was invaluable.

"Why didn't the Cains build up on the Bluffs like the Salters and Rutherfords?"

"They gave a lot of their fortune away to do good works. Their money was pretty much gone by the time Maude inherited this place from her mother."

"I see she was selling the house."

"She was old. I don't think she could handle the upkeep anymore."

"Okay, I'm going up. And, Molly . . ."

"Yeah?"

"Thanks."

As he walked to the staircase, he noticed the broken shards of porcelain, a few caked with dried blood, and the general destruction of the house. It didn't take a seasoned homicide detective to figure out that whoever killed Maude Cain had come looking for something. The question was what had they come looking for? And had it been found?

11

King got back to the motel room with a sack full of fast-food cheeseburgers, a liter bottle of Coke, a six-pack of Coors, and the local papers. King winced at the pine disinfectant smell and the artificial floral stench of the cheap soap that hit him in the face when he stepped into the room. He kicked the door shut behind him and shook his head at the look of the place. All done up in deep browns and mustard gold, the place hadn't seen new furnishings since the Carter administration, but they had to wait it out here only another day. Hump, his big body slouched across the ratty quilt, swung his legs off the bed at the sight of his pal. He muted the TV, the black preacher he'd been watching now silently waving his Bible around above his head like a machete.

"Here."

King flung the bag of burgers on the bed and put the bottle of Coke on top of the fiberboard-and-veneer nightstand. He popped open a Coors and took the papers over to what passed for a desk.

"This is Coke, King," Hump said.

"Yeah, and so what?"

"I wanted Pepsi. Didn't they have no Pepsi? Coke is too sweet."

"Hump, for chrissakes! You know how long it took me to find a fucking payphone. When I got to the store, I grabbed the first cola I found. Deal with it."

"Okay," he said, unable to hide his disappointment.

He felt a little better after inhaling two of the four cheeseburgers in the bag.

"King, there's two burgers left. You want —"

"Knock yourself out. I ate."

Hump liked that. He could've eaten a half-dozen more, but four was good for now. He took a big pull on the Coke and made a face.

"Why they make this stuff so sweet, King? Why do you think?"

"Like I give a shit."

"They find the old lady yet? What's the papers say?"

"Nothing."

"They ain't found her yet? Maybe it'll be a few days and we can get far away."

"Nah, Hump, they'll find her today, most likely. Even though we left the truck in Salem, the delivery company will just follow the route back to the old lady's house. Anyways, we aren't goin' anyplace. I set a meet for tomorrow."

"But we didn't find nothing in the house and we ripped the place all apart. Man, the walls in them old houses is tough to deal with. You can just punch through plasterboard, but those plaster-and-lath walls knocked the crap outta me."

"The man don't know we didn't find anything, right?"

"I guess."

"Then we're good. We'll get the money outta him."

"How we gonna do that, King?"

"You let me worry about that, okay?"

"I always do. So when they find the old woman, what are they gonna do to us?"

King snorted. "They gotta catch us first."

"I mean, it's not like we really killed her or nothin'. She just kinda died."

"I'm not a lawyer, Hump, but I don't think the cops'll see it like that."

Hump got agitated, jumping off the bed. "But we didn't try to kill her. And if she woulda just kept her yap shut, we wouldn'ta had to put nothin' in her mouth."

"Who you trying to convince?"

Hump didn't like that, balling his huge hands into fists so tight the blood seemed to drain out of them. The veins in his thick neck popped out.

"What's that supposed to mean?"

"Relax, pal. Go back to watching your preacher and finish your food," King said, finishing off his beer and popping open a second one. "When I'm done reading the papers, I'm going over to the office and see if they have a business center with a computer. This way I can find out up-to-the-minute stuff about if they found the body and what's goin' on."

Hump calmed almost as quickly as he had gotten riled. He unmuted the TV, opened up the wrapper on his third cheeseburger, and took a bite.

"Let us, brothers and sisters, turn to Leviticus 24:17–21 for an answer to the question of vengeance and repayment for our most egregious of earthly sins. 'If a man takes the life of any human being, he shall surely be put to death.' Notice there's no equivocation. No if, ands, or buts. No excuses. No guilty with an explanation. Now, what of a man at war as opposed to the greedy man who murders in —"

Hump couldn't shut off the TV fast

enough. His bite of cheeseburger went down hard. He took a big swallow of Coke. He stood up from the bed, looked in the mirror, and quickly headed for the door.

King was confused. "What's up? I thought you liked the burgers."

"I lost my appetite. I'm goin' for a walk. I can't breathe in here no more."

King rubbed the stubble on his cheeks as he considered the danger of Hump leaving the room. He decided not to try to stop him. He knew he couldn't have stopped him anyhow. Hump wasn't an easy man to stop once he got an idea in his head. Ideas weren't his strong suit, but when he got them, he hung on to them.

"Stay close. It's gonna take a few days to play our hand. We don't wanna attract attention."

But Hump was already out the door, heading to the office to ask about local churches.

12

Tamara Elkin was leaning over the body when Jesse stepped into the bedroom. He winced at the sour background odor of vomit. He'd been to countless crime scenes and witnessed bodies in all manner of decay, but rarely had he been as hungover as he was just then. Tamara turned to him, saw the look on his face, and smiled.

"What's the deal?"

"I can't say much without opening her up, but she definitely didn't die in this bed."

"Anything you can say other than that so we can get started? Right now, I'll settle for an educated guess."

"There's what looks like tape residue around her mouth, wrists, and ankles. There are some fibers stuck to the adhesive on the dermas proximate to her mouth, so if I had to venture a guess, I'd say whoever ransacked the house shoved some kind of gag in her mouth, then taped over it. She most likely vomited into the gag, but I can't say now whether that led directly to her death. She does have a split lip, which she received premortem. See the bruising there." Tamara pointed her gloved index finger at Maude Cain's face.

"Was she beaten or —"

"I can't be sure, but it doesn't look as if she was sexually assaulted and the bruising there around her mouth seems to be the only apparent damage. There's one other strange thing."

"Uh-huh."

"Someone cleaned her up a little and changed her clothes before placing her in here like this."

"Cleaned her up. Maybe to cover an assault?"

"I don't think so, but I'll know for sure when I get her on the table."

Jesse considered the things Tamara had just told him. Some killers, most often serial killers, presented bodies in certain ways either to satisfy some fantasy or obsession or as a display for the police. Sometimes it was a function of remorse. At this point, before the autopsy and forensic results were in, it was unwise to draw conclusions about motive. But Jesse knew his own gut, and what his gut told him was that this was more of a train wreck than the handiwork of some Hannibal Lecter wannabe. He was thinking it through when he heard heavy footfalls on the staircase.

"Hey, Doc. Hey, Jesse," Lundquist said, standing in the hallway just outside the bedroom. "Is it all right if I come in?"

Jesse saw echoes of Suit in Lundquist. A tall, sturdily built man with reddish hair, warm blue eyes, and a boyish *aw-shucks* smile, Brian Lundquist seemed as if he would have been right at home showing his prize pig at the Minnesota State Fair. Similarities in appearance to Suit notwithstanding, Jesse knew Lundquist to be an excellent detective, a cops' cop. You didn't rise to the rank of detective lieutenant because you were unfailingly polite or friendly. And they didn't make you acting head of Homicide because you were somebody's pal.

"Why don't you fellas talk somewhere else while I finish up in here?"

Jesse nodded to Lundquist that he was coming out.

"Okay, Doc. Lundquist and I will be downstairs if you need us."

When Jesse stepped out of the bedroom, he extended his right hand to the detective.

"My forensics unit's outside, Jesse. All I'm

waiting on is your say-so."

"Get 'em in here."

After Lundquist had given the go-ahead, Jesse detailed Tamara Elkin's preliminary findings. He explained that he thought the old woman's death didn't seem, at least on the surface, to be a purposeful act. Lundquist kept his thoughts to himself as they went down to the basement to talk the crime scene over with Peter Perkins, and Perkins got right to it.

"They had her tied up to this lally column with duct tape," he said, pointing at the tape still stuck to the metal pole. "I also think she probably died here." He pointed at stains on the slab at the base of the pole and held up an evidence bag containing the sock used to gag Maude Cain. "As to the mess upstairs . . . I don't know." He held up another evidence bag, this one containing the strip of tape used to cover the old woman's mouth. "Looks like there's blood on this, too."

Jesse spoke up. "ME says there's tape residue on the vic's mouth and that her lip was split. All right, Peter, the state Forensics Unit is here. Go upstairs and fill them in. Lend them a hand."

When Perkins reached the top of the stairs, Lundquist asked the question Jesse knew was coming: "What do you think went on here? The upstairs looks like a demolition team got hold of it, and it doesn't look any better down here."

Although Jesse knew homicide detectives were supposed to follow the evidence, it didn't mean their brains didn't work overtime once they got a good look at the crime scene. He had learned the hard way about the danger of falling in love with any single scenario before the evidence was in. Even then, he had seen colleagues ignore the facts in favor of their predetermined scenarios. He'd done it himself, but experience had also taught him not to completely ignore his gut. He looked around at the mess that was the basement. He remembered his first thought at seeing the chaos and blood upstairs.

"You've seen the house, how it was torn apart? The person or persons that did this were looking for something and they didn't know where to look for it. It takes a long time to go through a house like this, and they had to keep the Cain woman out of their hair while they searched. Maybe they got a little rough with her to see if she knew where it was before tearing the walls apart. My guess is the vic's death was, if not exactly an accident, unanticipated. Same as the delivery guy showing up."

"But neither thing stopped these perps from ripping the place apart."

"What's that tell you?"

"That whatever they were looking for is worth a lot of money."

"At least they think it —"

Before Jesse could finish, his phone vibrated in his pocket. He looked at the screen and excused himself.

"What is it, Molly?"

"The mayor's car is coming up the street."

"I'm heading out."

"Trouble?" Lundquist asked, as Jesse moved to the stairs.

"Uh-huh."

"The press?"

"Worse."

Lundquist laughed a joyless little laugh. "Only thing worse is a politician."

Jesse laughed, too. "You should have been a detective."

13

When he was sure Hump was well out of the room, King slipped the oddly shaped safety-deposit box key out of his rear pocket and ran his thumb over it again and again. The ridges of his thumbprint caught on the edges of the brittle Scotch tape holding the key in place against the yellowed index card. The key was tarnished with time and disuse, but it looked like a piece of heaven to him. A piece of heaven shaped like a pot of gold, blond hookers, and a Porsche. He'd had hookers before, all kinds, but never a Porsche. He'd always dreamed of having a Porsche. He had spent endless hours staring up at the photos of 911s and Caymans taped to his cell wall, imagining what it would feel like behind the wheel, the wind whipping his hair. His hair was mostly gone now. The dream remained.

King stared intently at the index card and spoke aloud the name of the bank that held the box as he read it off the card: "First Paradise Union Trust." He tried hard to decipher the age-faded numbers scrawled on the index card alongside the key. He thought he could make out most of them. He was unsure of one or two numbers in the middle and one at the very end. He wasn't particularly worried about the numbers, though, because it was the three capital letters handwritten in big block letters that had provided the magic. Tomorrow, before the meeting, he'd make an enlarged photocopy of the key and card and buy a magnifying glass. Then he would definitely be able to read the numbers. But if things went the way he hoped, the way they should, deciphering the numbers and getting access to the deposit box would be someone else's headache. If things went smoothly, his only problem would be figuring out how to carry his money and where to stash it.

King would make sure Hump got his share, not the pot-of-gold share. He'd pay him his half of the ten grand they'd been promised to do the job. He owed that much to his ex-cellmate. Poor, dumb Hump, he had no clue that King had found the key taped to the underside of a dresser in a second-floor bedroom. Good thing Hump had missed it on his first pass. Truth was that until King had scanned the papers looking for word on whether the cops had found the old lady, he wasn't even sure he'd be able to squeeze the original ten grand out of the guy who'd hired them to search the house. The old lady dying on them the way she had put them in a weak bargaining position. It was one thing for the cops to want you for assault and breaking and entering. Murder was a different beast altogether.

King was no lawyer, but he knew that even if they got it knocked down to manslaughter, the two of them were looking at a long bid. King didn't think he could deal with even another year back inside. Anything longer and he'd hang himself with a bedsheet or just cut his own throat. He'd thought about suicide many times during his life inside, but he was never more serious about it than he was right then. He'd already spent too much of his life in concrete-and-steel boxes, already depleted most of whatever soul he'd come into the world with.

He laughed at himself for his dark thoughts, given his turn of good fortune. He pushed the image of himself hanging from a makeshift noose out of his head. If he hadn't stumbled across the piece in the paper, King might've been willing to throw Hump to the wolves and barter the key away for a few grand and help getting out of the state. But now he didn't have to worry about sacrificing Hump to the cops or begging for scraps from his employer. His begging-for-scraps days were over.

King stood up and slid the index card into his back pocket. He ripped the article out of the paper, the one that answered his decades of unanswered prayers, and folded it into a neat little square. He put that in his other back pocket. He popped open another can of Coors, stared at it, and smiled. Before sucking it down, he thought, *No more Coors for me. No more Coors for the King.* Then he scooped up all the papers and went to find the Dumpster. Hump wasn't usually the newspaper-reading type, but King wasn't going to take any chances, not when he could almost feel the wind blowing through the new hair he would have transplanted with the money left over from the blondes and the Porsche.

After the papers were disposed of, King headed to the motel office as Hump had done not a half-hour earlier. Only he wasn't going there to Google local churches. He was going to Google blond girls and German sports cars. He imagined the price of both had gone up since the last time he'd thought there was a serious chance he might get close to either one.

Just as he got back to the room, his cell phone rang. The man on the other end was anxious.

"Write down this number."

King found the motel notepad and pencil and wrote the number down. "I got the number."

"How did it go?" the man asked. "Did you locate the package?"

But King didn't answer. He hung up. The Porsche and the blondes were now almost close enough to touch.

14

As Jesse passed Molly on the way out of the house, he told her to have someone start looking into locating the next of kin.

"She didn't have any family left that I know of, Jesse. She might have had an older sister, but she's probably dead, I'm thinking. Maude was in her nineties. Her husband died a long time ago. They never had any kids."

"We've got to try."

"Can't we officially ID her with dental records if we have to?"

"True, but we can't ask her dentist what the guys who wrecked the house were looking for. Maybe there's a relative who can shed some light on it."

"I never thought of that. I guess that's why they pay you the big money and you get to wear that fancy uniform."

Of course Molly was referring to the fact that her boss used the privilege of his title to make every day his version of casual Friday. Full uniform for Jesse usually consisted of his cop shirt — tucked in — with jeans, work boots or running shoes, and a blue baseball cap with the letters PPD stitched across the crown in white. In colder weather he wore his lined cop jacket.

"When the mayor cans my ass and you inherit the job," Jesse said, "you can dress however you like. You can wear your old high-school uniform for all I care."

Molly got a sick look on her face as if it never occurred to her that she would be Jesse's natural successor.

"No, thanks, Jesse. I'm happy right where I am. Besides, I gave away all my old clothes a long time ago."

"Shame." He winked at her, a smile on his face.

Still smiling, Jesse shook his head at her and immediately regretted it. His initial adrenaline rush was fading into a distant memory and the pills Tamara had given him were no longer doing the trick. If the mayor wasn't right outside, he would have gone back upstairs and begged a few more Fiorinal from the ME. Even with Her Honor so close, Jesse didn't exactly snap into action. Molly noticed.

"Jesse, don't you think you better get out there?"

"It's a crime scene. She can't come in without my say-so."

"Can't avoid her forever, and you really don't look any worse than anyone else who was at the wedding reception. The mayor was putting it away pretty good herself before she split."

Jesse said, "I didn't notice. Let me get out there. Remember, have —"

"I know, Jesse. I'll get someone working on next of kin."

Jesse stepped out onto the old wooden porch and noticed that the crowd around the crime scene tape had grown considerably since he'd entered the house. He also noticed the mayor scowling at Alisha, who was refusing to allow Her Honor to come beneath the tape. The mayor's new assistant and political adviser, Nita Thompson, a slick-looking early-thirtysomething out of Harvard who was working her way up the consultant ladder, was staring up at Jesse shaking her head at him. There'd been a bull's-eye on Jesse's back since she arrived.

Things between Mayor Walker and Jesse hadn't been great over the last several years. First there was the discovery of the remains of two teenage girls who'd gone missing from Paradise twenty-five years earlier, and an ugly spate of violence that followed. The violence had nothing to do with Jesse, who, in the end, solved the case and brought the last remaining killer to justice. It didn't seem to matter to the mayor. Crime focused the wrong kind of attention on Paradise, and whatever made Paradise look bad made her look bad. Their relationship really deteriorated after Diana's murder. That violence *was* directly tied to Jesse. When rumors about Mayor Walker's political ambitions began circulating and a political consultant showed up in town, Jesse knew he was in for a hard time. It was pretty clear that Nita Thompson meant to hang as much bad baggage around Jesse's neck as possible.

He called down from the porch. "Alisha, let the mayor up. Only the mayor."

Jesse didn't have to see the look on Thompson's face to know her eyes were burning a hole right through him. He had other things to worry about, like the mayor racing up to him, a less-than-friendly expression on her face.

"Chief Stone, why is your officer keeping me off —"

"Chief Stone?" He cut her off. "Yesterday during our dance it was Jesse. Have we broken up?"

"Not funny, Chief. Not funny. And as I was saying, why —"

He cut her off again. "Because Alisha was doing her job as she's been trained to do it. This is a crime scene, almost certainly the scene of a homicide and a serious assault. Evidence is being gathered by our people and the state Forensics Unit. The ME is still upstairs with the body. We need to limit the number of people who might unknowingly contaminate the scene."

Mayor Walker was unmoved. "I'm the mayor of Paradise, Chief Stone. You had better instruct your officers, old and ridiculously new, that when I want access to anything in this town, I expect to get it. And why did I have to find out about this from the fire chief and not the chief of police?"

Because, Madame Mayor, I am not interested in kissing your ass.

"What are you smiling at, Stone? Did I say something amusing?"

"Was I smiling? It must have been a random thought. Sorry."

"Answer my question."

"Before I alert you, Your Honor, I need to gather information and have my facts straight. I was in the process of doing that."

Just then, the two men from the ME's office came up the front steps, one carrying

86

an empty body bag under his arm. Jesse and the mayor stepped aside. After they passed, the mayor gestured toward the crowd that had gathered around the house, as well as the satellite dish–equipped news vans that had pulled to the curb.

"Well, we need to tell them something," she said, pointing at the vans. "So give me the facts you have."

"We wouldn't have had to tell them any-thing yet if your people hadn't called them."

"Are you accusing me of something, Chief Stone?"

"Yeah, of being a politician. And don't worry about the press," he said, now smil-ing broadly at her in spite of his pounding head. "I'll handle the press."

With that, he turned and walked down the porch steps.

15

Exhausted and still hungover, Jesse fell back on his black leather couch. He stared across the room at the bar, at the neat chessmen-like assembly of glasses: the cut-crystal rocks glasses that broke up the light like static kaleidoscopes, the frosted highball glasses that Suit had given him for his birthday five years ago, the hand-blown wineglasses that rang long and loud if you tapped them just right, the squat shot glasses with the single air bubbles in their thick bases, and the sleek champagne flutes that mostly collected dust. Functional alcoholics like Jesse found romance in all the aspects and rituals of drinking. To think otherwise was like believing that sexual pleasure was strictly about the act itself.

No, the clinking of the ice in the glass, the pour of the rich amber fluid, the peaty aroma, the hiss when he twisted the bottle cap, the glug of the soda pour, the swirling of the glass were as much foreplay as anything else. It was also, as Dix had pointed out, as Jesse knew deep in his soul, a distraction. It was a way for him to fool himself that since Diana's murder, he really didn't want to just grab the bottle and pour the Black Label down his throat until the relentless guilt and hurt and emptiness dulled a little.

It was worse than in L.A., worse than when Jenn had cheated on him. He loved Jenn, but it was almost like he had been in love with the idea of Jenn rather than who Jenn actually was. From the outside, Jenn was everything Jesse had ever wanted: beautiful, blue-eyed, and blond; an actress; more social than he was ever comfortable being. But inside she was never who he imagined her to be, and that wasn't really her fault. The sex between them was good, never great. And only after years of separation, divorce, and therapy did he come to realize what had actually drawn them together was a kind of unhealthy yin/yang. Jenn could be terribly needy and Jesse was born to be needed by a beautiful woman. He was born to fix things. His career was about that, about righting wrongs, doing justice. In the end it turned out their pas de deux bound them together more powerfully than love ever did, and it took a very long time to undo the knots.

It was worse now because Diana, an ex–FBI agent, had been the real deal, inside and out. And if Jesse ever had a soulmate, she was it. He was thinking about that now as he stared at the bar, about how Diana really was a match for him in every way in spite of the fact that their relationship had started as a lie. Hers, not his. In some sense, that was one of the ways he knew she was it for him, that their love outlived the lie. It was as if their love had a kind of life of its own and wouldn't be denied. It was worse than with Jenn, because there would be no reconciliation. Death doesn't compromise, didn't make accommodations for love, and the ties that bound them together were now his and his alone.

He couldn't take it anymore and leapt off the couch, grabbing the new bottle of Black Label he had purchased on his way home.

"You're getting to be my best customer, Jesse," said Karl Benton, who ran the wine-and-spirits store in town. "Would you rather have me just have a case delivered to your house? I'll give you a good price."

Jesse thought about it. After hesitating for a few seconds, he told the shopkeeper that he would do his scotch buying the old-fashioned way for the time being, though he was tempted to take Karl up on the offer. Purchasing bottles one at a time was a way of limiting his consumption.

Jesse grabbed the bottle off the bar and held it up to the light. He laughed because he even liked the way the bottle felt in his hand and how the scotch looked in the light. He'd moved his right hand to twist off the cap when his front bell rang. He thought about having a short one straight from the bottle before answering the door. It would relieve the headache and make it easier to deal with whoever had come calling. He put the bottle down when the bell rang again.

Tamara Elkin was standing on Jesse's welcome mat. She looked tired but otherwise much better than Jesse — though, minus the political bullshit, her day had been as long and as hard as his was. She was wearing what she always wore when she came over — beat-up cowboy boots, tight jeans, and a low-cut lightweight sweater. Her hair was still damp, so that her curls were loosened. Jesse was always amazed at just how long her hair was when it was wet. And he could smell that grassy and crushed-herb perfume she wore when she was off the job. In spite of that, it was what Tamara was carrying that got most of his attention.

There was a beige folder cupped in the long, slender fingers of her right hand.

"Preliminary autopsy results?" he said.

"Yes, sir."

"Then you'd better come in."

16

Tamara reached over to the other side of the bed, and just like every other time she'd slept over, Jesse wasn't there. But this time was different. This time it was of her own doing. The room was still black with night when she swung her long legs over the edge of the bed. Instead of moving, she sat there in the dark, going over the evening's events and second-guessing herself. She had been so patient, had waited so long. It had all gone so well . . . until it didn't.

She had come to his house determined to finally satisfy her curiosity about Jesse and to scratch her own itch. She was tired of being the good, loyal friend. Tired of being Jesse's sympathetic ear and comforting shoulder. Tired of stepping aside, first for Diana and then for her ghost. After dancing with him yesterday, after seeing what a wreck he'd been this morning, she'd convinced herself she no longer cared about being plan B or a drunken conquest and that the autopsy results were just an excuse to get in the door. Tamara wasn't a born martyr. She had no delusions that their being together was going to heal Jesse or make him forget Diana. She didn't even know if there would be a second time. She would worry about that later.

At the moment she was too busy reliving it all in her head, remembering how she had strolled into the living room and set the file out across the coffee table. How she had asked Jesse to pour her a drink. She laughed there in the dark to herself, thinking that she was about the only person in the world who would have made autopsy photos and results a prelude to sex. But that was the point, really. If she had come over and made her intentions clear, Jesse's radar would have picked it up and he would have reflexively backed off. She wasn't going to let him back off this time.

After they had discussed the results and gone over the photos, they'd sat around for a while, talking about the case. Then when she got up to leave, she kissed him hard on the mouth. She had tried this before, to no avail. Jesse always backed her off, gently, muttering some kindnesses about how it wasn't the right time or how he was committed to Diana or how it was too soon after Diana. But this time it had taken him a little bit longer to push her away. His protestations sounded hollow, so she kissed him again. The difference this time was that she backed him off.

"Jesse, I can't do this," she thought she'd heard someone say, as she pushed away from him. "I can't go through with it."

He tilted his head at her. "Why not?"

"I thought I could. I thought I wanted this. But I guess I'm not willing to sacrifice what we have. It means more to me than I thought it would. You're the best friend I've ever had, Jesse Stone."

"That doesn't have to change."

"Yes, it does, and somewhere you know that, too. It'll change everything. It always does, no matter what we say or think."

Whether out of some misplaced sense of obligation or to see if she really meant what she said or to test his own resolve, he made a half-hearted attempt at kissing her again. Maybe it was as simple as too much scotch, though that had never been a factor in the past. And when he kissed her, she slid her lips off his and asked him to just hold her for a little while. Now in the dark of the bedroom, Tamara tried remembering the flurry of thoughts that had gone through her head as he'd held her. But all that came back to her was the memory of her inner voice damning her for her sudden and unexpected surge of honor.

"I'm going up to the guest bedroom, Jesse, because I'm in no shape to drive. You need to get some rest yourself."

"You're sure about this?"

"Hell, no, but it's the right thing for us."

He'd nodded, knowing it was true.

"And listen to me. Hear me, please," she'd said, her voice cracking as she spoke. "You've got to stop doing this to yourself. You weren't responsible for what happened to Diana. There was only one person responsible for that. If you're going to blame yourself, then you have to blame her, too. You want me to come over and keep you company, you call me anytime. You know I'll be there for you, but until you slow yourself down I won't be coming over to drink with you."

He didn't like that. She didn't expect that he would, but she figured she might as well use her newfound strength to tell him the truth. Of course the first thing he did was pick up the bottle and pour himself another drink.

Tamara had walked slowly past him toward the staircase, making certain not to look back. Even as she made her way up to the guest bedroom, she knew that looking back, regretting or not regretting, would be for later.

Later was now, and playing it over in her mind yet again wasn't going to change a thing. She got off the bed, went into the bathroom, and got dressed. She crept down the stairs as quietly as possible and let herself out. As she drove away at the first glimmer of dawn, she could not help but look back and wonder what might have been.

17

Unlike regular people, cops didn't even think about it when they walked into a hospital. In fact, cops usually have pleasant associations with them, having to do with nurses. There's a certain inescapable commonality between their experiences. During his days with the LAPD, Jesse had dated a fair share of nurses and had had a serious relationship with one or two of them. But that wasn't what he had on his mind as he walked through the doors of Paradise General. He was thinking about the last time he'd been there.

Everyone in the room knew Diana was dead. There was an unmistakable quality to death. Yet as distinct and recognizable as death is to people familiar with it, none of them could have explained it to you. Jesse had given it a lot of thought over the years and the best he could come up with was that there was a vacancy and stillness in death that couldn't be faked or re-created. Though he knew she was dead, Jesse insisted on Diana being brought to the hospital. Although he knew as well as anyone that Diana was dead, he just couldn't stand the thought of her being brought directly to the county morgue.

In the corridor now, the odd mix of odors — disinfectant, ammonia, the metallic tang of blood — odors he had once gone nose blind to, were getting to him. He didn't cry. He didn't get nauseated. It wasn't his way. Jesse Stone didn't turn himself inside out for the world to see. That was, in part, what his drinking was about, about control, at least according to Dix. He and Dix had gone round and round about the subject. Dix always coming back to the same question: Did Jesse use alcohol to help control who he really was, or to free himself from who he wasn't? As Jesse walked up to the nurses' station, he noticed his hands were shaking. This time, he couldn't pretend it was all about alcohol.

"Is Dr. Marx available?" Jesse asked, his hands in his jacket pockets.

The nurse looked up from the computer screen, smiled at Jesse, and asked him to wait while she paged the doctor.

When the short, stocky man with the

jaunty walk, dressed in blue scrubs under a white coat, came up to the nurses' station, Jesse was on the phone, leaving a message for Tamara. As he approached Jesse, the smile disappeared from Dr. Marx's face. It was Marx who had been in the ER the day Diana was brought in.

"Chief Stone," Marx said. "I'm so sorry about —"

"No need, Doc. There was nothing you could do. I know that."

"You're here about Mr. Walsh."

"The MassEx guy, yes. Officer Crane tells me he's pretty banged up."

"He's actually quite seriously injured and another blow to his head might have killed him or caused permanent brain trauma. As it is, he's sustained a serious concussion."

"But I *can* talk to him?"

"Briefly and under the condition that you speak softly and try not to get him agitated. Have you ever had a concussion?"

Jesse nodded that he had. His memory of it wasn't a happy one.

"Then you'll understand that you must try not to trigger or exacerbate any of his symptoms."

"Uh-huh."

Marx ushered him into a quiet, darkened room, the doctor indicating that Jesse should stay by the door. Marx walked over to the bed and whispered to Walsh, but just loudly enough for Jesse to hear.

"Okay, Chief Stone. I'll leave you to it. Please don't raise your voice, open the curtains, or —"

"I've got it, Doc."

After Marx left, Jesse sat on a cushioned stool next to the hospital bed.

"Mr. Walsh, I'm Chief Stone of the Paradise PD, but call me Jesse."

"I'm Rudy," the MassEx guy said, his voice a rasp, the words slurred. "I'd shake your hand, but."

Jesse lightly patted Rudy's shoulder, leaving his hand there. "No need. I have a few questions for you about what happened to you on Saturday."

He felt Rudy tense. "Saturday? What day is it today?"

Jesse remembered his concussion after he got beaned during a game in A ball. He didn't actually remember getting hit, but he remembered the confusion, the headaches, the general sense of unease he felt in its wake.

"Relax, Rudy. It's Monday. Can you recall how you came to be here in the hospital?"

"Some of it, but I'm not sure how much

of it really happened and what I'm mixing up."

"That's okay. Let me worry about what's real and what isn't. Just tell me what you can."

"I was working my route in Paradise. I remember that, and I think I was in the old part of town by Pilgrim Cove. Is that right? Was I?"

"Uh-huh."

"I remember that Mrs. Cain was waiting for a package, but I'm not sure if I delivered it there. I think I did, but I'm not sure. Did I?"

Jesse patted Rudy's shoulder again. "Listen, you just talk, and then afterward we can discuss things. I don't want to color your answers. Understand?"

"I guess."

"So . . ."

"I think I remember a guy with like a shirt over his face coming at me. He broke my fucking nose. He broke my — ow, my head."

"It's okay, Rudy. If you get too worked up I'm going to have to stop. So take it easy, please. Let me ask you some questions. Answer with the first thought that comes to mind. Don't worry about it being right or wrong. Don't think about your answers. Okay?"

"Okay."

"The guy who broke your nose, was he white, black, Asian, or Hispan—"

"White."

"Tall, short, average?"

"Average."

"Hair color?"

"None . . . I mean he was mostly bald. Whatever hair he had was gray. He was older, but not old."

"Fat, thin, medium?"

"Thin."

"Anything else? Do you recall how he sounded or —"

"There were two of them? I heard them talking when I came to a little."

"Can you remember what the other one looked like?"

"I think so. He was big and white. Ugly, too. The big guy called the older guy King. And the big guy was called Hump. That doesn't make much sense, does it, Jesse? A guy called Hump."

"You let me worry about that, Rudy."

"Jesse, I don't feel so good right now. My head is killing me and I'm feeling pretty sick. I'm sorry."

"Don't be. You've been a real help."

Jesse pressed the call button and kept patting Rudy's shoulder until a nurse arrived.

He didn't have to be told to leave. At the nurses' station, he asked to have Dr. Marx give him a call when it was convenient. He'd done better with Walsh than he had expected, given the deliveryman's injuries. Two names or nicknames and a partial description. He'd made cases on less. It was a start.

18

Jesse headed into Boston to speak with Roscoe Niles about Terry Jester and the mysterious album Stan White had alluded to. At least that's what he told himself, though he knew when he was done talking to the DJ, he'd be making another stop before heading back to Paradise. That stop was the real reason he'd driven the fifteen miles south to Boston. He'd already spoken to Molly, relaying to her the descriptions Walsh had given him and telling her to see if the names King and Hump rang any bells with Lundquist. It was a long shot, but if they could get a jump on the forensics, it was worth it.

The offices and studios of WBMB-FM Boston's Rock School Radio were in a face-less office park on the outskirts of town. It was strange, he thought, how distinctive-looking Boston was, but that these damned office parks with their stucco, concrete, steel, and glass were indistinguishable from one another. WBMB-FM was on the second floor, and as he rode the elevator up he went over the questions he'd have for Roscoe. Jesse knew who Terry Jester was, even had some of his CDs. Normally, when dealing with a homicide, Jesse wouldn't have given something like this Terry Jester business a second thought, but he got the sense that with Mayor Walker on the warpath he'd better cover all his bases.

The woman at the reception desk gave Jesse a cursory smile and sent him back to the studio. As Jesse walked down the dimly lit hallway, he came upon two glass-paneled studios on either side of him. The one to his left was empty and completely dark, with the exception of small red and green lights flickering on the equipment. In the studio to his right, seated before a control panel and microphone slung from a spring-loaded arm, was a big man. He was thick around the arms, neck, and belly, and wearing a The Jam T-shirt that fit him twenty years and forty pounds ago. He seemed preoccupied with the magazine in front of him, but when he looked up and noticed Jesse, he waved him in.

"Jesse Stone, as I live and breathe," said the DJ at the console when Jesse stepped into the studio. "Come in, sit down. Just give me a second here." He pulled the mic close to his mouth and in a deep sonorous voice said, "This is Roscoe Niles, the Teacher and your afternoon headmaster at WBMB-FM, Rock School Radio, Boston. Here's that new Eastern European sensation Bocaj Slivovice doing David Bowie's 'Starman.' " He turned to Jesse, pulling a bottle of Johnnie Walker Red Label off the floor and half filling a rocks glass. He leaned toward Jesse. "Technically, they should fire my fat ass for drinking in here, but everyone plays dumb." He shook the bottle at Jesse. "Want one?"

"No, thanks, Roscoe."

"On the wagon again?"

"On duty?"

"When'd that ever stop you?"

Jesse laughed without an ounce of joy in it, noticing his hands were a little less shaky today.

Roscoe, like Jesse, was a transplant. An ex-Marine, he'd once been big other than just around the waistline. For almost five decades beginning in the sixties, he'd had one of the highest-rated overnight FM rock shows in New York City. But his station was bought by a giant media conglomerate and the format was changed to songs that were one step harder-edged than elevator music.

"The fucking program director considered The Carpenters subversives," Roscoe had confided to Jesse a few years back after too many Red Labels. "He fired me when I played a set of Rancid, the New York Dolls, and the Dead Kennedys. Asshole had no sense of humor. After that, I got this gig up here, and I've been here ever since. The pay is crap. The ratings suck, but they let me play what I want."

Jenn, Jesse's ex, had introduced them at a party when she was doing the weather for a local TV station, and they immediately took to each other in spite of their divergent tastes in the Johnnie Walker universe of label colors. When Diana came into Jesse's life, the three of them would sometimes hang together on the weekends Jesse came down to visit her. It had been months since they'd seen each other or spoken.

"Sorry about Di, man. She was something else," Roscoe said, taking a big swallow of his scotch. "How you holding up?"

Jesse ignored the question, sort of. "Let's change the subject."

"Okay. I hear Jenn got hitched to some rich SOB."

"Hale Hunsicker, yeah. He's not as much of an SOB as you'd think, with all that money. Now, don't you have to spin some records or something?"

Roscoe laughed. "It's all digital, my friend. Most of the staff here thinks turntables are for turning pottery. I'm like a pilot in a modern cockpit. All I do is like monitor the equipment and say something every now and then to let the listeners know I'm alive. I've got a new car spot coming up in about two minutes." He shook his head in disdain. "Time was I'd let you read the copy on air and the station would've loved it. Not anymore, man, not anymore. I should let you do it anyway and get my ass fired. It wouldn't matter."

"Why's that?"

"History's repeating itself. The station's been sold to one of those big conglomerates. Doesn't pay to be an indie station anymore. They think I don't know about it, but I've been around too long to fool. Too many people being let go and getting replaced by unpaid interns. Only reason I'm still here is that I'm relatively cheap. It's like a ball club dumping salary and trimming the roster for the new owners."

"Sorry to hear it."

"I'll land on my feet. I always do. So why'd you really come here, Jesse? Not that I'm not happy to see you and all."

"What can you tell me about Terry Jester?"

Niles smiled a beaming smile. "They don't call me the Teacher for nothing. Jester was born Terence Jacobivitz to a schoolteacher mother and doctor father in Boston in the forties. Left college, moved to the village in the sixties, and was part of the folk duo Terry and Stan."

"Stan White?"

Roscoe was impressed. "You know that schmuck?"

"Met him a few days ago. He's throwing a big birthday bash for Jester in Paradise next month."

"Real piece of work, Stan is. We used to be buddies, Stan and me. He was a smart guy. He understood that he had to get out of Terry's way, that Jester had the looks, the voice, and the talent. It was Stan's idea to change Terry's name. Sharp, because as names go, Jacobivitz is even less appealing to the Christian masses than Zimmerman. But that's not what you're asking, is it? You know Jester's music. Everybody does."

"I know his greatest hits, sure. But White referenced something that I didn't understand. He said something about *the album.* Do you know what he was talking about?"

Roscoe Niles sucked down the rest of his drink and nodded. "It's the stuff of legend, my friend."

"What is?"

"The Hangman's Sonnet."

Niles excused himself, once again pulling the mic close to his mouth. He read the car spot as smoothly as if he had it memorized, then hit a button on the console, pushed the mic away, and poured himself another scotch. He fiddled around with a laptop keyboard, tapped the screen, grabbed the mic, and hit the talk switch.

"Okay, folks, the Teacher's changing the lesson plan. My apologies to Difford and Tilbrook for the interruption. We'll let Squeeze get back to pulling mussels a little later on. In the meantime, here's side one, when there was such a thing, of Terry Jester's classic album *Minor Angels and Two-Eyed Jacks.*"

The DJ turned his attention back to Jesse, Terry Jester providing the background music. "Where were we, man?"

Jesse said, "The stuff of legend."

"Right on. So after Jester's first album ran

up the charts, he moved back to Boston and did all of his future recordings at Vagabond Sound on the Cape. Don't ask me why. Maybe he felt like the place was a good-luck charm for him or something. Who the hell knows with musicians? His first two albums did great guns and then he recorded this classic," Roscoe said, pointing at the studio speakers. "But his fourth album was uninspired. His fifth was downright awful. Suddenly all the adulation, the comparisons to Dylan and Donovan, vanished. Then, so did he. Stopped touring. Stopped recording. Pretty much became a recluse. There were all sorts of rumors about his disappearance from the scene: bad acid trips, a sailing accident, a smack OD, schizophrenia, a pilgrimage to India to study meditation with some nutty guru. One rumor, my personal favorite, is that he was a passenger in the car when Paul McCartney bought the ranch. Man, I miss those days. You could say anything, crazy things, and people believed it."

Jesse tapped his watch crystal. "Sometime today, Roscoe. Remember, the stuff of legend."

"My bad. Sorry, man. So flash-forward to 1974 and there are new rumors, only these are positive ones. Word is that Jester was back in the studio recording an album that was more mature, deeper, more intense and poetic than his old stuff. That it was going to blow everybody's mind. By the next year, word had leaked from the record-label people about the album's title —"

"The Hangman's Sonnet."

"You should have been a detective."

"Wiseass."

"According to my ex, my ass is the only part of me that ever had any brains. Otherwise I would've been in a business where I made some real scratch."

"So . . ."

"So the deal was that the album was thematically based on a sonnet written in like 1882 in Wyoming or some such place by an anonymous guy who was about to be hanged for murdering the woman who done him wrong."

"Sounds interesting."

"Doesn't it, though?"

"I sense a 'but' coming on."

Niles guzzled some scotch and laughed. "Funny, I think I'm one of a very few people who's ever heard it. Back when we were friends, Stan White invited me to the studio to hear the master before they turned it over to the record label."

Jesse was losing his patience. "But . . ."

"The master tape disappeared."

"It's been my experience that things don't just disappear."

"Okay. Stolen, then. Kind of beside the point, because one way or the other that tape did an Elvis and left the building and it's never been recovered."

"I'm no expert, but why not remix the album from the other tapes."

"There, my friend, is the rub." Niles took a sip of his drink. "They didn't remix it because there was only ever just one master tape. They brought the musicians for one day of rehearsals and then recorded the album live on tape, twelve songs straight through over two days. The only editing done was to be the countdowns and the banter between songs. The version I heard still had those things on it."

Jesse asked, "But why not rerecord it?"

"I guess part of the answer to that is the roster of musicians who played on the album. They were like an all-star who's-who band of people who were admirers of Jester, people who had rearranged their schedules for this onetime deal. There's some argument about who was really there, but I'm pretty sure Stephen Stills and Glen Campbell were on guitar, Booker T. on the organ, Leon Russell on piano, Jim Keltner on drums, Charlie Daniels on the fiddle, Earl Scruggs on banjo, and, get this, Paul McCartney on bass. The backup singers were James Taylor, Jackson Browne, Joni Mitchell, Judy Collins, Mavis Staples, and Linda Ronstadt. But here's the best part: None of them has ever admitted to taking part in the sessions. Very mysterious, like they signed nondisclosure forms or something, or maybe none of them has wanted to be associated with a musician's worst nightmare. Bad karma and mojo.

"But I suppose the better answer is that, unlike the rumors in the sixties, Jester did actually go flip city when the tape walked out the door. He couldn't bring himself to remake the album, couldn't even get out of bed. I hear he was catatonic for a spell. When he came out of it, he went into total seclusion, and I do mean total. Greta Garbo had nothing on him. And the lawsuits!" Roscoe threw up his hands. "Everybody was suing everybody else — Jester the recording studio, the record label Jester, Jester the record company. It was a free-for-all."

"What happened?"

Niles shrugged. "Who knows? History swallowed the details, but I guess some monies exchanged hands eventually, though the suits dragged on for years. In the end, no one came out happier or better for the experience. I do know that Vagabond's rep was shot and they went belly-up. Every ten years or so, some music journalist or investigative reporter latches on to the story and rides it for what it's worth. There was a story in the Boston paper yesterday. So, is there anything else I can help you with, Jesse? Not that I don't love shooting the breeze with you, but I do have to do something here besides bending my elbow."

Jesse stood and shook Roscoe's hand. "Thanks for the time. One more thing, Roscoe. How much would that master tape be worth if it ever resurfaced?"

"Several million, at least. You know, there are probably Terry Jester fans out there who run tech companies, people who could drop a few mil without thinking about it." The DJ let go of Jesse's hand and hugged him. "Don't be such a stranger, man. Come down one weekend and we'll tear it up."

"Sure, Roscoe," he lied.

As Jesse moved to the studio door, Roscoe called after him. "Do you miss her?"

"Every day."

There was nothing else either man needed to say.

Eight hundred forty-five thousand dollars! That was the number running through King's head as he made his way to the meet with the man who had hired him to do the job in Paradise. Eight hundred forty-five thousand dollars, the price of a new Porsche 918 Spyder. He swore he could feel himself harden when he scrolled through photos on the net of the sleek, gunmetal-gray beauty. Still, as much as he loved the car, there was no way he would blow all of his potential windfall on it. Besides, he didn't much care for paddle shifters. Paddle shifters were for wimps, the kind of guys who spent ninety grand on a 'Vette with an automatic transmission. King was a stick man all the way down to his DNA. You were one with the machine when driving a stick. When he drove on jobs, he always insisted on a stick. But even if the 918 came with a stick, King had other plans for his money. The blondes.

He hadn't forgotten about the blondes. Blondes were way more available than stick shifts or Spyders, blondes of every size and shape and hourly rate.

He downshifted the stolen red-and-white Mini as he got off Route 1 and onto U.S. 93. He'd boosted the Mini from the Walmart parking lot three blocks from the motel. In a few minutes, he'd be at the Whole Foods where the meet was to take place. King had made sure to set up the meet in a public place where he would be protected from ambush, but not one where the exchange of money would be noticed. It was also a store situated at the confluence of U.S. 90 and 93. If he had to split in a hurry, he had lots of options. He could head into Southie on the streets or backpedal to Route 9 if need be. It would make following him or setting a trap nearly impossible. He was proud of himself for that.

On the other hand, he wasn't particularly proud of keeping Hump out of the loop. True, Hump was as dumb as a bag of hammers, but he was about the only friend King had anymore, and his time inside would have been much worse if Hump didn't have his back. Dumb as Hump was, he knew the rules of the game. Honor among thieves was a load of crap, and just like in the boxing ring, you had to protect yourself at all times. If Hump had forgotten how it worked, well, that was on him.

King pulled into the lot. He was sure to be ten minutes early so he could check to see if he could spot anything that didn't fit or seem to belong, but what the hell did he know about fitting or belonging? He'd been inside for so long he always seemed to be out of place. The thought made him self-conscious about his clothes — a pair of ill-fitting secondhand-store jeans, Payless running shoes, a Wham! T-shirt, and an Old Navy hoodie. He took a deep breath, counted to ten, and got out of the car.

Once inside he circled the store, stopping to pull jars and cans off the shelf, pretending to read the labels, dropping some in his handbasket. By the time he got to the produce department, he saw his employer was right where he was told to be, standing by the mangoes and pineapples. King liked mangoes. He loved the way they smelled so sweet and how slippery they were when the pieces slid down his throat. He watched his employer pick up three of the green-and-red fruits, prod them, hold them up to his nose, and put them back.

"They're best when they're slightly soft to the touch and when they smell sweet," King said, walking up behind him. "But they shouldn't smell too sweet or give too much when you poke them."

"They teach you that in the prison kitchen?"

"We never got them inside. You got the money?"

"Right here." His employer patted his jacket pocket.

"Come on, let's shop a little."

As they moved out of the produce section, King's employer said, "Did you find anything?"

"First I'm gonna put my basket down and then you're gonna drop a can off the shelf. When you bend over to pick it up, drop the money in my basket. Then we'll talk."

The employer sighed in disgust. "Who are you, James fucking Bond?"

"Just do it."

A minute later, there was a thick brown envelope in King's basket. They strolled some more.

"Here." King handed a piece of folded white paper over to his employer.

As the man unfolded the paper, he said, "And, Jesus, did you have to kill the old broad?"

"She croaked. We didn't kill her. Just look at the paper."

"What's this?"

"It's a photocopy of a safety-deposit box key and the account number . . . Well, most of the account number. I took the trouble of blotting a few of the numbers out. Now, are you gonna bitch about the old lady giving up the ghost?"

The employer's eyes widened. "So what? For all I know, the old lady was keeping her pressed flowers in the box."

"This has to hold what you're looking for. Truth is, we almost missed it. Tore the whole damned house apart and I got lucky and looked a second time."

"Okay, you've got your money. Hand it over."

King snickered and shook his head. "No. What I got in the basket there is a small down payment. Maybe if I didn't know what was in the box, I would take the envelope and walk away, but the problem is I know and I got a pretty good idea of how much it's worth to you and how much it's worth to me."

"Oh, yeah? And how much is it worth to you?"

"A mill."

The employer laughed. "Get the fuck outta here."

"Nice try, boss. The thing is, if it's worth

122

a lot to you, it'll be worth just as much to other buyers. Right now, you've got exclusive bidding rights. You walk outta this store without making a deal with me and you're outta the bidding."

"Don't be stupid. You're in a box yourself. You're wanted for murder and assault. You don't know anyone in the business. You may have the goods, but you've got no juice, no contacts."

"Don't worry. I got all the contacts I need, and I got the key. The clock's ticking, boss. Tick tock, tick tock."

"Fuck you!"

King picked up his basket and walked away. His employer waited a beat to see if King would stop, but he didn't. He caught up to him in the parking lot.

"I can't do a million. I swear on my mother's grave."

"Bullshit."

"I swear."

"Okay, then, eight hundred forty-five thousand bucks. Not a penny less."

"What the hell kinda number is that?"

"It's your magic number and mine. Deal?"

"It's going to take me a day or two to get it together."

"Call me tomorrow and we'll set up the swap."

King smiled, shoving the envelope with the ten grand into his pants. "Okay. Tomorrow. You try any slick stuff or try to squeeze me and I go find another buyer," he said, feeling now like he was the boss. "Understood?"

"I know when I'm beat. Call me."

King got in the Mini and split. He was in too much of a hurry to see his employer clap his hands together and look up to the skies.

21

Hump was going stir-crazy in that motel room. Made sense. Being inside for half his life had trained him to hate confined spaces. But inside you didn't have a choice about it, so you lived with it. You couldn't just slide the bars back or swing the cage door open and step out. There were a million rules governing everything you did inside — written and unwritten, official and unofficial, guard rules and prisoner rules. When to talk. When to wake up. When to sleep. When to do everything. Who to look at in the eye. Who your friends could be and who they could never be. Rules enough to choke an elephant.

The fact that he could open the motel door and leave if he wanted to made it all worse somehow. There was something about freedom that gnawed at his gut, always had. He didn't understand why. Hump had never been good with understanding the why of things. That was the reason he kept finding friends like King, inside and out of prison. Men who understood things and could explain them when he asked. What Hump never needed anybody to explain to him was how he felt, and he felt itchy in there.

King had warned him about spending too much time outside the room until he got back with the money. He guessed he understood that. There was a chance maybe that the cops had gotten a line on them as more than a day had passed since what they'd done in Paradise. At the same time, he didn't understand why King didn't say anything about him going to church yesterday. It was almost like King was happy to have him out of the room. Hump looked at himself in the mirror and shrugged. It wasn't like he didn't trust King. When you spend so much time locked up with someone else, alone time becomes special. People on the outside didn't understand that. Inside, the only things that really belonged to you are in your head and heart. Truth was, Hump had liked his alone time, too. The first few hours with King gone felt good, but now it was wearing on him like a belt sander dragged across his face. The sound of the TV became a shrill and constant howl. Even after he turned it off, he could hear it in his head.

He looked in the mirror, pinched his spare tire, slapped his belly, and made a disgusted face. His midsection used to be tight as a snare drum. That was something else being inside gave you, time for crunches, sit-ups, push-ups, dead lifts, squats . . . Maybe he'd take some of his money and join a gym. He stepped away from the mirror, went to the window, pulled back the curtains, and made sure no one was coming. Even after that, when he saw he was as alone as he was ever likely to be, he looked over his shoulders just to make sure. Then and only then did he reach into his duffel bag, find the right pair of socks, and take out the dragonfly ring.

King had made him promise before going into the old lady's house on Saturday that he wouldn't take anything out of the house except what they'd been paid to take. That was all part of the deal King had set up with the man who had hired them.

"Remember, Hump, if we don't find what we come looking for, we don't take nothing. We're getting a nice payday for the work, so we can't afford to get caught fencing stuff."

"Yeah, yeah."

" 'Yeah, yeah' ain't good enough. Promise me."

"Jeez, King, what am I, five freakin' years old? What's with this 'Promise me' shit all of a sudden? We spent five years together. Ain't I always had your back?"

"Promise me."

He promised and he meant it when he said the words, but after the old lady kicked he figured all bets were off. There was no guarantee they would get paid after that. Given the risks, the guy who'd hired them might just blow them off or disappear. And Hump figured he needed to get something out of it, especially if he was looking at manslaughter or murder two. He knew people thought he was stupid. He guessed maybe he was, but he had an instinct for survival. Even insects and the dumbest animals had that, an instinct to survive.

Hump ran his thumb over the stones on the dragonfly's wings. He liked the way the edges and facets of the gems felt against his skin. He held the ring up close to his eyes, moved it around so that the light made the red and green stones sparkle. But it was the two big diamonds that were the dragonfly's eyes, the way they seemed to make the light dance and break up like a rainbow, that he loved most. He didn't know much about jewelry. He was mostly good at breaking things, at being muscle, but he knew something worth a lot of money when he saw it. And he was staring at something worth a lot of money. He'd found it in the old girl's bedroom, in a box under the bed that King must've missed. He liked thinking about how the old lady must've worn it when she was young. He liked thinking about the man who had loved her enough to shell out all the money it must've cost. He never loved nobody that much and nobody ever loved him that much. Nobody ever loved him at all.

He plopped himself onto the bed and thought about how much he could get for the ring. He tried sliding it onto his pinkie, but he couldn't even get it over his nail. He laughed at himself for trying. He stopped laughing when he remembered the old lady was dead and the way she smelled before he cleaned her up and put her back in her bed. He put the ring in his pocket and wondered where King was. It felt like he'd been gone a really long time.

22

As trying as it was to see Roscoe Niles again because of his connection to both Jenn and Diana, this was harder. He took a few deep breaths before turning his Explorer off the Concord Turnpike and into the parking lot. The lot belonged to the adjacent bowling alley, and Vinnie Morris ran his crew out of the place. Jesse and Vinnie went way back and had been connected through the late mob boss Gino Fish. Even before Fish's death, Vinnie had broken away from Gino to go out on his own, though he never stopped kicking a percentage upstairs to Gino out of love and respect for the old ways.

Jesse asked for Vinnie at the front desk, and the kid played dumb.

"Vinnie *who,* mister? What you say his last name was again?"

Jesse shook his head. It was the same routine every time.

"Do you guys have to learn a script?"

"What?"

"Look," Jesse said, showing the deskman his shield. "I'm chief of police in Paradise. I've known your boss since before you were out of third grade. Call back and tell him Jesse Stone is here to see him."

"Paradise, huh? I didn't think you'd need cops in Paradise."

"You'd be surprised, kid. I'll be at the bar."

Jesse sat at the bar, staring at the neat array of scotch and Irish whiskey bottles, but he ordered a club soda and lime. The bartender laughed.

"On the wagon, bud?"

"What is it today? I got a drunk sign over my head?"

"C'mon, buddy, you kiddin' me or what? You're sitting here staring at them scotch bottles like you'd like to take 'em to a motel and then you order club soda and lime. It's the dry drunk's favorite cocktail." He shrugged. "Am I wrong?"

Jesse didn't answer because he heard the sound of Vinnie Morris's handmade Italian shoes on the floor behind him. Vinnie was an impeccable dresser. Jesse imagined that Vinnie and Bella Lawton could blow a lot of money if they ever went shopping together. He doubted either of them had ever been to the outlets. The thought made him smile, but neither the thought nor the smile had a very long shelf life.

"Been a couple a months at least, Stone," Vinnie said.

"Uh-huh."

"Joe, get the man a Black Label. I'll have one, too."

Jesse didn't put up a fight. They took their drinks over to one of the unused lanes way down away from any of the bowling. They sat on the plastic bench, clinked glasses, sipped. Both men faced the pins at the end of the lane, their eyes looking into the not-so-distant past. When Gino Fish was alive, Jesse and Vinnie had a kind of respect and admiration for each other's talents and toughness, but now they were bound to-gether in darkness forever.

"Don't tell me you're here about that thing I did," Vinnie said. "That scumbag killed your girl, and even though he didn't pull the trigger exactly, he killed Gino. Nobody ever deserved killing more than that piece of shit. You saw what I did to him?"

"I didn't look at the pictures you brought me, Vinnie. I trust you. It's not why I'm here."

Vinnie looked relieved. "Good. So what brings you here? You come for chitchat or to bowl?"

"A little chitchat. Had a B-and-E in Paradise on Saturday. An old woman died while she was tied up and the two guys who did it beat the crap out of a MassExpress delivery guy."

"Good. Those MassEx fuckers never deliver my supplies when they're supposed to. Sorry about the old lady. But what's it got to do with me?"

"Nothing. But I got two names or nick-names of the perps. I thought maybe you could ask around."

"Sure thing. What are the names?"

"King and Hump."

Vinnie made a face. "Hump?"

"Hump. That's what the MassEx guy said."

"Okay, I'll see what I can do. But Stone, you didn't come all the way down here just for this favor."

"I was visiting Roscoe Niles over at —"

"You know the Teacher?" Vinnie was impressed.

"My ex introduced me to him years ago. We've been friends since."

"I love that guy. Always sounds half in the bag when he's on air. So what were you talking about?"

"You really interested?"

"Stone, you ever know me to ask questions or to say anything I don't mean?"

"We were talking about Terry Jester."

"Boston's Bob Dylan." Vinnie was curious. "What about him?"

"His manager's throwing him a big birthday party on Stiles Island in a few weeks and I wanted some sense of what I was in for. Then we got to talking about some missing recording."

Vinnie laughed. "He told you about the *Hangman's Sonnet* tape."

"Somehow you don't strike me as a Terry Jester fan."

"I'm not, but I'm a big fan of money. That tape would be worth a lot of 'scarole to the person who finds it." Vinnie rubbed his fingers together. "When Gino was alive, he tried hard to get a line on that recording. He came up empty. And it wasn't only Gino. When there were all those lawsuits about the theft of the tape, somebody hired a PI I've crossed paths with to look into the whole thing. He came knockin' on Gino's door. Gino told me that the cops used to come around asking him about it, too."

Jesse said, "I guess a lot of people used to come knocking on Gino's door. So how are you doing?"

"Not like how it used to be out there, Stone."

"How so?"

"Joe Broz was far from a saint and Gino had his moments, but these foreign gangs have no respect. They'd just as soon shoot your grandma and your puppy as you if it got them another square foot of territory."

"Uh-huh."

"You watch out, Stone. See if I'm not right. These clowns are in Boston now, but they'll be in Paradise, too. Maybe sooner than later."

Jesse and Vinnie finished their drinks in silence. When they shook hands good-bye, they looked deep into each other's eyes. Neither spoke. Eventually, Jesse just turned and left.

23

Jesse hit rush-hour traffic on his way back to Paradise. Traffic was a fact of life in L.A., but he'd been away from there for a long time. Paradise had changed him. Diana's murder had changed him. He just wasn't sure exactly how. Not yet. Except for the occasional reminder — a call from Jenn or the odd interleague visit from the Dodgers to Fenway Park — it almost felt like L.A. had happened in another lifetime. Even when he worked a case like he was working now, relying on all the savvy he'd gained in Robbery Homicide Division, Jesse could separate the knowledge from his memories of his time on the job in L.A. He had come to put things in distinct mental boxes: Jenn here, experiences on the job there, Paradise over here.

He was thinking of L.A. now, but it wasn't only the traffic. It was the rain. The roiling blanket of clouds that had all day hung like an ultimatum above eastern Massachusetts had made good on its gray threat. The skies opening up while he was inside the bowling alley with Vinnie, lightning snapping at him, tearing at the early dusk as he got into his Ford. In L.A. rain didn't come and go like it did here. It didn't throw just one or two big punches and leave by morning. When it came, it stayed. It stayed for days at a time. It hit you and hit you in the mouth and kept hitting you. And when it left, it left scars behind it on hillsides and riversides and in people's lives. As Jesse listened to the rain pinging on the roof of his Explorer, he remembered having to be out on patrol in the relentless rain. It was odd, he thought, that he had lived in so many dry places — Tucson, Albuquerque, L.A. — and how rain was so much more dangerous in dry places. How it could rise up and swallow you. He'd heard that L.A. had dried out, that all of California had, that the rains didn't come to stay anymore.

But Jesse hadn't dried out. He had been able to resist Roscoe's Red Label, but had succumbed to Vinnie's offer of a drink without any fight at all. He could still taste the scotch at the back of his throat and began jonesing for more, the real reason the traffic was getting to him. L.A. drivers, crazy as they were, knew how to handle rain the way the people here could handle snow. Around here, rain slowed the world down, and Jesse wasn't in the mood to be slowed down. He wasn't in the mood for anything except his sofa and a few drinks. He knew his drinking partner, Ozzie Smith, would be there waiting for him, defying gravity, suspended in midair. Ozzie's silence could be damning, but could be a comfort, too.

The pinging on the roof, the low radio, and his thoughts were rudely blotted out by the ringing of his phone coming through the speakers. He looked at the screen, hoping it wasn't Tamara Elkin calling. As if hoping had anything to do with it. He didn't know what to make of what had happened between them, not yet. Tamara, for all of her laid-back Texas attitude and upbringing, was born in New York, raised by New Yorkers, and had worked in New York. She was intense in everything she did and yet, after seeming to want him since the day they met, she'd backed off when given an opening. For all of his savvy, he thought he would never understand women.

"What's up, Molly?"

"I got a line on next of kin and maybe an idea of what those guys were looking for in the house."

That got Jesse's attention.

"Let's hear."

"I spoke to someone at the library, Mary Henderson, and she says that although the Cain family had pretty much run through all of their money, that they did own a jewelry and watch collection. All custom-made pieces by famous designers like Tiffany and Piaget. There were also some items they had purchased over the years. She said she was sure that a few of the pieces must have been sold off or donated, but that Maude Cain must have kept some of the pieces. Maybe the guys who ransacked her house got wind of it."

"Sounds like it. Did you get any information on the value and —"

"She said you'd have to talk to Mr. Wilmott; he runs the museum part of the library. He's the man who would know about the value of the Cain family collections, what they had donated, and any other information. He would know if Maude might have kept anything in the house. She also says she's sure the museum and library have some photos of the Cain collections stashed somewhere in storage."

"Good work, Crane."

"The only kind of work I do."

"Not for you to say," Jesse said, a smile in

his voice.

"Somebody's got to say it occasionally."

"I just did."

"Last time you said it before that was . . ."

"I'll write myself a note to say it at least once every six months. You said you got a line on next of kin."

"It's not much to go on, but I was right, Maude had an older sister, Mercy Updike. Deceased. Died seven years ago in Vermont. She left Paradise before I was born. Mary Henderson says she and Maude weren't close. Barely spoke. But she believes that Mercy had one child. She's looking into it."

"Given the strain between the sisters, I doubt we could count on any relatives for ID. I'll talk to the ME and the town attorney about handling it through dental records. You got those, right?"

"Yes."

"Good work. See, I said it again. Does that count toward my six-month quota?"

"You're a funny man, Jesse Stone."

"I'm a man of many charms."

"Charm? Ha!"

There was a click and a two-note electronic tone denoting that the call had ended.

24

Jesse finally relaxed as he drove down the road leading to his house. He didn't even mind the rain-battered FOR SALE sign swinging in the wind at the edge of his property. It usually ate at him, the fact that he hadn't gotten a reasonable offer for the place since he put it on the market. He had wanted to move back into town before Diana's murder. Now his desire to be less isolated was even more intense.

His moment of relaxation was short-lived. In spite of Jesse's thirst and his sofa's siren song, they would have to wait. Tamara Elkin's Jeep was parked in front of his house. This far outside of town, the ME's presence was no coincidence. Whether or not he could make any sense of what had happened, or, more accurately, what hadn't happened, between them didn't matter. Jesse, his windbreaker collar up against the rain, got out of his Explorer, rapped a knuckle on Tamara's driver's-side window, and nodded for her to come inside. He didn't wait for her.

Jesse didn't bother taking off his windbreaker. Instead he went straight to the bar and poured two Black Labels, his with soda, Tamara's with one ice cube. He raised his glass to Ozzie and took a big swallow. Ozzie didn't seem interested in damning or consoling. Jesse was putting more scotch in his glass when he heard the front door close and the deadbolt click.

Tamara came into the room, her tangled hair hanging damp and long over her shoulders. On his drive back from Boston, Jesse had gone over some things he might say to Tamara the next time they were together. He just hadn't anticipated the next time coming around so soon.

He held her drink out to her, but she didn't take it.

"No, thank you, Jesse," she said. "I don't think I'm up for it."

Jesse shrugged and put her glass down.

"This about last night?" he asked, taking a sip of his drink.

"You don't beat around the bush, do you?"

He took another sip. "What's the point in doing that?"

"No point, I suppose."

Tamara, like Jesse, had been distracted during the day, imagining what she might say and how she might say it. One of the reasons she hadn't gone through with things last night was that she hated the thought of any awkwardness between them. They had always been so comfortable together. And yet neither of them seemed capable of actually saying something meaningful for the awkwardness. Jesse filled the emptiness by pouring Tamara's untouched drink into his glass. That seemed to be the spark she needed.

"Jesse, sit down," she said, pulling the drink out of his hand.

He wasn't sure he liked that, but he sat down on the sofa.

"There's always been an 'us,' I think, from the day we met, even if that 'us' existed only in my own head and heart. Even when Diana was still alive, I thought of the two of us as a pair, not like a couple, exactly . . . I don't know. I meant it when I said I was never anybody's Miss Right and I don't want to be, but I thought that two loners like us, we might be able to be something more than friends and less than . . . that we were good together. This isn't coming out right."

"Say what you've got to say."

"I used to dream about being with you."

"Then why didn't you —"

"I don't know, maybe because I'm a fool."

"You're a lot of things, Doc, but a fool isn't one of them."

"Then because lovers have always been easy to come by for me. I've never had trouble getting men in my bed, but I've never had a lot of friends. I've never had any like you."

He laughed. "Not sure how to take that."

"As a compliment, you ass." She shook her head at him. "I guess I'm not willing to risk what we have. Because no matter what you might say, I'd be your rebound girl and that's how you would think of me. I don't think I could stand that."

"But last night doesn't have to mean anything more than it was. We can go back to what we were, you showing up at my door and drinking, talking."

"You see, Jesse, I don't think we can go back. I don't want to."

"But you just said —"

"Last night when you kissed me, I think it kind of woke me up. It made me realize some things."

"Like?"

"Like I'm not willing to let you drink yourself to death anymore. At least, I'm not

144

willing to be part of it anymore. After what happened to Diana, sure, I understood your drinking. Hell, I was over here half the time drinking with you. All of us understood how you felt and we were willing to look the other way. But not me, at least not from now on. If I was willing to give up sleeping with you to save our friendship, I sure am willing to give up drinking with you."

"You done?"

"Almost."

"What else?"

"Just because I passed up my opportunity doesn't mean I can't get a little jealous. I heard about that woman who was in your office the morning of Suit's wedding. I heard she'd make Venus green with envy."

"Bella Lawton," Jesse said, smiling. "How'd you know about her?"

"I have my sources." She leaned over and kissed Jesse on the cheek. "I'm heading out now that I've had my say. Oh, I almost forgot. It's definite. Maude Cain died of a myocardial infarction, a heart attack, plain and simple. I can't say the stress of what they did to her induced it, but it sure didn't help."

25

After stopping at the donut shop for coffee, Jesse took a detour away from the station and backtracked the few short blocks to Berkshire Street. He had taken a quick look at the reports from Molly, Alisha, and Gabe Weathers after they had spoken to the residents living on Maude Cain's block. It had netted them very little information. But canvassing, knocking on doors and talking to neighbors, was real police work. More cases got closed with worn soles and bruised knuckles than by DNA or deduction. The thing was, Jesse had learned that it often paid dividends to knock on the same doors more than once. That people weren't robots, they were imperfect, and sometimes, with a few days for their minds to focus on other matters, they would recall things they had forgotten or give you information they weren't even aware they had.

There were dangers in it, too. The human

mind is a curious thing and it can conflate events or even create memories to fit scenarios according to what it's heard or read. It isn't malicious or intentional, and Jesse accounted for the possibility. One of the ways he protected against it was to catch people off guard. That's why he was standing on the porch of 20 Berkshire Street at seven a.m., his finger pressed to the doorbell. Unlike Maude Cain's house, which was directly across the street, 20 Berkshire was well maintained and updated. It was a pumpkin-orange and forest-green farmhouse, Victorian without much of the fussiness of the more elaborate Victorians up on the Bluffs.

Jesse backed his finger off the bell, knowing that when the door was eventually answered, the person on the other side wouldn't be very happy. He was right about that.

"For chrissakes almighty! Who the hell is getting me out of bed at this hour?" An angry woman's voice cut through the wood-and-glass door as if it were made of tissue paper. "Who is it?"

"Chief Stone, ma'am, of the Paradise PD."

Two locks clicked open and the door pulled back. Standing there in the vestibule was a slender woman in her early sixties with short, slightly disheveled gray/brown hair. She had a thin, handsome face that was probably much more welcoming with a smile on it. She was dressed in a beat-up white robe and had bare feet.

"What can I do for you, Chief?"

"I'm here about Maude Cain."

Her face went from anger to sadness. "Terrible thing. Terrible."

"You're Mrs. Lynch, is that right?"

"Sharon Lynch, yes. Come on in, Chief. I'll make us some coffee."

Jesse followed her into the kitchen and sat quietly, listening to Sharon Lynch make small talk as she put on the coffee. He was careful not to speak unless she asked a specific question. He was anxious to hear how she filled the void.

"I don't know what I can tell you that I didn't tell that pretty officer of yours who was here on Sunday. Beautiful black woman. What was her name?"

"Alisha."

"Alisha, right. Like I said, I'm not sure what I can add, Chief. How would you like your coffee?"

"I'll have it the way you're having it."

That made her smile, as he knew it would. She placed the coffee down on the place mat. "Here ya go." She sat directly across from him.

"What was it you said to Alisha? I haven't had a chance to study the reports."

She didn't like that and made a face. "Ralph, that's Mr. Lynch, and I were going to go down to Boston to visit our kids, Jeremy and Jill. And —"

Jesse cut her off. "Where is Ralph now?"

She liked that even less. "Work. He owns a construction business. He's an early riser and is out of the house most days before I get up. Like I was saying, we were going down to Boston and were going to get an early start, but one of his men called and he had to go into the office to put out a fire."

"Did you or Ralph notice anything out of the ordinary Saturday?"

"Like we told your officer, we didn't notice a thing. Maude has kept to herself lately and didn't come out of the house much these days."

"What was Maude like?"

"Nice woman. A very proud woman and one ahead of her time. She kept her own name. Pity, though."

That got Jesse's attention. "What's a pity? Her dying?"

"Of course, but that's not what I mean, Chief. Their family had more money than the Lord himself, but poor Maude needed to take in boarders for years in order to pay

149

her bills. You'd think the people in the family would have planned better for their own. Charity is a good thing, but at the expense of your own . . . I just don't see it."

"Boarders?"

"Boarders, yes. Lodgers, you know. But not for the last few years," Sharon said. "She couldn't handle it any longer. Still, until about five years ago she was still taking them in . . . mostly in the summer."

Jesse thought about questioning her further but decided he could always come back another time. First he wanted to knock on some other doors. Then he wanted to have a talk with someone at town hall.

26

Jesse had hoped to avoid the mayor completely, but her black Suburban was parked in its official spot. He knew that once he set foot inside the building, word would leak back to her. So now the best he could hope for was to put off seeing her until after he had spoken to Dick Bradshaw, the town code enforcement officer. Bradshaw's car, with the Paradise town seal painted on its doors, was in its spot, too. He laughed to himself. One for two wasn't bad. You bat .500 in baseball and they'd build you a separate wing in Cooperstown.

Jesse rapped his knuckles on the wavy glass panel of the code enforcement office.

"Come in."

Dick Bradshaw was sitting behind an ancient metal desk cluttered with files and papers, a computer monitor off to one side. Bradshaw's white uniform shirt fit him about as well as Roscoe Niles's T-shirt had fit him. Dick had put on some poundage since Jesse had moved to Paradise, and his hair, what was left of it, anyway, had turned a wiry steel gray.

"Jesse!" Bradshaw said, a big smile on his face as he looked up from his coffee and egg sandwich. "Been a long time since we've seen you in here."

Jesse nodded to his left, toward the mayor's offices.

"Yeah, the mayor certainly has no love for you. What did you ever do to her to make her dislike you so much?"

"I didn't have to do anything, Dick. I just had to be who I am."

"True. You never were much for playing ball by the politicians' rules, were you?"

Jesse shook his head.

"Sit down," Bradshaw said. "Sit, sit."

Jesse sat across from Bradshaw, shaking his hand as he did.

"Want some coffee, Jesse? I can brew us up another pot."

"I'm fine."

"So what is it I can do for you, or is it the chief of police I'm speaking to?"

"Don't sweat it, Dick. This is off the record."

"Okay, shoot."

"Maude Cain."

Bradshaw's smile vanished. "Awful news. She was a fine lady and this town wouldn't be what it is without her family."

"Sorry I never met her."

"But you're not here for a testimonial, are you? Makes me wonder what you want with the code enforcement officer."

"Relax, Dick. It's that I hear Maude took in boarders. Don't you need a license from your department to do that, a food-and-health license from the commonwealth, and a safety inspection certificate from the PFD?"

Bradshaw shrugged his big round shoulders. "What can I tell you, Jesse? She was already doing it when I took over from Hurley and he told me to just let her be, that she and her family had helped make this town and that I was to lay off or it would be trouble for me. And what was the harm, really? We didn't have much of a tourist industry back in the day. So when people passed through town there was only the hotel or the few unofficial places where people rented out rooms. If there were going to be tax issues, they would be hers and hers alone, not that anyone in Paradise was going to drop a dime on her. There weren't even any B-and-Bs in town. You wanted to stay in one of those, you had to go to

Marblehead."

"Uh-huh."

"Anything else I can do for you?"

"You said it was unofficial, Dick, but did you make her keep any sort of records at all? Did she have to report to you in any way?"

"How do you mean?"

"Did she at least have to keep a guest-book or a roster of guests, anything like that?"

"Sorry, Jesse. No records, no complicity. We couldn't risk being held accountable. You know how it works."

"I do."

"So what is it, Jesse? You think the people who did this to Maude had once stayed with her?"

"Maybe. At this point, I don't know anything for sure, but it makes sense to look into all possibilities. You never know if some guy who stayed at the house ended up in jail or prison. Guys on the inside talk a lot of garbage, spin all sorts of bull. One says something about the old lady who had a safe in her house or gold bars. Believe me, it wouldn't be the first time."

"Man, I would hate to think that, but it makes sense. Makes you think twice about letting strangers into your house."

"So," Jesse said, "you can understand why a guestbook would be helpful."

"What can I say, Jesse? I don't know of one. Maybe you should have someone go through the house."

"Thanks, Dick. I'll do that, but thought I'd come here first."

"Where you headed now?"

As he stood, Jesse pointed to Mayor Walker's office.

"Once more unto the breach, huh?"

"Yeah, I might as well get it over with before they come looking for me. And, Dick, keep this conversation strictly between us for now. Anyone asks, make something up."

Jesse gave a half-salute to Dick Bradshaw and left, but Nita Thompson, Mayor Walker's hatchet woman, was there waiting for him.

27

Mayor Walker was smiling a predatory smile at Jesse when he walked into her office, and Nita Thompson trailed over his left shoulder. He knew the mayor's game, what the smile was meant to do, how it was intended to unsettle him. It didn't. Even if it had, he would never have shown it.

"Sit, Jesse," she said, gesturing at the black leather chair in front of her desk. "I have some things to catch up on."

He sat. "Thank you. Nice to hear you calling me by my first name again. Does this mean we're back together?"

She didn't respond, turning her head down and making a show of signing some papers while he waited. Some people, he thought, enjoy their power way too much. Jesse had had a commander in L.A. who used to pull the same crap. A real self-important prick. He'd call you into his office and make you sit there while he pretended to be busy. While you waited, he wanted you to look at the walls, at his medals and commendations, at the photos of him with Kareem and Magic, with Jack and Warren Beatty. He wanted you to be impressed by his power. More than that, he wanted you cowed by it. Jesse being Jesse, he never looked. Just kept his eyes straight ahead, staring at Pinkston, turning the tables on his commander, making *him* uncomfortable.

"You're an icy bastard, Stone, you know that?" the commander had once said. "Get the hell out of my office."

Jesse took it as high praise.

So now he sat there in Walker's office, looking straight ahead at the mayor as she pretended to be busy. If it wasn't for Diana's murder, he wouldn't have even given the mayor's recent machinations a second thought. He didn't resent her ambition. He resented her trying to scapegoat him. From day one on the job in Paradise, there had been friction with one politician or another. Usually he bit his tongue and moved on, working with the selectmen or mayors because it was better for the citizens of Paradise if they all worked together. But Jesse would have a hard time forgiving the mayor because of how she had come at him when he was most vulnerable.

Finally, Mayor Walker looked up from her make-believe work.

"So, Jesse, you weren't going to leave the building without stopping by to give me an update on your progress on the Cain murder, were you?"

"Murder? I wasn't aware the DA had decided on what charges he would bring."

"He hasn't, but he will. About you leaving the building . . ."

"No, it was never my intention to leave without stopping in, Madame Mayor. In fact, I was in Dick Bradshaw's office looking into a potential line of investigation."

"Really?" The mayor made a show of tilting her head in curiosity. "I'm listening."

"With all due respect, Mayor Walker, I'm uncomfortable sharing details of any investigation at this stage. I am particularly reluctant to do so in front of persons without official standing."

Jesse could see the mayor's displeasure as plain as day. He felt Nita Thompson's eyes burning a hole right through him.

"I take full responsibility for Miss Thompson."

"Can I have that in writing? Because we both know that if there's a leak and the case falls apart, it's not your door the press will be knocking at."

The mayor said, "Chief Stone, you're being insubordinate."

"No, Your Honor, I'm doing my job. We have the names of two potential suspects. Probably aliases or nicknames."

"And the reason you were in seeing Bradshaw?"

"Sorry, Your Honor, I'm not ready to discuss that. I can't afford for any possible suspects to discover how I might locate them."

"You don't fool me, Stone," Nita said. "You're covering your ass."

Mayor Walker didn't like Thompson coming directly at Jesse that way, because it gave him an opening. He stood up and faced the mayor's political adviser.

"You ask your boss if that's what I'm doing, Miss Thompson. From the day I was hired by Hasty Hathaway and his minions who hoped I would screw up and be easy to manipulate, I have never tried to spurn responsibility or hide behind anyone else." He stepped close to Thompson. "I understand why the mayor doesn't like me. We've had our skirmishes over the years from when she was a selectwoman and during her tenure as mayor. But I don't get your beef with me."

Thompson tried hard to keep her mouth shut, but Jesse had just gotten even deeper under her skin and she couldn't contain herself.

"Personally, Chief Stone, I don't give a damn about you, but you're a drunk and a cowboy. And I've heard the rumors."

Jesse's guts tightened. Sure, he had crossed the line in the name of right more than a few times, but there was one transgression that could get him sent to prison for life: handing Diana's killer over to Vinnie Morris. He played it cool.

"Rumors?"

"Everybody in the state knows about you and the motorcycle gang in Helton. How you shot up one of the gang members' Harleys and then walked away while another member of the gang beat him bloody. One version of it says the guy was beaten to death."

"Nice story. Any proof? Witnesses?"

Thompson gave him a dismissive wave. "You think you can do as you please without consequences. You're a throwback. Your presence is a weight around the mayor's neck, a political liability."

Jesse smiled at her with his mouth. His eyes remained cool. "A political liability?" He turned back to the mayor. "Congresswoman Walker, Senator Walker, or Governor Walker, which one is it to be, Your Honor?"

But it was Nita Thompson who answered. "Whichever one she chooses, but first there needs to be a little housecleaning around here. Someone needs to clean out the attic and take the garbage to the curb."

"Too bad your parents didn't teach you how to talk plainly," he said, tweaking her. He about-faced. "Is that how you feel about it, Madame Mayor?"

Walker cleared her throat. "I might not have used such a regrettable metaphor, but essentially, yes."

"Nice to know where we all stand. I'm leaving now. I have a case to handle before someone tries to take me to the curb for morning pickup."

"One last thing, Chief," Walker said.

"Uh-huh."

"I want you to fully cooperate with Bascom, Mr. White, and Miss Lawton. That party could mean a lot of press for Paradise and I want it to all be positive. Is that understood?"

Jesse laughed. "That's amazing."

"What is?" The mayor was confused.

"I didn't know Miss Thompson was a ventriloquist, too. Good day, ladies."

Jesse walked out of the mayor's office without turning back.

28

Back at the station, Molly sensed something was up with Jesse. She stood, walked over to him, and inspected his face.

"No blood or bruises," she said. "But I know you, Jesse Stone. You've got that look on your face."

"What look?"

"The one where you look as if you've just had a fight."

"You do know me, don't you, Crane?"

"To the extent that you're willing to let me know. It hasn't been easy."

"What fun is easy?"

"First man I've ever heard ask that question."

"I'm special."

She laughed. "That's one way of putting it. So stop stalling."

"I was over talking to Dick Bradshaw."

"About what?"

"About what you're going to assign someone to do or do yourself."

Molly rolled her eyes. "I can't wait."

"Did you know Maude Cain let out rooms?"

"A lot of people in town did before we got touristy and the B-and-Bs started springing up. The hotel was too expensive for some folks because it was the only game in town."

"Did your family do it?"

"C'mon, Jesse, you've seen the house I grew up in. There wasn't even enough room for us. Where were we going to put them, in the crawl space? But some of the kids I went to school with, their parents did it."

"Can you remember any of the kids who did it?"

"Where are you going with this, Jesse?"

"First, send someone over to the Cain house and see if they can locate a log book, ledger, or guestbook where Maude might have kept an accounting of who she rented rooms to. If we get hold of that, we're going to see if we can't track down some of the people who stayed with her. But if we don't come up with the guestbook, maybe we can find some folks who stayed at Maude's one week and then someplace else the next."

"Long shot."

"Very long shot, but till we get a hit on the fingerprints or something else, it's a place to start."

"Any luck in Boston?"

He shrugged. "We'll see. If Vinnie Morris calls, put him through no matter what."

Molly's expression was a cross between fear and fury. Although Suit, Healy, and Jesse were the only people who knew for a fact what Jesse had allowed to happen in the immediate wake of Diana's murder, Molly had always suspected things hadn't quite happened the way the official story went. She had trouble believing that a convenient coconspirator had somehow swooped into the room, grabbed Diana's killer, and vanished before Jesse, Suit, or Healy could stop him. She didn't know that Vinnie Morris had anything to do with what had gone down, but she had never quite approved of Jesse's closeness to him or Gino Fish. No matter how many times Jesse explained how big-city policing meant sometimes making allies of the bad guys, she didn't like it.

"I thought after Gino Fish died, you would —"

"Let's not do this again, Molly. Call Alisha in, and you and Peter go over to the Cain house."

"Perkins, too?"

"You know Peter. Sometimes his obsessiveness has a benefit."

She laughed, recognizing the truth in Jesse's words.

"Sometimes," she said, "I think he put the O in OCD."

"I'll tell him you said that."

"You do and you'll pay."

"Threatening your superior officer?"

"Promising, not threatening."

"Get out of here, Crane."

"I'll wait until Alisha gets here."

"Fair enough."

"What are you going to do?"

"I suppose I should go over and talk to Bascom to see what's up with the security arrangements for Terry Jester's big party. The mayor sees this as a big photo op for her. Fine. It means I can get everybody overtime. She's also going to push the DA to charge the perps in the Cain case with murder two."

"What's with her lately, anyway? She can be mayor here forever. Why is she —"

"That's the problem, Molly. She doesn't want to be mayor of Paradise forever."

"Ambition." She shook her head. "It's worse than jealousy."

"I've seen it eat people alive. Like desperation, it causes people to make dumb choices."

He patted Molly on the shoulder, signaling that their talk was over. He watched as she walked away from him and wondered if she really understood how valuable she was to him and to Paradise.

29

It was a very short trip over the bridge to Stiles Island. Stiles was quite a beautiful place in the way that things in the Northeast could be. In the desert, where he'd grown up, things changed, but subtly. The changes were small ones, so that only someone with local eyes would notice them. Sure, the desert might bloom after a rain, but mostly it would seem always the same to the uninitiated. It could be like that in L.A., too. In the Northeast even a blind man could track the change in seasons. Here the seasons were scented distinctly. They had distinct sounds, distinct weather. Stiles Islanders also had the benefit of the ocean and the coves. It's why the rich built summer homes here. Jesse had always thought Stiles was at its best and most alluring in summer. Now he was less sure. The brown grass and the silence, the desolation of winters on the island, suddenly held more appeal for him.

Jesse pulled his Explorer up to the doorstep of the security building. He remembered how, when he first came to Paradise, there wasn't even a security building on the island, just a flimsy military-surplus Quonset hut tucked out of sight behind some hedges. Now the security offices were nearly as elaborate as the Paradise police station. It was certainly more modern and better equipped in terms of electronic surveillance. There weren't many places you could travel on Stiles that weren't visible to the people inside the security building. The building itself was a long way away from that flimsy old hut. With its robin's-egg-blue clapboards, white fish-scale shingles, and bluestone driveway, it might easily have been mistaken for a gate house at one of the larger estates on Stiles. The Island, upscale to begin with, had really gone big. The homes went for millions, and that was due, in part, to the owners' reluctance to part with them. When a Stiles house or a piece of property went on the market, there tended to be a feeding frenzy. Even during the crash, the houses on Stiles held their value.

Jesse walked through the front door and strolled right by two uniformed security men who were too busy with the array of video screens in front of their faces to pay any mind to him. All the house alarms were wired into the buildings. After the siege, resident participation in the network was no longer optional. If you bought on the island, you had to agree to be part of the network. Jesse understood that private security had its purpose, that cops couldn't be everywhere, couldn't guard everything for everyone, but they still made him uncomfortable. Their loyalties were bought and paid for, not a matter of duty, not a matter of right and wrong. And right and wrong were as essential to Jesse Stone as his spine.

When he made it down the hallway to the threshold of Bascom's office, he was stopped by a tall guy in a light blue blazer with eyes to match, a white shirt, and a red tie. His light brown hair was short, gelled flat, and perfectly parted on the left side, as if he had escaped from an episode of *Leave It to Beaver*. His vibe couldn't have been more ex-military if he were wearing camouflage. Jesse knew all of Bascom's personnel. They were required to register with the PPD and produce their carry permits and prove they had met the same shooting certification Jesse's people did. He didn't know this guy and that didn't sit well with him. It wasn't because he felt Bascom had tried to put something over on him. It was more a reminder of how sloppy Jesse had been in his administrative duties since Diana's death. He was a drunk and he hated things that made it impossible for him to deny it. On the other hand, Blue Blazer knew who Jesse was.

"Chief Stone," he said, putting out his right hand, smiling a cautious smile. "I'm Dylan Taylor, Bascom's new second. Happy to meet you."

"Nice meeting you. Call me Jesse, please."

"Will do, sir."

Jesse smiled at him for that. "How long have you been out?"

"A year now, sir."

"Jesse."

"A year now, Jesse."

"Bascom around?"

"No, sir — no, sorry, Jesse. I believe he went over to the Wickham property. Is there something I can help you with?"

"No, I think I'll head over there. You want to give him a heads-up, go ahead. Nice meeting you." Jesse started to turn, then turned back around. "Dylan, who did you deal with at the PPD when you registered?"

A careless smile washed over Taylor's handsome, clean-shaven face. Jesse recognized the look.

"Alisha."

"How'd you know?"

Jesse shrugged. "Lucky guess."

Once outside, he just stood in the sun for a minute, eyes shut, letting it warm him.

30

The Wickham estate was on the ocean side of the island and it was nothing so much as large. The main house was one of those faux old New England houses with Cape Cod–gray shingles surrounded by a six-foot-high, new-to-look-old stone wall. The house was meant to give someone coming upon it a warm, rustic feel, but was, in fact, the size of an aircraft hangar and about as cozy as a solid-state drive. Jesse had been inside a few times and knew its interior was all granite, tile, marble, and exotic woods. Grant Wickham, who owned a specialized software company in Boston, had built the house about eight years earlier and had since moved on to bigger, better houses spread across the country. He let friends or business associates use the place for a few weeks at a time or rented it out while he was in Aspen or East Hampton or Jackson Hole.

Whether it was the warmth of the sun or

because he just felt like it, Jesse decided to have a little fun. He liked the notion of sticking it to Roger Bascom. Bascom was quick to tell anyone who would listen that island security was beyond reproach and that Jesse's cops were no more than glorified ticket-givers. Jesse knew better. If there was one thing he'd learned over the course of his career, it was that nothing and no one was ever completely secure. As Jesse approached the Wickham place, he pulled in between some trees, got out of the Explorer, and lifted its hood as if something was wrong with the engine, and then walked around to the front of the Ford. The trees and the raised hood blocked him from view of the security cameras. He was over the stone wall without much effort, though his wrecked right shoulder barked at him.

Jesse had come over the wall behind the pool house and cabanas. Some pool house. The thing was the size of a three-bedroom ranch. Jesse figured he'd come along the pool, scout out Bascom's location, and walk right up behind him. But when he came around the side of the pool house, it wasn't Bascom he saw.

Bella Lawton was faceup, sunning herself on a chaise longue at the side of the infinity pool. Other than her sunglasses, the PR flack was wearing only what she had been born into the world with. This might've been a thirteen-year-old boy's dream, but it was more than a little awkward for Jesse. Awkward because he'd just climbed over the wall and because it was difficult not to stare. He wasn't going to run or to climb back over the wall. He wasn't a man to run or hide.

Instead, he cleared his throat loudly enough so that Bella would know he was standing there. But if Jesse expected her to grab a towel and cover up in embarrassment, he'd been wrong. She smiled, raising up the back of the chaise.

"Chief Stone — Jesse."

"Bella."

She reached over to the Adirondack chair next to her and patted the seat. "Sit."

He sat.

"It's okay to stare, Jesse. Men have been staring at me since I can remember. Women, too. I like it. I like the attention. Do you think that's weird?"

"Sometimes I played ball in front of thousands of people. Sometimes in front of hundreds. I liked the thousands better. But I'm a cop, Bella, not a shrink. If you're happy, I guess that's what's important."

The smile that had been on her face disappeared. "I didn't say I was happy." She took off her glasses, turned, and stared Jesse in the eye. "Do you think I'm beautiful?"

"Uh-huh."

She beamed at that. "Good."

He let that go. "Look, Bella, it's lovely to see you —"

She smiled again.

"What I mean to say is that you're not why I'm here."

"Then why are you here?"

"To see Bascom."

She made a sour face, made a show of looking for him under her chaise. As she did, she made sure Jesse got a good look at her.

"Sorry," she said. "As you can tell, he's not out here. No offense, but don't you think you might have had better luck coming in through the front door? It's more traditional."

"But then I wouldn't have seen you."

She liked that a lot. "I think he's in the house. He and Stan have been bitching at each other all morning like an old married couple."

"About what?"

She shrugged, her round, firm breasts rising and falling as she did. "Who knows?"

"How's the promo going for the event?"

Her smile did its vanishing act again. "Not great. Something better happen soon or I'll be begging C-listers to come."

"Good luck with that," he said, standing up. "I better go find Roger."

"Jesse, if you ever want to go to dinner . . ." She didn't finish her sentence.

He stared down at her. She *was* beautiful and under most circumstances would have been almost impossible to resist, but these weren't most circumstances. Bella's beauty only served to remind him of Diana's and how much he missed her.

31

Jesse could hear their voices as he walked through the restaurant-sized kitchen and toward the cavernous great room. Bella's assessment was spot on. Though Jesse couldn't hear what was being said, Bascom and White were definitely not pleased with each other. He hadn't thought much of White when they'd met, but given how he was getting under the usually unflappable Roger Bascom's skin, Jesse thought he might have to reconsider. Anybody who could get Bascom to react this way deserved a second chance. Bascom's back was to Jesse, White looking over the security man's shoulder. Unlike with the sunbathing Bella, Jesse didn't need to clear his throat to be noticed. White's eyes got big with something that looked like a cross between panic and anger.

"Chief Stone!" White said too loudly, as if

to cue Bascom to shut up. "Come in. Come in."

Jesse wondered what it was White didn't want him to hear. Maybe it was what Bella Lawton had already confessed to him, that this gala for Terry Jester wasn't coming together as expected and that the big party was going to be a big bust instead. Maybe it was something else. When Bascom turned to face Jesse, there was no confusing the meaning of his expression. He was pissed.

"Stone! How the hell did you get in here?"

"Through the kitchen."

Stan White grinned at Bascom's annoyance, but Bascom was unamused.

"That's not what I'm asking and you know it."

"Maybe you better check with the guys manning the video monitors. I guess they think I'm still looking under the hood of my Explorer."

The grin was gone from Stan White's face, as he realized he wasn't sure how much of the argument Jesse had heard.

"Never mind how you got in here, Chief," White said.

"Jesse. Call me Jesse, Stan."

He liked to discombobulate people with that line. There were times, in their confusion, that they'd say things they hadn't

179

meant to. This wasn't one of those times. White composed himself before he spoke again.

"Yes, Jesse, I'll remember that. Like I was saying, never mind how you got in here. No one likes having their private conversations overheard, even when that someone is the chief of police."

Jesse said, "Maybe especially not by the police chief."

White shook his head. "Don't be silly, Jesse."

"Was it a conversation? Sounded more like an argument to me."

"No disrespect, Jesse, but my conversations or arguments with Mr. Bascom about security on the grounds of this estate are our business and not your concern."

"True."

Bascom had had enough of the polite banter.

"What are you doing here in the first place, Stone?"

"I'm on a mission for the mayor."

"A mission." White was curious. "What mission?"

"She has big plans for your big party. She seems to believe this will reflect well on her. She wants to bask in the glow of all the celebrity star power. Thinks it will give a boost to her career."

Bascom didn't like it. "What does that have to do with you?"

"Ask Nita Thompson," Jesse said. "But I suppose they want to make sure everything goes off without a hitch. The mayor isn't fond of egg on her face."

The security man bristled. "I've got it handled. All I need your cops to do is manage the traffic . . . if there is any."

That got White's attention. "What are you talking about? There'll be lots of traffic. There'll be traffic jams of TV news vans alone."

Jesse caught Bascom rolling his eyes. Bascom had even less patience for dolts than Jesse did, but Jesse was still curious about what the two men were arguing about.

"So what were you guys arguing about?"

Bascom opened his mouth to answer, but Stan White cut him off.

"Arguing, sure we were arguing. Some of the big names, they have their own security people and they aren't fond of dealing with Mr. Personality over here." He nodded at Bascom. "Look, Roger is good at his job, but he isn't used to dealing with artists. I know what they're like. I've dealt with them for fifty years already. The rich have their quirks, but rock stars and actors . . . oy!"

Jesse didn't know whether to buy it or not. He knew White was bullshitting about the big names because of what Bella had told him about scrounging for C-listers, but he knew from his time in L.A. that actors and rock stars could be difficult to deal with.

"If that's all, then I guess I'll leave you to it. Just remember that the mayor wants me to be part of things." Then in a deadly serious voice, with his best cop face, Jesse said, "No surprises, gentlemen. Do we understand each other?"

White was quick to answer. "Sure, sure, Chief — Jesse. No surprises."

Bascom nodded and turned his back. Jesse took that as his cue to leave but decided to head out through the front door. He didn't feel like going another round with the birthday-suited Bella Lawton, nor did his right shoulder much feel like doing any more wall climbing.

32

They met for dinner at the Lobster Claw. The Claw had been open for a few years but had never managed to catch on like the Gull. Jesse couldn't figure it out. The only decent food choices at the Gull were sandwiches and salads, and while the rest of the menu wouldn't put you in the hospital, the best thing you could say about their hot dishes was that they were usually hot. Jesse mentioned his confusion to Tamara. She shook her head at him.

"You know, for the best cop I ever met, you sure can be thick sometimes," she said.

"How so?"

"It's that small-town thing. You still don't get it, do you, even after that thing with the missing girls?"

"But this isn't about dark secrets. It's about a restaurant."

"I agree with you, Jesse, the food's better here, but it's not about the food, it's about

183

comfort. Small towns like their comfort. It makes them feel safe. It insulates them from 'out there.' " She gestured with both hands.

"When did you become an expert on small towns?"

"You ever see Texas on a map? Next to Alaska, there's not a better place to study small-town life than in Texas. You learn that early on. The more this area becomes an extension of Boston, the harder people are going to cling to places like Daisy's and the Gull. Someday, maybe sooner than you think, this town and the others nearby will be very different places."

Jesse took a sip of wine, consternation on his usually inscrutable face.

"What?" Tamara asked. "Something wrong with the wine?"

"The wine's okay. You're the second person in the last few days to say something like that, about how Boston would start encroaching on Paradise. Something wicked this way comes."

"It's inevitable, I guess, with more people moving up here and commuting to the city. Who was the first person to mention the subject?"

Just then, Jesse's phone buzzed in his pocket. Being chief had its perks, but they came at a price. He didn't usually have the luxury of blowing off calls. And when he saw who this particular call was from, he knew he was going to pick up.

Tamara was curious. "Who is it?"

"The person you were just asking about. I'll be back in a minute," he said, standing up and heading for the Lobster Claw's outside deck.

"Stone, you there?"

"I'm here, Vinnie. You have something for me?"

"Maybe."

"Maybe? This a negotiation?"

"That's up to you."

"What's it going to take, Vinnie?" Jesse asked, looking out into the blackening ocean. He remembered two years earlier, standing on the deck just after the Lobster Claw had opened. He had a Black Label in his hand that night, not a cell phone. Although he had been drinking wine to appease Tamara, the prospect of bargaining with Vinnie Morris was making the thought of a double Black Label neat very appealing.

He repeated Jesse's question. "What's it going to take? Nothing too crazy. Just an understanding between us."

"What sort of understanding?"

"The same sort you had with Gino. A

favor done is a favor earned."

"This wouldn't have anything to do with —"

Vinnie cut him off. "Never. You got my word on that. That thing was something I did for us both, and it wasn't business. What I'm talking here is business, good business for us both. Always worked for you and Gino."

"Until it didn't."

"Yeah, until it didn't. But that's not going to happen to us, Stone. And just to show you I mean what I say, this one's on the house. You got a pen and paper handy?"

Jesse reached into his back pocket for the notepad he'd always carried since his days in uniform in L.A. and into his front pocket for a pen. He looked around to make sure no one was in earshot, then put the phone on speaker and placed it on the deck rail.

"Shoot."

"Kirk Kingston Curnutt. Goes by King. Petty thief who's good at boosting cars. Last stretch was for pistol-whipping a gas-station attendant. Got out a few months ago. His cellmate was a clown named Humphrey Bolton."

"Hump."

"See, I knew there was a reason you're chief. Word is you don't want to tangle with him. Country strong and good with his fists. They're both in the system."

"Thanks, Vinnie."

"Remember, Stone, this one's on the house. Next time it's business."

"Uh-huh."

"You know what I like about you, Jesse?"

"No."

"Most of the time you talk even less than me."

The phone went quiet. Jesse scrolled to Lundquist's number but got voicemail. He left a message that included the information Vinnie Morris had just given him. Then he called the station and had Alisha look up Curnutt and Bolton in the system and put together a packet for him to present to the mayor and the DA. He also had her make up two photo arrays that included the suspects. He supposed he could have had her alert the state and local authorities, but he didn't want to get ahead of himself.

When Jesse got back to the table, dinner was waiting for him. Tamara, too. A brick-sized hunk of lemon-scented salmon over arugula and watercress was in front of the ME and a skirt steak over mashed sweet potatoes was at Jesse's place. The ball of rosemary butter atop his steak had nearly melted away. Tamara took one look at Jesse and knew. She also knew it wasn't another homicide or her cell would have gone off as well.

"Don't worry," she said, waving the waitress over. "Can we have these wrapped separately to go?"

"I'm sorry, Doc. It's business."

"I figured. You mind telling me what's up."

He leaned over and whispered in her ear the information he'd received about the two likely suspects. She made a face halfway between a smile and a frown. When the waitress returned, Tamara said, "I'll take care of the bill. Take yours and go on and git."

Jesse Stone was old-school, and the thought of Tamara paying bugged him, though he knew better than to show it. Instead he focused on something else Tamara had said.

" 'Git'! Your Texas is showing."

She folded down her middle and ring fingers on her left hand, holding them down with her thumb, and raised her index finger and pinkie. "Hook 'em horns. I bleed burnt orange."

33

Jesse's first stop was the station. Alisha had already done as he had asked, putting together two packets on the suspects and two photo arrays. What Alisha didn't do was ask Jesse where he'd gotten his information from. She was wise that way, and every time she displayed those good cop instincts, he felt better about hiring her instead of some old-pro city cop. Gabe Weathers was good, but he'd been on the job in Boston for only five years before hiring on in Paradise. The problem with who the selectmen and the mayor had wanted him to hire was that retired big-city cops came with all sorts of baggage. They always knew better and their attitudes were hardwired. You had to spend as much time untraining them as training them, and even then you couldn't beat the big city out of them. And if the last few years had taught him anything, it was that policing a small town came with different challenges. To Jesse, the savings on pension and benefits wasn't worth it.

"What should I do now, Jesse?"

"Call the mayor and tell her I've got two potential suspects, but that I have to talk to Rudy Walsh first."

"The MassEx deliveryman? To get a positive ID?"

"Exactly. Tell Her Honor that if Walsh IDs them, I'll be by first thing in the morning. By the way, Alisha, you've got an admirer over on Stiles."

She turned away from Jesse in embarrassment.

"Dylan seems like a good kid," Jesse said. "Maybe you should give him a chance."

She smiled at him. "Maybe I already have."

Jesse plucked one of the two packets on the suspects and a photo array from in front of Alisha and headed out the door.

Before he had gotten a block, the radio went off and the ringing of a phone came through the speakers of his Explorer. It was Lundquist.

"Jesse Stone."

"You want to tell me where you came up with these two guys?" Lundquist asked, sounding a little bit annoyed. "We haven't gotten the DNA results back and we didn't find a single fingerprint. You'd also be amazed at how many cons have the nicknames King and Hump. Still somehow you found out it was these mutts."

"Does it matter how? I'm on my way over to the hospital to see if Walsh can pick them out of photo arrays."

"Healy always said you had connections. Never bothered him, but I always wondered what price you had to pay or what you had to trade for their information."

"Healy never let it bother him too much, Brian. You've been at this long enough to know that good information doesn't come from the sunny side of the street."

Lundquist let that go. "So what's the plan if he IDs them?"

"Then I have to go to Mayor Walker with it. She'll want to do a press conference, but if Walsh IDs them, I'll give you a heads-up. We can't let these guys get away because of my mayor's political aspirations."

"I'll be here."

But then he wasn't. The familiar two-tone hang-up chime sounded in the Explorer and the music came back on. It was Terry Jester singing "King to Pawn," one of Jesse's favorites. He even caught himself singing along.

Deborah Holt, the nurse in charge of Rudy Walsh's floor, was less than pleased to see Jesse Stone. They'd crossed paths before, usually when Jesse wanted to break hospital rules.

"I'm sorry, Chief Stone," she said, putting her palm up to cut him off, "but Mr. Walsh is probably asleep and his concussion symptoms haven't abated as quickly as Dr. Marx had hoped."

Jesse took a deep breath. Normally he wouldn't have pushed, but this wasn't normally.

"I'm sorry, but I've got two potential murder suspects out there, the two men who put Mr. Walsh in here to begin with. I need him to make a positive ID so we can get after them."

She didn't like it and it showed. This was always the nature of her interactions with Jesse Stone. He always wanted to cut corners but always came armed with a valid reason to do so. The last time they'd done business, she had had to help the chief sneak a man who'd been hit by a truck out of his room.

"The best I can do is to call Dr. Marx. If

he says you can go in, then I won't stop you."

"Fair enough."

Jesse waited. He could tell by the expression on Nurse Holt's face that Marx had given his blessing for him to show the photo arrays to Walsh. And if that didn't give her away, her slamming down the phone certainly did. Even her stride was angry.

"The doctor says that if Mr. Walsh is awake and agrees to see you, then you are to be permitted to talk with him, but that if he is asleep or doesn't feel up to it, you are to come back in the morning. Understood?"

"Uh-huh."

Sixty seconds later, she waved Jesse into Walsh's room.

The room was dark. Jesse had had a concussion or two and knew that bright light and loud noises could trigger awful headaches. But he couldn't risk Walsh misidentifying the suspects or leaving any doubt in his identifications because the lighting was poor. So he stood beside Walsh, laid out each array on the movable food table, and shone his keychain LED flash onto the photos. He made sure to keep direct light out of Walsh's eyes. The photos were all the same size and were all in color. The subjects were all roughly the same size in the photos, the same race, and within a fair age range. Jesse had seen judges throw out IDs because the arrays had been done in such a way as to influence the witness's choices. Not in Paradise, not on Jesse's watch. And just to make doubly sure, he had Nurse Holt stay to confirm the IDs.

"This guy was the guy who clocked me," Walsh said, pounding his index finger on Kirk Kingston Curnutt's photo. "He tried to hide his face with his shirt, but it slipped off him and I got a good look. And this fella here, he's the one who tied me up." This time Walsh was pounding Humphrey Bolton's head shot. "I hope you find an excuse to shoot these two bastards."

Jesse let that pass without comment. Instead he wished Walsh a speedy recovery, thanked Nurse Holt, and left. He had calls to make and business to do.

34

King was on his way to the meet, visions of blondes and Porsches dancing in his head. The man on the other end of the phone hadn't sounded pleased at having to cough up all that money. That was just too damned bad for him, King thought, smiling as he downshifted the stolen Outback and turned past the WELCOME TO PARADISE sign at the edge of town. When his contractor demanded they get together back in Paradise, King was tempted to up the payoff back to a million dollars. But impulsiveness had gotten him into trouble before and he wasn't going down that path again. Not this time, not when he was finally going to hit it out of the park. He shook his head, remembering how he'd done time in various state pens for boosting cars on the spur of the moment or the one time he pistol-whipped a gas-station attendant over seventy-eight dollars. *Seventy-eight freakin' dollars!* Even his greed had been small-time. Petty and small-time . . . not anymore.

That was not to say he wasn't totally pissed off that the exchange was happening in Paradise. It was risky and just plain dumb for him to go back to the town where he was likely going to be charged with felony murder. He had hoped that the DA would see the old biddy's death as an accident and that they had meant the woman no harm. But he guessed the cops had spotted her split lip and that their attempt to clean her up and to place her back in her bed hadn't gone a long way in putting things right. With all that was hanging over his head, there was only one option: make the exchange and get gone.

He'd left Hump behind earlier that day while his ex-cellmate was snoring up a storm. King left him a note with two grand extra from the ten thousand they'd earned. He'd already given Hump his five large for the job. Surprisingly, King felt crappy about leaving Hump on his own with just seven thousand dollars and cutting him out of the big money, but prison friendships went only so far. Truth be told, he hoped the extra two grand would encourage Hump to do the favor King had asked of him in the note. He wanted Hump to stay in the motel room a few more days and to keep as low a profile as possible. Besides, Hump was a guy who could make seven grand go a long way. He was an uncomplicated man without a lot of needs.

He drove slowly along the roads leading to Paradise and kept under the speed limit once he'd gotten into town. He didn't know Paradise. He'd been to town only once, and it wasn't like that had gone according to plan. He figured that if he got collared for the old lady's death he could probably plead it down to manslaughter and save the commonwealth the expense of a trial, but if he got pulled over by a cop and had to use his gun, he was screwed. There was no pleading down killing a cop. Do that and they hunt your ass down no matter what, and they might even find a way to kill you before you ever got to see the inside of a cell.

King slowed to a stop and turned left onto the road that led into the wooded area of town north of the Bluffs that ran along Sawtooth Creek. From what he could tell downtown, Paradise wasn't a hive of activity, but it was Times Square compared to the road he was on now. The trees were so thick that the canopy nearly blotted out the moonlight. When he spotted the metal gate for the access road, he stopped and got out of the Subaru. The gate was unlocked, as he was told it would be. He swung it open, got back into the car, drove up the road to the utility shed, and parked.

As he'd done at the meet at the supermarket, King had come early to make sure this wasn't a trap, not that he thought his employer capable of such a thing. He'd known guys like him all his life, inside and out of the joint — street-savvy users, tough in their way, but not hard. Setting a trap of the kind where someone winds up dead took more sand than people thought. King hadn't ever killed a man, though he'd been mad enough at the gas-station attendant to crack his skull. Whether the guy had the stuff to set a trap or not, King did his due diligence.

Turning the car in a slow circle, using its headlights, he looked for cars hidden in the darkness or for a silhouette that didn't belong. All he saw were some tiny pairs of glistening eyes, eyes that were there one second and then gone the next.

Out of the car, he had a look inside the utility shed, a flimsy old wooden structure that held nothing more than a broken rake handle and a million spiderwebs. He looked for tire tracks that didn't belong to the Subaru. And he listened. It was a waste of time. All he could hear was the faint sound of flowing water and the chittering of insects. About ten minutes later he heard the distinctive sound of tires spitting out rocks on the dirt road and he caught the sweep of headlights coming his way.

King poked his head back into the car, checked the dashboard clock, and clapped his hands together. "Right on time."

But even before the car came to a stop, King felt something wasn't right. The car wasn't right. The man who'd hired him wasn't the four-door-sedan type, and when he saw the stranger get out of the car, King knew there might be trouble. So when King got out of the Subaru, he came out with his nine-millimeter pointed right at the man's mid-section.

"Relax, tough guy," the stranger said, raising his empty hands to the sky.

"Who are you?" King asked.

"I'm the guy with your money." And then, as if anticipating King's next question, he said, "You didn't think our mutual friend was really going to drive around with nearly a million in cash in his front seat, did you? He strike you as the kind of man to do that?"

"Let's see it. And, mister, if you know what's good for you, reach back into the car slow, very slow."

The man did as King demanded and pulled a big leather satchel out of the sedan. He swung it, tossing it so that it landed about ten feet in front of King's car. "It's all there, but go ahead and check."

King, keeping the nine-millimeter raised, took slow, measured steps toward the bag. "Stay right where you are."

"It's all there."

"So you said."

"You don't recognize me, do you?" the money man asked. "How do you think the shithead who hired you found you?"

King waved his gun dismissively. "I got no time for this. Don't matter to me who you are."

Then, finally, with the money tugging him to his knees like a magnet, King lowered his gun and unzipped the satchel. "Hey, what the f— ? Newspapers! Goddamned news-papers. You mother —"

King swung the nine-millimeter back up, but it was already too late. When he looked up from the leather bag, he saw something that confused him into inaction. It looked like an orange oil filter. Then he noticed it was attached to the end of a gun. Just as he made sense of it, there was a flash. He was already dead by the time the soft bark of the shot reached his ears. Good thing he was dead, too. As hard as his head hit the rock in the dirt beneath him, it would have really hurt.

35

For the first time in Jesse's recent memory, Nita Thompson and the mayor seemed pleased to breathe the same air he did. He knew better. It wouldn't last. In fact, the mayor was trying her darnedest to poke holes in their détente, even as Nita Thompson was working the phones with the Boston media.

"You're one-hundred-percent positive these are the men?" Mayor Walker asked, biting her lip in anticipation.

"No."

"No!"

"These are the names given to me by a confidential informant and Rudy Walsh picked both men out of separate photo arrays. Am I sure these are the men? Yes. Am I a hundred percent sure? No."

"I'm going to go in front of cameras and microphones in an hour and I don't intend to look foolish when I do so, nor do I want to be proved a fool later on."

"Prisons are full of innocent men and women. Just ask anyone inside. But there are actually a few who don't belong there, and that's not right. No doubt the people who put them in there were sure they were guilty. Maybe they were a hundred percent sure."

"Save the sermons for Sunday school, Jesse. Give me an answer."

"I'm as sure as I'm going to be until I get a voluntary confession."

"This confidential informant. You trust him?"

"I didn't say it was a him."

"Don't be obstinate, Jesse."

"I trust my source and there was no doubt in Rudy Walsh's mind. He didn't hesitate for a second. Went right to both of them."

Nita Thompson put down the phone and stepped between the nearly warring parties, finding herself in the unlikely position of peacemaker.

"What's going on?" she asked. "This is a good day all around. A win for the mayor and for the Paradise PD."

Jesse said, "When we bring them in, it'll be a win."

The mayor pointed at Jesse. "And he can't say he's a hundred percent sure these are the perpetrators."

That displeased Thompson.

"Look, Stone, the mayor is going to put herself on the line here. So you better be damned sure about your facts."

Jesse had reached his politics-tolerance threshold. He had been through this same two-step in L.A. with a few high-profile homicide cases. Ones where there was a lot of public pressure to solve the cases and/or a load of political capital to be gained. The pols and the commissioners were always hot to parade any piece of good news in front of the media but never wanted to risk blow-back if the details turned out to be less than rock-solid. He'd been through it on an almost yearly basis here in Paradise. If it wasn't the mayor, it was a selectman who wanted to reap all the benefit while letting Jesse take all the risk. His job had been threatened so many times, he'd lost count. He stared directly into Nita Thompson's eyes.

"No, Nita, you look. You want the mayor to take a lap of honor before we even have these guys in custody and have a chance to question them, that's on you."

Thompson withered under Jesse's gaze, her upper lip twitching slightly. She didn't like it, but she knew he was right. The mayor screwed up her face, opened her mouth to say something. Nita Thompson stopped her by speaking first.

"What do you suggest, Chief?"

"Let the mayor make a brief statement. Something about her commitment to keeping Paradise safe for its citizens, but noncommittal in terms of the suspects. Then let her turn the announcement about the potential suspects over to Lundquist and me. She gets face time on camera, but it's the staties and the Paradise PD who'll take the lumps if I'm wrong."

Nita Thompson fiddled with her fingers and her lips as she listened. "I'll never underestimate you again, Chief," she said. "You're better at this game than I imagined."

Jesse shook his head in disdain.

"What's that about, Jesse?" the mayor wanted to know. "Nita just gave you a compliment. The polite thing to do is to say 'Thank you.'"

"Game? Polite thing to do? This is where people like you, Miss Thompson, and I part ways. You see this as a game, as a lever to boost your career or a club to beat mine down. I played a game for a living for a long time. I know what a game is and I know what police work is. I never get them confused. When you decide how you want the press conference to go, call me."

He turned and headed out of the mayor's office, making sure not to slam the door shut behind him.

36

There was a lot more media in the room than Jesse would have believed for an announcement that just as easily could have been put out in a succinct press release, but he realized this was how it was going to be until the mayor ran for whatever office was the next rung on the ambition ladder. The one thing that gave him hope was the clause in the Paradise charter prohibiting a current officeholder in town to run for county, state, or national office without first resigning from their position in Paradise. Not that Jesse thought he'd click his heels on the day Walker resigned and left town with Nita Thompson. Politicians came and went, but one was much like the other. When the crime rate was low, they took the credit. When it ticked up or particularly when there was violence, they came looking for a scapegoat. Chief Scapegoat was Jesse Stone's unofficial title.

Mayor Walker raised her hands to shush the crowd. She stood in front of the microphone-laden lectern, Jesse and Lundquist behind her left shoulder. Nita Thompson lurked off to her right.

"Good afternoon, ladies and gentlemen. I'm going to make a very brief statement," she said, "after which I am going to turn the lectern over to Paradise chief of police Jesse Stone and Brian Lundquist from the state police. They will answer all of your questions."

As the mayor spoke of keeping Paradise safe for its citizens and visitors, Jesse noticed Nita Thompson studying the crowd, checking out members of the press, taking a head count of who had shown up and who hadn't. He also imagined she was trying to figure out which members of the press were ready to pounce. Jesse understood that the calculus of digital media and modern politics meant there were no longer any unimportant public appearances. The least noteworthy elected official in the smallest town in the most remote reaches of the nation might turn up in a viral video on YouTube if he or she made a big enough ass of themselves. These days, even the local dog catcher had to seem presidential on-air. It was also why Jesse was happy he didn't have to run for office and why Nita Thompson had advised the mayor to take Jesse's advice and let the cops take all the risks. That was a cop's job, wasn't it, to take the risks?

Thompson looked over at Jesse and nodded. Jesse nodded back. It was a familiar if unexpected show of mutual respect. It was what happened on the baseball field when you faced a player you hated but admired for his skill and competitiveness. It had been a long time between those kinds of grudging looks for Jesse. And Jesse wasn't big on doffing his cap to murderers and thieves. He knew that most career criminals were losers, lazy men and women who lacked impulse control and who sometimes got lucky. Criminal masterminds were for TV and books. The movies, too, probably, but Jesse enjoyed only Westerns.

He had come across very few exceptions to the lazy-loser profile. There was Crow, of course, Jesse's dark opposite number: cool, self-contained, supremely competent, and irresistible to women. He grinned, thinking of Crow. It didn't last, as Jesse thought of the other exception he'd encountered in Paradise. That exception had murdered Diana. The sting of that encounter would stay with Jesse for the rest of his life. In fact, he was so distracted by reliving that awful moment that he didn't hear the mayor call his name. It was only when he noticed Nita Thompson nodding furiously at him and he felt Lundquist tap him on the shoulder that he came back to the present. But even as he came most of the way back into the moment, all he wanted was a drink. No, not a drink. Lots of drinks.

Jesse had been able to hold the memories at bay for the last few days, distracted by the case, by the mayor's machinations, and by whatever was going on between him and Tamara. But now it was back, all of it, the scene playing over in his head even as he stepped up to the microphone. He had fooled himself that he could hold the memories at arm's length and that as long as he could, he could control his drinking. As he started to speak, he thought he could hear Dix laughing at him.

When the press conference was over, after Jesse had identified the two suspects and Lundquist had said his part, after they had answered all the questions — mostly the same three questions asked in different ways: *How do you know these are the two men? How close are you to arresting them? Are they dangerous?* — and the press had left town hall to go file their stories, Jesse took off. But of all people, it was Nita

Thompson who tracked him down before he could get into his Explorer.

"Are you all right?" she asked with what sounded like real concern in her voice.

He lied. "Uh-huh. Why?"

"Because for the first time since I've met you, you seemed shaken up there. In my few months here with the mayor, I've studied you, Jesse Stone."

"Like a lab rat?"

"Hardly. I'm interested to know what makes a man like you tick."

"Batteries."

"Very funny, Chief."

Given where he was headed and what he meant to do when he got there, Jesse wasn't about to argue with her. But she had his attention.

"Why the shift in strategy?" he asked. "Tired of playing the bad cop?"

She didn't flinch. "I'm not playing the bad cop. I'm doing my job. But this isn't strategy and I'm not working now."

"People who do your job are always on the clock."

"Most of the time, that's true."

"What's different now?"

"I'm tired of being alone here," she said, digging a cigarette out of her bag and lighting it. "I could use some company other than the mayor."

Jesse had to admit she sounded sincere and that under other circumstances he might have asked her to join him in his plunge down the rabbit hole. In some ways she resembled Abby, another woman who had met a bad end because she was close to Jesse. That realization about Thompson's resemblance to Abby only increased Jesse's thirst and his desire to get out of there. He raised his arm and pointed south.

"What are you doing, Jesse?"

"Boston's fifteen miles that way. Easy not to be lonely there."

Thompson took in a deep lungful of smoke and let it out slowly, a wry smile on her face.

"I take it that's a no," she said.

"It's a not today."

She flicked the cigarette down and tamped it out under her shoe. "Fair enough."

He nodded and pulled open the Explorer's door. When he got in, Thompson tapped on the driver's-side window. Jesse lowered it.

"You're wrong about Boston," she said. "I went to school there. Sometimes it can be the loneliest place on earth."

Jesse watched her retreat back toward town hall and thought about how hard most people worked at hiding who and what they really were.

37

It was the phone. It sounded far, far away, and when it stopped ringing he wasn't sure he hadn't dreamed it. Its ring, real or imagined, roused him just enough to make him aware of the pounding in his head and the intense nausea welling up in him. He thought about trying to get up to get water, to swallow some aspirin, or to just throw up. But he couldn't move, pinned to the sofa like a bug catcher's specimen waiting for the jar or to be framed for a spot on the wall next to Ozzie.

Ozzie. Ozzie had been his only company last night as he slowly drank himself into the state he found himself in now. He forced his eyes open. That hurt almost as much as the pounding in his head, but he had to look at the poster. Jesse liked the sight of the soft-handed, acrobatic shortstop suspended in midair, liked to imagine how he might've handled the same play. He was a different kind of shortstop than the Wizard of Oz. Jesse's hands weren't as soft. Nobody's were. He hadn't been nearly as acrobatic, and though his range was above average, it couldn't touch Ozzie's. But as all the scouts had said of him, Jesse had the most powerful infield arm they had ever seen, better even than Shawon Dunston's. That meant Jesse could position himself more deeply in the hole and had more time to make the hard plays than other shortstops. He remembered thinking he couldn't get more deeply in the hole than he already was when he slipped back into unconsciousness.

This time it wasn't the phone that roused him, but someone shaking him. *Tamara? No, it had been just Ozzie and him last night. Had he misremembered?* He went into fight-or-flight mode. For Jesse it wasn't ever much of a choice. It was always fight. He jumped off the sofa, swinging his left arm in front of him to sweep away the immediate threat and to create space between himself and his attacker. Only the actions that seemed to him to be lightning-fast were, in fact, laughably slow and disjointed. His left arm missed his perceived attacker by a mile and his leap off the couch was more of a stumble and fall over the coffee table. And when he hit the floor, the pain in his head nearly split him in two.

"Jesse! Jesse! Get up! Get up." He heard a woman's voice call to him from the top of the well into which he'd fallen.

"Jesse. Jesse." Another woman was at the top of the well, calling to him.

Then he blacked out.

When the cold water hit him he startled. He reflexively shook his head, but the pain of it nearly drove him back into his stupor, cold water or not. The water stopped.

"Jesse, for chrissakes, c'mon. Get up!"

When he didn't open his eyes, the water came back on and stayed on until Jesse opened his eyes and they stayed open.

"All right. All right. Shut it off," he said, holding his right hand up in front of his face. "Shut it off."

The water stopped.

"You among the living now?" Molly asked, kneeling down beside the tub in Jesse's downstairs bathroom.

He didn't answer, his eyelids flickering, shutting. When they shut, the water came on again and Molly let it run until Jesse had lifted himself up onto his knees. And when he got on his knees, that sensation he hated hit him. It hit him hard, the bathroom spinning off into space. He climbed out of the tub, crawled over to the toilet, and heaved up the contents of his stomach.

"You can wait for me in the living room," Molly said to someone standing beyond the bathroom door.

Now Jesse lay on the cold tiles, grabbing his head, but at least the spins had stopped. Molly picked up Jesse's head and cradled it in her lap. She opened his mouth and slowly poured a bottle of water into him. He coughed some up, but he got most of it down. When that one was finished, she poured another one into him.

"Aspirin," he said, pointing to the medicine cabinet. "Aspirin."

"Here. Take these. The ME said they'll do you more good than aspirin or any of that other stuff."

Jesse swallowed them with more water, but they still went down hard. He sat up, gingerly, leaning his back against the tub.

"Who else is here?"

"Alisha."

"You shouldn't have brought her."

"And you shouldn't need me to wake you up out of a drunken stupor to save your job. It's not like I had a big choice about who to bring."

"Wait a second," he said, rapidly blinking his eyes as if to shake the cobwebs out. "The ME gave you those pills. When did you see

—" He didn't finish the question.

"That's right, Jesse. We've got another body. This one's in the nature preserve along Sawtooth Creek."

"Another body? Who?"

"Gunshot. One to the head. One to the heart. Small-caliber. No exit wounds. Male, white, in his fifties. It looks like it's one of the suspects."

"Which one?"

"Curnutt."

"King?"

"I think so. Can't check the body for ID until the ME's done with him."

Jesse asked, "How long ago?"

"Doc says it looks like he's been there for twenty-four hours plus."

"No, Molly. How long since somebody called it in?"

"About an hour. I've been calling you on both phones since. After the way you looked at the press conference today and when you didn't pick up, I figured you must've tied one on. When the ME showed up at the scene, I told her what I was thinking about you and she gave me those pills."

"Alert the staties and then get back there. I'll be there soon as I can manage."

"I'm leaving Alisha here to drive you. Don't even argue with me, Jesse. You're in no shape to get behind the wheel of a vehicle and you won't be for a while."

He didn't argue.

Molly stood, asked, "Should I call the mayor's office?"

"You leave the mayor to me. I don't want you to have to lie to cover for me."

"Since when did that bother you?"

"What's that supposed to mean?"

"You know what it means, Jesse."

She didn't bother explaining. Instead, she gritted her teeth and left.

38

The sun was just coming up as Alisha turned Jesse's Explorer toward the nature preserve. He got an uneasy feeling in his already knotted gut when they turned past the open gate and onto the access road. In his drunken, hungover fog, he hadn't given much thought to why Kirk Curnutt had been murdered way out here. He wondered if this had been the handiwork of Curnutt's partner, Hump. It had been Jesse's experience that honor among thieves was as sturdy as tissue paper and that it was easily torn apart by greed and self-preservation. But those two things cut just as sharply in the straight world as they did among thieves. He'd seen plenty of violence done in Bel Air, Brentwood, and even Paradise for the same reasons it happened in East L.A. or Skid Row.

When the Explorer came to a stop next to Tamara Elkin's Jeep, Jesse turned to look at

Alisha. They hadn't spoken at all on the ride over. Even now, Jesse didn't speak, not right away.

"What is it, Jesse?"

"If there's trouble, I don't want you to lie to cover anything up. Not for me or for Molly. Molly's pension and benefits are secure and they won't do anything to her anyway, but you're still in your probationary period. You can be fired for cause."

"But —"

"That's an order. Someone from the mayor's office or the Board of Selectmen makes an inquiry, you tell the truth. You're going to make a helluva cop and you're not going to screw that up on my account. Understood?"

She nodded.

"Okay. Now get out of the car."

When she was gone, Jesse drank another bottle of water, took some deep breaths, and stared at himself in the visor mirror. He supposed he looked as good as he was going to look. The early hour was about the only thing working in his favor. Not many people were at their best or looked their best at this time of the morning. He'd showered and rubbed some Bengay onto his bad shoulder. It wasn't that his shoulder hurt. For once it actually didn't, not even after his fall over the coffee table. He hoped the intense menthol odor would help overwhelm the stink of his scotch sweat. He'd brushed his teeth hard enough to take off the enamel and used mouthwash until it burned his throat.

The early hour had helped him in another way. The mayor was dead asleep when he called and seemed almost as foggy as he had been. He was careful not to offer up too many details, not that he had many. Nor did he give her a story about how much time had elapsed between the discovery of the body and his arrival at the scene. What she didn't know wouldn't hurt her . . . or him. He didn't want to risk tripping himself up. If those sorts of questions ever came up, he'd be better equipped to handle them when he was less hungover. He did give her the news that the body, pending verification, was likely that of one of the suspects in the Maude Cain case and that he'd apparently been shot to death. She'd gone silent for a second or two after that.

"Do you think it was his accomplice who killed him?" she asked, some of the sleep gone from her voice.

"It's possible, but so is anything else. We should know more soon."

That seemed to placate her. "Keep me

updated, Chief. I've got to make some calls" was all she'd said before hanging up.

Now that he was here, he figured he had at least a little while before Nita Thompson, the mayor herself, and the media began to show up. For the moment, the only people on scene were Jesse's allies, so there was no need for him to pretend he wasn't nursing a wicked hangover. The body-bag boys from Tamara's office were in their van waiting for the okay to take the body to the morgue. Jesse called Gabe over to him.

"Gabe, take Alisha to the station, then get back here."

Weathers didn't say anything, turning on his heel to go. Jesse watched him walk away, tap Alisha on the shoulder, and urge her toward his cruiser. She turned back and looked at Jesse over her shoulder. Her expression was no happier than it had been when he gave her the orders about telling the truth. But when Gabe's cruiser kicked up a cloud of dust on the dirt road, the time for hesitation was over.

After trying unsuccessfully to stretch the hangover achiness out of his body, Jesse approached Molly and Lundquist. Both of them were sipping coffee against the slight morning chill. Molly reached down by her feet, grabbed a second cup, and held it out to Jesse.

"Morning, Jesse. I think it's still hot," she said, as if she hadn't already seen Jesse earlier. "But don't make me swear to it."

He grabbed the cup from her and took a sip. "Hot enough." Coffee had never tasted so good. "Who called it in?"

"Anonymous male," she said. "Blocked number called in to the station, but not on the nine-one-one line."

Jesse didn't like that. "So there's no recording of it. Who took the call?"

"I did. Peter was the responding officer. Good thing, too, because he preserved the crime scene and began doing the evidence search as soon as he called me back to confirm it was a homicide. I called the ME and then you." Molly kept up the charade that it had only taken a call to get Jesse to the crime scene. She didn't know Lundquist well enough to trust his attitude toward Jesse and his drinking.

39

With the near-empty cup in his hand, Jesse stood at the boundary of yellow tape strung in a wide, misshapen circle around pine trees, oaks, and maples. At the far side of the circle were Tamara Elkin and the body of the man presumed to be King Curnutt. Inside the circle to Jesse's right was a blue Subaru and an old, weathered toolshed, its door flapping in the morning breeze. Peter Perkins, in a Tyvek suit and booties, was taking photos of the car.

"I need to talk to the ME," Jesse said, calling to Perkins. "Get me a pair of gloves and walk me over to her and fill me in."

Peter came to where Jesse was standing, handed him gloves, and lifted the tape. Jesse limboed under it, wincing as he did. Taking careful, measured steps, the two of them made their way slowly toward the ME. As they went, Perkins pointed to some tire tracks. *Car's stolen from some small town near the New Hampshire border. One set of tire tracks are definitely from the Subaru. Don't know about the other.* He pointed at faint impressions in the dirt that vaguely resembled footprints. *I'm pretty sure one set belongs to the vic, but there are lots of imprints around because runners use this area.*

"How was he killed?" Jesse asked.

"Close range. One to the head, one to the heart. I couldn't see any exit wounds. Another thing, Jesse," Perkins said. "If he used an automatic, the killer collected his brass.

"Something else. The vic was armed. I've bagged a Glock Nineteen that I found in very close proximity to the body. Killer must've surprised him."

"Or Curnutt knew him," Jesse said as they reached the ME and the body.

"Thanks, Peter."

"No problem. I'm almost done anyway. Just have to pack up and make some notes."

Jesse waited for Perkins to leave before kneeling down.

"You look almost as bad as him," Tamara said. "At least you smell a little better."

Jesse gave a slight nod toward the body. "I don't feel so well, either, but let's talk about him."

"I'm sure Peter already told you."

"Uh-huh. Been here for a day-plus. Killed by two at close range."

"Probably a .22 caliber," she said. "Small entry wounds, no exit wounds. None that are visible, at least. I'll know more when I get him on the table and cut the clothes off him."

"Can I pat him down?"

"One more thing, Jesse. The body was moved. Rolled over, I think, at least once," she said, pointing at a small patch of dried blood on a smashed-down area of brown grass and dirt to the left of the body.

"You think it was my man who moved him?"

"Unlikely," she said. "Perkins is too OCD to do that. My guess is it happened shortly afterward."

"Thanks, Doc. That it?"

"Now he's all yours. I'm going to go give my guys the okay to come get him. Your car here?"

Jesse stared up at her, puzzled. "Why?"

"I'll leave some pills for you in your front seat."

"Thanks."

He turned back to the body, but Tamara wasn't quite finished.

"Jesse."

"Yeah."

"Slow down. For goodness' sakes, please, slow down."

He knew what she meant. She knew he would, but she didn't want to stay to argue about it.

The body was on its back. The head wound *was* small, though obvious enough against the dead man's bloodless pale skin. The chest wound was less obvious, but that wasn't Jesse's concern at the moment. He checked the pockets of the dead man's cut-off sweatshirt and the front pockets of his jeans. No wallet. No ID. Nothing. He ran his gloved hands along the front, outsides, and insides of the victim's legs, and felt around his ankles. Again nothing. But he didn't come up empty when he gently turned the body over and patted down the vic's back pockets.

"Peter," Jesse said. "Bring an evidence bag over here."

Perkins didn't ask why, just carried a bag over to his boss. "What is it, Jesse?"

"An old index card with some letters and numbers written on it. Log it in and then bring it over to Lundquist. I think the state lab should get a close look at this asap."

"You think it's significant?"

Jesse didn't answer immediately, continu-

228

ing to pat the victim down to see if there was anything else on him. When he was done he looked up at Perkins.

"Significant? I don't know, but it's the only thing he's got on him."

"No wallet?"

"No nothing except that faded old card. Tell Lundquist I'll be right over."

When Jesse was done, he looked hard at Curnutt's remains. As far as Jesse could tell, what was left didn't amount to much. He hoped the same wasn't true for the index card.

40

The sun had finally taken a seat low in the sky about the time Jesse got to where Lundquist and Molly were waiting, Lundquist holding the evidence bag with the index card.

"Is this all he had on him?" Lundquist asked, waving the clear plastic bag in the air.

"One second, Brian." Jesse walked past him and went over to where Peter Perkins was packing away his equipment.

"What's up, Jesse?"

"Did you see the blood off to the side of the body?"

"I did. I got a sample of it, marked it in my notes, and got photos of it." Perkins tilted his head in confusion. "Why you asking?"

"You didn't move the body, did you?"

"You know I know better than that. All I did was check for a pulse to make a hundred percent sure he was dead. Then I backed away and followed procedure."

Jesse smiled as best he could, given how lousy he was feeling, and patted Perkins's left biceps. "Good work. I had to ask."

When Jesse got back to where Molly and Lundquist were standing, Lundquist repeated his question. "Is this all he had on him?"

"All I could find."

"An old index card. Not much to go on."

"I'm not so sure," Jesse said.

That got Molly's attention. "Not sure about what?"

"Something doesn't feel right about this."

"What feels right about murder?" she asked.

"It's not only that," Jesse said. "That car was stolen from up north. Why come back to Paradise? Why would he expose himself like that?"

Molly spoke first. "Maybe he had no choice, Jesse. Maybe he had left something behind in that shed on his way out of town, money or something he took from Maude's house we didn't know about." Jesse remained silent.

"More likely he was meeting someone and whoever it was didn't feel like sharing, possibly his partner," Lundquist said.

231

Jesse shook his head. "Maybe. I don't like it."

Molly pointed over Jesse's shoulder. "Well, you're going to like this even less."

When he turned, Jesse saw the mayor's black Suburban pulling to a stop. He had hoped he might be able to get away from the scene before the mayor showed, if only to shower again, shave, and shut his eyes for an hour.

"Brian," he said, turning back to Lundquist. "See what your lab can do with that. I'll have Peter send the rest of the stuff over as soon as possible."

"Okay, Jesse, but we're not done talking about this crime scene and what you don't like about it."

"Fine. Go ahead. We'll talk later," Jesse said. "Molly, you too. I'll deal with the mayor."

"You sure, Jesse?"

"Always. Now get out of here."

But as he watched Lundquist and Molly retreat to their vehicles, he noticed only Nita Thompson getting out of the Suburban, two large cups of coffee in her hands. There was no sign of Mayor Walker. As she got to Jesse, Nita handed him one of the cups.

"I think this is how you like it," she said. "But you look like you could use it whether it's how you like it or not."

He took a big sip of the steaming coffee, the smell of it filling his head. He was almost as thankful for the aroma as he was for the taste of the coffee. "Thanks. Where's Mayor Walker?"

Nita ignored the question. "Rough night?"

"I've had rougher ones. The mayor?"

"Right. Sorry. I advised her not to show her face here until we knew what we were dealing with."

"That's why the media hasn't shown up. You don't know how to spin this yet."

"I don't know why I ever underestimated you," she said. "Is it him, Kirk Curnutt?"

"Looks like him, but he had no ID on him and the car was stolen. We'll be certain as soon as we run the prints."

"So what else do we have, Jesse? I mean, who would kill someone out here, of all places?"

"I'll tell you that when we have some idea about the evidence."

"C'mon, Jesse, give me something."

He thought about that for a second before answering. His instinct was to say nothing. He still didn't trust Nita as far as he could throw her, but he also knew that having her in his debt for once might not be a bad thing.

"There's something not right about this."

She laughed a laugh disconnected from amusement. "Not right! Nothing's right about this."

"That's not what I meant. I've done a fair amount of homicide investigations. I've been to a lot of murder scenes and this one just feels wrong."

"Wrong how?"

Again, he hesitated. He didn't want to say anything that she might be able to turn against him later if his sense was wrong.

"Just this," he said. "If you were Curnutt, would you come back to Paradise? And it was called in by an anonymous caller, not to nine-one-one, but to the station landline. Someone wanted us to know the body was here and wasn't waiting for a jogger to find him."

"You think it was the killer?"

"Maybe."

"Jeez, Jesse, do you think you have some kind of psycho on your hands?"

Nita's use of the word *you* didn't escape Jesse's notice. Jesse had given her all he was going to. "I think a lot of things right now. That's why I have to see what comes of the evidence."

Nita Thompson shook her head. "Two murders in town in less than a week. It's a nightmare for all of us."

Jesse understood that the biggest nightmare was his. Nita and the mayor's nightmare was about how to spin the news and control the fallout. His was solving the murders and saving his job.

41

Jesse didn't particularly enjoy using his authority in a threatening way, but there were times he just had to. He hated bullying people. Hated bullies. Hated them as a kid, as a ballplayer — even when they were teammates — and as a cop. As a cop most of all. He had his share of run-ins with them since his arrival in Paradise. It never ended well for the bullies. And so it was with very little enthusiasm that he warned the guys who worked for the ME's office about not revealing the exact location of where the body had been found.

"Not a word," he said, giving them both an icy stare. "Not to your wives, not to your kids, not to your friends. No one. You do and you'll answer to me."

He'd asked Tamara to reinforce his message. She agreed, but was curious.

"What's the point, Jesse?"

"Until I know what's really going on here,

I don't need any other headaches."

"You know, Jesse, it's impolite to lie to your friends. What's the real reason?"

"I don't like speculating about crimes, especially murders, but my hunch is that the person who killed our vic called it in."

"Why, and why wait a day?"

"Good questions. The obvious answer is that he wanted us to know. The less obvious reason is why he wanted us to know. Why wait a day? My guess is that he was hoping a jogger or someone walking their dog would stumble across the body. When that didn't happen, he got impatient."

"Sounds more like he needed you to find the body more than wanted you to," she said.

Jesse smiled at her. "Exactly. It's like he needs the attention of the press. So I want to starve him of the attention as much as we can. Things work best when everyone's agendas line up. At the moment, I don't want to deal with the press any more than the mayor does. And if the killer's trying to screw with my department . . . good luck with that."

"What if you're too successful with robbing him of attention and he kills again?"

Jesse ignored the question. "When will I get the autopsy results?"

"Voilà!" she said, handing him the file. "It's him, by the way, Curnutt. We printed him and sent the prints to Lundquist and your office. Got an immediate hit."

"Good. And don't worry about another body turning up. Curnutt's wasn't an impulse or random killing."

"You look more human than you did this morning, and you smell a lot better."

He answered without looking up from the file. "Molly gave me a few hours' cover and I got some sleep and some food in me. Amazing what a shower, shave, and some cologne will do."

"Okay, Jesse, leave the file and get out of my office. I've got work to do."

"Thanks, Doc," he said, put the file down on Tamara's desk, and walked to the door.

"Jesse," she called after him. "You can't keep drinking this way. You just can't."

"Why not? Afraid my liver will explode?"

"There's that, too, but no. You can't keep on like this because it's selfish and you're not a selfish man."

Tamara's parting words rang in Jesse's head louder than the hammer that had pounded in it earlier that day. So loud that he could barely pay attention as he sat across the table from Lundquist at Daisy's. He did

have the wherewithal to introduce Lundquist to Daisy when she brought the cof-
feepot over to their booth. She was her usual
diplomatic self. Which is to say it was a good
thing Lundquist wasn't easily offended.

"Lundquist, huh? Norwegian?"

"Swedish."

"Too bad." She didn't elaborate.

Jesse said, "He's taken over Captain
Healy's job."

"Healy. I liked Healy. He was a good tip-
per. Swedes good tippers?"

"Depends," Lundquist said.

Daisy sneered at him and shook her head.
"Wrong answer, son. Wrong answer."

"She always so charming?" Lundquist
asked when she walked away.

Jesse said, "On her good days, yeah. You
read the autopsy report?"

"It's Curnutt."

Jesse wanted to know, "Anything else in
the report catch your eye?"

Lundquist didn't answer right away. He
reached for his coffee mug instead, put in
an obscene amount of sugar and a few
drops of cream. Halfway to his lips, he put
his coffee mug back on the table. "Wait a
second. Is this right? There were traces of
filter paper and metal fragments in the
wounds not from the bullets dug out of the

body. Holy sh— crap, the killer used a homemade sound suppressor."

"Looks that way."

"What's that tell you, Brian?"

"It's evidence of premeditation."

"What else?"

"He used a homemade suppressor. Tells me he was an amateur."

"Or not. Maybe he just wants us to think he is."

Lundquist rubbed his left hand across his cheek. "You think this guy is playing with us?"

Jesse didn't say anything. He just sat there drinking his coffee.

42

This time, the press conference was held at the police station and Mayor Walker was nowhere in sight. Even Nita Thompson hadn't gotten closer than a TV screen in her office. If Jesse's plan to starve the media of information went wrong, it would blow up in his face and his face alone. It would also supply the mayor with the excuse she'd been looking for to make Jesse an issue. Nothing like firing someone to look like a woman of action and to draw attention away from the real issue at hand.

Jesse understood the risks. He knew that Nita Thompson hadn't gone along with his plan out of the goodness of her heart. He still wasn't sure she had a heart. No, she had gone along with it because there was only an upside for her client. It was a win-win situation for the mayor, no matter how things turned out. But why had Jesse done it if all the risk was his? That was simple.

He'd bought himself and his cops room to maneuver. In the end, what mattered to Jesse wasn't losing his job or looking good in the press. What mattered was catching the bad guys.

What had become pretty clear to him, even if it wasn't yet clear to anyone else, was that the ransacking of Maude Cain's house, her death, and Kirk Kingston Curnutt's murder were a continuation of the same crime. In spite of Jesse's own rules about jumping to conclusions, he knew there had to be a connection. The bigger question was: Why murder Curnutt in that spot? Why murder him in Paradise at all? The answer seemed an obvious one: to draw as much attention as possible. For the moment, there was nothing to do on Curnutt's homicide until some of the forensics results came back.

"Molly, come into my office," he said after the press had cleared out.

She wasn't happy. "What is it, Jesse? I'm exhausted."

"Give me five minutes."

"Five minutes! I gave you two hours and I've been on the clock since . . . Jeez, I don't even remember which shift I started on."

"Think of the overtime pay."

"Right after I stop thinking about strangling you. You drink and I suffer. How does that work?"

"Believe me, Molly, I suffered. I'm still suffering. I'm probably going to suffer all night if I don't take a —"

"Woe is you."

"Molly!"

"I'm sorry, Jesse Stone. I love you, but I'm done with risking my ass for you."

"Come on, Molly."

"It's not funny anymore. I've got two of the girls in college, and my pension, good as it is, wouldn't cut it."

"I'm sorry, Molly. You know what I think of you."

"It's not even me, Jesse. When Suit helps me with you, it's one thing. Okay, he looks up to you. He would risk anything for you. He has. That was his choice. But you made me put Alisha at risk, and that's where I draw the line."

And there they were again, Tamara Elkin's words about Jesse's drinking, his selfishness going round and round in his head.

He nodded. "It won't happen again."

Molly was skeptical, but she had already said more than she wanted to. She didn't have any energy left for a fight.

"All right, I surrender, Jesse. What did you want?"

"Maude Cain's house."

"What about it?"

"Remember I asked you to go through it and look for a —"

"A log book or registration books. Right."

"Well?"

Without a word, Molly stood up from the chair across from Jesse's desk and left the office. She came back a minute later carrying an evidence bag. Inside the clear plastic was what seemed to be three old-fashioned composition books, the kind with the rigid black-and-white cardboard covers and the black fabric binding. The kind Jesse had used as a kid in school but were no longer very common.

"In all the excitement, I forgot about it," Molly said. "I found them in the basement. They're pretty beat up and they're more about financial recordkeeping than they are registration books, but there are plenty of names in them."

"Recognize any of them?"

Molly shrugged.

"All right, get out of here. Come in tomorrow when you want, but once you're here, you're going to get all the overtime you can handle . . . for the right reasons."

She left without another word. When the door closed behind her, Jesse reached into his drawer for some gloves. But before examining the notebooks, he stood, looked out his window at the water, at Stiles Island. When he turned back around, he reached for his desk phone and dialed Dix's number.

43

He hadn't seen Dix for months. They had spoken on the phone once or twice since Diana's murder and Dix had made some noises about the possibility of Jesse coming in to talk about what had gone down. He had offered the sessions free of charge. It wasn't standard operating procedure, but most cops don't become psychotherapists. Dix had a unique perspective. He understood the kinds of risks cops and those close to them live with day to day and, for that reason alone, he was willing to waive his fee. But Jesse couldn't bring himself to do it. He'd made an appointment and canceled it a few days before he was to go. That was two months ago. Now here he was again, finally.

They shook hands, Dix holding on to Jesse's hand a little longer than usual. He stared into his eyes a little deeper than normal. Jesse understood that this was Dix's way of expressing his sorrow beyond the words he had spoken to him over the phone last night. Dix gestured to the chair Jesse had sat in for most of his previous sessions and Jesse took it with little ceremony. They sat there in silence for a few minutes, feeling each other out. This was how it went unless Jesse came in to discuss a case in the guise of coming for a real session. Dix got paid either way.

"You called me, Jesse," Dix said, prodding his patient. "That means you've got something to talk about."

"Uh-huh."

"A case?"

"No."

Another two minutes passed before Jesse broke the silence.

"You think I'm selfish?"

"Do you?"

Jesse smiled at the corners of his mouth, not because Dix was funny, but because he answered Jesse's question with a question. This was how it went with them, and Jesse found some small comfort in Dix's predictable responses, even if they often infuriated him.

"I don't usually think about it."

"But you're thinking about it now?"

"Yesterday, Molly and Tamara Elkin —"

"Tamara Elkin?"

"The county medical examiner. I've mentioned her before . . . I think. Both Molly and Tamara told me I was selfish."

"Do their opinions matter?"

"I'm here."

Now it was Dix's turn to smile. "You pay more per spoken word than any other client I have ever had, and that's saying something."

"They didn't say *I* was selfish, not exactly, and it was more than what they said."

The light of understanding went on behind Dix's eyes, but all he said was "Go on."

More silence. Then, "They said my drinking was selfish."

"You're drinking heavily again?"

Jesse made a face that betrayed his feelings, which, for Jesse, was out of the ordinary. Part of his whole self-contained aura was that he didn't give away what was going on inside him. He supposed he paid a price for that, but it was how he was wired. Even Dix was surprised by it.

"I know you think some of my questions are obvious ones," Dix said, "but why don't you put that expression into words?"

"If I wanted to do that, I wouldn't have made the face."

"Okay, I'll do it for you, Jesse, since we're already being a little unconventional today. Your expression says to me that the woman you loved and had asked to marry was murdered in front of you and that you blame yourself for it. So only an idiot would ask if you were drinking. That about sum it up?"

"About."

"But see, Jesse, here's the thing. Not everybody would be drinking heavily again, not even all alcoholics."

"Well, they're not me."

"Nobody is. Would anybody want to be?"

"Getting metaphysical on me now, Dix?"

But Dix wasn't having it. "What happened that made these two important women in your life choose yesterday to tell you your drinking was selfish?"

Jesse explained about how, during the press conference at town hall, the guilt and grief had crept back in, how Nita's looks and manner had reminded him of Abby, of Abby's murder. He explained how that started a chain reaction that resulted in him reliving Diana's death. He talked about how he had guzzled himself into oblivion. He recounted how Molly and Alisha had probably saved his job.

"Do you think your drinking is selfish?"

Dix asked again.

"Yes."

"That's always the easy part."

Jesse furrowed his brow. "What is?"

"Recognition."

"What's the hard part?"

Dix laughed. "Deciding what to do about it."

44

Hump had done what King asked in his note and hadn't ventured out of the motel room for the last few days. It was easy enough. Flush with his seven grand cash, he'd ordered in Chinese food and pizza, but only from places that had Pepsi bottles or cans. He was pretty sure some chick at a Chinese takeout place had cursed at him after he told her to skip the order if they didn't sell Pepsi. She kept telling him "Only Coke. Only Coke," her voice getting louder and louder until she was screaming at him, "Only Coke!"

Looking in the mirror now, finger-combing his hair after getting out of the shower, he thought that she wouldn't have screamed at him if he was standing right in front of her. *No, she woulda shut her stupid mouth and offered to go next door to the deli and buy him some Pepsi. Woulda paid for it, too.* And he had also splurged on some movies. He had watched some of them three times. He liked the one about the guy trapped on Mars. He liked that one a lot. When you've been inside, been in solitary, you understand what that's like. Except that inside, hope runs out before the bad food. He also watched some skin flicks. He didn't like them as much because they only frustrated him. He had a better chance of getting trapped on Mars than getting to be with any of them girls. Then he looked at the wad of cash on the dresser and realized that even a guy with a face like his could get anything with enough money.

Hump clicked on the TV, figuring he'd lay low for one more day and then move on. He could go a long way on what was left of his seven grand. Plus he still had some of his release money stashed away. He thought about where he might go. He thought about going someplace hot and dry, someplace where it didn't rain a lot. He didn't like rain. Hated it. It was always bleak inside, but there were times the rain darkened the place so, he thought about killing himself or killing someone else just to make the rain in his head go away. He wanted to get as far from the rain as he could get. Tomorrow, he thought, when he left this dump, he'd get himself some maps of the Southwest, buy himself a bus ticket, and just go. But first he had to see about selling the dragonfly ring.

He pulled out the drawer, grabbed his bundled-up white socks, and carefully pulled them apart. He slid his hand down into one of the socks, the one with the tear above the ankle, and felt for the ring. Inside, you learn about how and where to hide things. You also learn to hide how you feel. It was always safer to never give away your feelings. You never wanted the other guys to know what you were thinking, but Hump couldn't hide the smile when he felt the ring there where he had left it. He held it up to the light as he did each time he looked at it. It was a beautiful thing to behold. He imagined it on a woman's red-tipped finger, the long tail of the dragonfly curling around her pale skin. The four jewel-encrusted wings spreading slightly across her pinkie and middle fingers. He hadn't ever had much beauty in his life and had certainly never had beautiful things.

Watching it sparkle in the light, he thought he might not fence it. He wanted to have one precious thing to hold on to, even if it was a fancy lady's ring that he couldn't wear or show to anyone. He knew that even the best deal he would get would only make him pennies on the dollar. Maybe less, because besides the big diamonds that were the dragonfly's eyes, he had no idea about what kind of stones were in the setting. Rubies, sapphires, and emeralds, he figured. But even if they were, so what? He didn't know what they were worth, didn't know what the diamonds were worth. The gold setting had some value, though that was the least of it. He placed the ring back into the sock, bundled the socks back together. And placed the bundle back in the drawer.

He rubbed the thick stubble that he'd let grow on his face since the day the old lady died. By tomorrow, he thought, it would almost be a beard. Between a beard, sunglasses, and a hat he'd be okay. He sprayed some Right Guard under his arms, threw on some clothes, and reached for the clicker. He plopped himself down on the bed, thinking King would know what the ring was worth. King was smart like that. But King would lose his mind if he found out Hump had taken the ring. Even though no one was there to see it, Hump shrugged his shoulders. Maybe they'd hook up again someday. They were good together, on the inside and out.

He slid his index finger over the clicker buttons, searching for the ones that would get him to the paid movie channels, but when he looked up at the screen he stopped moving his finger. Stopped moving at all. Stopped breathing for a second, because there on the screen was Hump's booking photo, next to King's booking photo. Then King's photo was enlarged, completely displacing Hump's photo. Then King's photo disappeared and was replaced by the image of a tall, good-looking cop standing before a row of microphones. Hump turned up the sound so he could hear what the cop was saying. When he heard, he turned off the TV.

He and King hadn't been partners, not like some guys they'd known inside who worked together for years. They weren't part of a crew. They were just two guys who had shared a cell for a few years and got along, each watching the other's back. King was older and smarter, but he was as big a screwup as Hump, maybe even a bigger one. Still, King had been his friend, and now his friend had been murdered. Hump knew he should walk out of that room and never look back. He should fence the ring and just get on that bus to the place where it didn't rain. Instead he clicked off the TV and searched the drawers King had used for his stuff while he'd been there.

45

Jesse waited for Henry Wilmott in the lobby outside the curator's office. The Cain Library was at the center of what used to be all of Paradise. What the townspeople now called Old Town. It was where most of the quaint shops were, the ones that catered to the folks who came in spring for the garden tours and tours of the Victorian houses, the ones who came in summer for the regatta, and the ones who came in the fall for the changing of the leaves. These shops that had once been home to the butcher, baker, dry-goods store, greengrocer, and cobbler were now leased by cafés, antiques stores, art galleries, and tourist shops that sold souvenirs, sunblock, old-timey whaling paraphernalia, and plastic scrimshaw. Old Town wasn't far from Pilgrim Cove and the old Cain house.

Jesse got tired of sitting. Between his visit to Dix and the press conference, he was full of the kind of energy he got charged with when he did unsettling or unpleasant things. Though his visit with Dix went as he had expected and the press conference had gone off without a hitch, he was wound up. He thought it might be a rebound effect from the day before and that in a few more hours he would begin to feel the drag on his body from the drinking, the nausea, the coffee, and the lack of sleep. It was an edgy, brittle kind of energy he was feeling as he strolled through the museum displays. Although it was called the Cain Library, the building also housed the Cain Museum. The museum told the story of the founders of Paradise and housed collections of art, finery — clothing, jewelry, silverware — family histories, and things like small stained-glass windows removed from their grand houses on the Bluffs before demolition.

"Jesse, Jesse, forgive me," said Henry Wilmott, scurrying toward him, his right hand extended. "I'm so sorry, but I was on the phone with the broker for one of the Salters. They want to make a contribution."

Wilmott was shorter than Jesse but not by much, though his hunched posture made him appear smaller than he actually was. His wispy gray hair, wire-rimmed glasses, and papery white skin gave him the look of a Dickens clerk. Jesse wasn't fooled. Henry Wilmott had a handshake like a vise.

"No problem, Henry."

"I saw the press conference on the local news at noon. This is a bad business. I mean, between poor Maude and this fellow. Awful stuff. Just awful."

"Uh-huh."

"So, Jesse, how can a lowly curator and librarian assist the chief of our local constabulary?"

"Molly tells me you're the man to talk to about the Cains."

"I believe I am. Yes, indeed I am. What about the Cains?" Then he talked over himself before Jesse could answer. "Poor Maude. I'm afraid she was the last in the line of a wonderful and generous family. Did you know her?"

"I did not."

"A shame. She was a lovely woman, really."

"So, Henry, I was wondering if you knew whether Maude kept any valuables in her house. Something either she or her family hadn't donated to a good cause or to the museum?"

Henry thought about it for a few seconds, then a light seemed to go on in his gray eyes behind his glasses. He made a hook of his index finger and waved it at Jesse.

"Come with me."

Jesse followed him back past the waiting area, past Wilmott's office, down two half-flights of stairs, and into an area that, unlike the wood-paneled walls and creaky-planked floor of the museum and library, was all concrete and steel. Wilmott reached into his pocket for a key and opened the large steel door before them. Inside, a ceiling light popped on. Wilmott tapped a code on a keypad affixed to the wall just below the light and motion sensor.

"Precaution, you know," he said, turning to Jesse. "We store our most valuable small pieces in here that are not currently on display. We store our artwork at a different facility. Please, have a seat."

Running down the center of the window-less room was a long, black marble-topped island. Six high stools on poles bolted to the floor were on either side of the island. At the center of the island were six magnifying lamps mounted on spring-loaded articulated arms. The walls of the room were actually drawers of varying sizes. Each drawer had a keypad on its face. Wilmott walked over to a large drawer opposite Jesse and punched in a code. A buzzer sounded, a lock unlatched, and Wilmott pulled out the drawer. He reached in and pulled out a foot-square blue velvet–lined tray and placed it before Jesse.

Featured on the tray were a pair of earrings, a necklace, a brooch, a bracelet, a decorative hair comb, and three bangles. All of the pieces were of a dragonfly motif, but the brooch was especially beautiful. All of the jewelry was exquisitely crafted in gold and featured diamonds, rubies, and emeralds.

"Breathtaking, aren't they? René Lalique himself designed these pieces for Zachariah Cain Junior, who presented them to his wife, Emma, as a birthday gift. Emma left them to Maude, who donated them to the museum in 1973."

Jesse had no idea who René Lalique was, but the beauty and craftsmanship of the pieces were undeniable. He noticed something else: an empty spot on the tray. He pointed that spot out to Henry Wilmott.

"Yes, the ring. It was the one piece in the set Maude could not part with. We are to receive it upon the execution of her will." Then Wilmott made a face, not a happy one. "Oh, no, Jesse. Are you telling me you haven't found the ring among her possessions? What a tragedy. You see, the endowment the Cains left to us has been drained away over the years as a result of foolish spending and poor investments. The auctioning off of this set was to infuse the endowment with new cash. With the ring, the complete set would be worth millions."

"But even without the ring —"

"Yes, it is still a valuable collection, no doubt. But the ring and the brooch are the stars of the set. It would be like *Casablanca* with Bogie and no Bergman. No, no, the ring is of premium importance to the set and the future of the museum. We must get it back. We simply must."

"Have you got an image of it?"

"I do. Come up to my office."

Following behind Wilmott, Jesse asked, "Do you know why Maude was selling her house?"

"She was too old to manage any longer and it was falling into terrible disrepair. She knew it was time for her to take whatever funds she could get out of the place and find an assisted-living facility."

"Did she have any takers?" Jesse supposed he was thinking as much about his inability to sell his place as he was about the late Maude Cain's prospects.

"You'd have to ask her agent. The fate of the house wasn't part of our concern."

Back on the street, Jesse stared at the image of the ring. He hadn't had the heart to tell Wilmott that the chances of recovering the ring intact weren't very good, though that wasn't what was troubling him at the moment. None of what Jesse had learned from Henry Wilmott, nor the questions that information raised, had done a thing to dissipate the buzz of negative energy he'd felt while waiting outside the curator's office. If anything, it made it worse.

46

Back at the office, Jesse was working off some of his energy by pounding a hardball into the pocket of his old glove. Then, as suddenly as he had started, he stopped and called Alisha into his office.

"What is it, Jesse?" she asked, closing the door behind her.

"I'm sorry about yesterday. You shouldn't have been put in that situation."

"You don't have to apologize to me, Jesse. Where would I be if you didn't hire me? I know I wasn't who they wanted you to hire. I was happy to help. Proud that Molly trusted me enough to ask."

"I'm grateful, but that's not the point, Alisha. It's not your job to babysit me. It's not Molly's, either. I'm sorry."

"Apology accepted."

There was a knock at the office door and it opened before Jesse could answer.

"This a private party or can anyone join?"

Molly asked, stepping in and closing the door behind her.

Alisha said, "Is that all, Jesse?"

"Sure."

Molly was curious, but waited until Alisha had gone back to the desk. "What was that about?"

"Yesterday."

"Oh."

" 'Oh' is right."

"If you're going to bite my head off for —"

"Relax," Jesse said, interrupting her. "I was apologizing to her."

"Why? I was the one who got her in the middle of the situation."

"But there shouldn't have been a situation. I was responsible for that."

Molly wasn't going to argue with him, so that's where they left it.

Jesse asked, "Are you in for the day?"

"For as long as you need me or until the overtime budget runs out. I've cooked enough food for my family for the next two days and everyone knows where they can find me."

Jesse waved Molly over to his desk and handed her the photo of the missing dragon-fly ring.

"My goodness, it's gorgeous." Molly held

264

out her left hand next to the photo as if imagining the ring on her finger.

"It's also missing from Maude Cain's house."

Jesse told Molly about his visit with Henry Wilmott. As he explained it to her, he could see Molly's wheels turning.

She asked, "You think Curnutt and Bolton ripped Maude's house apart to find this ring? It would explain why one might kill the other if they found it."

"In L.A. I handled more than one case where friends killed each other over pocket change, so something worth as much as that ring would be reason enough."

Molly saw the look on Jesse's face. "But this isn't L.A. and that ring isn't pocket change. I can tell you don't like it."

"You do know me."

"Too well," Molly said with a laugh. "So what's bothering you about it?"

"Everything."

"That narrows it down."

"Okay, how do two low-rent guys like Curnutt and Bolton know about this ring? You read their sheets. Either one of them strike you as a master jewel thief?"

"You know what it's like inside. All those guys do is talk about big scores."

"But only a very few people even knew

she had the ring or about her deal with the museum."

"Maybe someone hired Bolton and Curnutt."

Jesse smiled. "I like that better, but unless you suspect Henry Wilmott, Maude's lawyer, or Maude herself, who hired them? And it doesn't explain why Bolton would make Curnutt come back to Paradise to kill him."

"Maybe they never left town and maybe Bolton just picked the wrong place to get rid of his partner."

"And maybe he just happened to decide to call it in to the police to make sure the body was found. I'm also pretty sure the person who called it in to the station was the killer. Why would Bolton do that?"

"Okay, so then what?"

"I don't know. I read the ballistics report," Jesse said. "The bullets that killed Curnutt were .22s, most likely fired from a Walther."

"Yeah, Jesse, I read it, too. The slug recovered from the head was badly distorted, but the one recovered from the chest was in pretty good shape."

"We recovered a nine-millimeter at the scene with Curnutt's prints all over the gun and ammo. Either Bolton or Curnutt strike you as types to carry .22s or to bother with homemade sound suppressors?"

Now Molly was wearing the same skeptical face as her chief. "Okay, Jesse, so if the ring is missing but no one hired these guys to find it and the job wasn't their idea —"

"It means they were looking for something else."

"But what?"

"You tell me."

47

Mayor Walker's invitation to dinner at the Gull was a polite one, but Jesse Stone understood it was a command performance. It was just the three of them at the table by the floor-to-ceiling windows overlooking the marina and Stiles Island. Although Jesse had gotten to the restaurant ten minutes early, he was the last to arrive. Just like with the polite invitation, he knew what that meant. The mayor and Nita were back at it, looking for every possible edge. They wanted to pick the table, to pick the chair he'd sit in. They wanted to see if he staggered a little when he approached. Jesse didn't think Nita's recent thawing toward him was all an act, but he understood her priorities.

He removed his PPD baseball cap as he approached their table, bowed his head slightly. "Your Honor. Miss Thompson."

"No need for the formality tonight, Jesse," the mayor said, smiling up at him. "We all seem to be on the same page these days, if not quite the same team."

Jesse nodded, put his hat down on the seat next to him, the one without the place setting before it. "Okay, Connie."

The mayor waved for the waitress.

"I'll have a very dry martini with three olives." She turned her head to her aide. "Nita?"

"Jim Beam Single Barrel. One ice cube."

Jesse didn't need prompting. "Club soda, lime, in a tall glass."

The mayor and her adviser gave each other a look. They both seemed to want to say something, but neither did.

"So, Jesse," Walker said when the waitress was out of earshot. "Nita tells me I owe you a debt of gratitude. That it was your idea to keep most of the information out of the media's hands as to where this Curnutt fellow's body was discovered and who may have called it in."

"I didn't want to deal with a media feeding frenzy any more than you did, Connie. How's it working? I've been busy today and haven't had time to catch the news."

It was Nita who answered. "So far so good. No one on our end of things has said anything and none of the reporters have worked it out yet. They've all been focused on Curnutt's connection to the Cain incident and speculating about whether his partner killed him and why."

The drinks arrived. The waitress asked if they wanted to hear the specials before they ordered, but the mayor shooed her away.

"Give us some time. I'll call you over when we're ready."

The waitress didn't need to be told twice. The three of them raised their glasses to the others, but without uttering a word. None of them, least of all Jesse, believed this was the beginning of a beautiful friendship.

"Where were you this morning, Jesse?" Nita asked. "I tried you at your house several times."

"I had to go into Boston."

Nita seemed to want him to give her a more complete answer, but Jesse had said all he intended to say. Molly and Suit knew about Dix. Healy had known, too, but Jesse didn't want to broadcast to the world that he went to therapy. He was old-fashioned in that way. In spite of all the good seeing Dix had done for him, he had never gotten over thinking needing help was a sign of weakness.

"And then I tried your cell later in the day," she said, immediately regretting it when she saw the confused look on the mayor's face.

Jesse let her off the hook. "I spent some time with Henry Wilmott."

Nita was confused. "Who?"

Mayor Walker put down her martini and said, "The curator of the Cain Library and Museum. And what did you and Henry discuss, Jesse? Henry doesn't strike me as much of a Red Sox enthusiast."

Jesse explained about Maude Cain's missing ring. He took out his cell phone, tapped the screen, and scrolled. He showed them the image of the ring. They both gasped at the sight of it, but it wasn't beauty the mayor had on her mind.

"A motive." The mayor clapped her hands together. "That's why those men tore poor Maude's house apart. They were looking for the ring."

Jesse was tempted to rain on her parade. He decided against it. He didn't believe that's what had happened, but he couldn't disprove it.

"So one partner killed the other to take the ring for himself," Nita said. "It all starts to make sense now." She took a sip of her bourbon, then pulled out her cell phone. "Let's get this out there. Let the press know we're making progress."

"No," Jesse said, not shouting, but making it very clear it wasn't up for negotiation. "Lundquist and I have already alerted all the PDs, pawn shops, and jewelry dealers in New England, New York, and southeastern Canada. We've let our other contacts know that it would be in their best interest to alert the authorities if that ring walks through their door."

"But —"

"Can't do it, Nita. For now Hump Bolton thinks the ring is his meal ticket. He thinks he can unload the ring to a fence or a dealer and be gone. But the second this becomes public knowledge, we lose him and the ring. He'll toss the ring in the closest body of water and run. This way we have the advantage. We can get Bolton and get the ring back. You can't trade that in for a day of good press."

"I'm afraid Jesse's right, Nita," Walker said, gently pushing Thompson's phone hand down toward the white linen tablecloth. "Let's see how it plays out. What are you doing to sew the case up?"

"We received the ballistics report earlier and the forensics results should be coming in within the next few days. We also discovered some documents in the Cain house that might help us track down some of Maude's former lodgers and —"

One of the martini olives seemed almost to turn rancid in the mayor's mouth, her tone of voice reflecting the foul taste. "But not two minutes ago you told us you know who perpetrated these crimes and why. I'd say it would be irresponsible of you to waste further resources pursuing unnecessary lines of investigation." She guzzled her drink and signaled furiously to the waitress for another.

"Actually, Connie, I didn't. You and Nita came to those conclusions yourselves. I don't have the luxury of relying on reasonable guesses. The PPD has to be able to prove what we suspect. Until we have enough proof to shut down other lines of investigation, we'll keep digging."

Mayor Walker tried unsuccessfully to smile but stopped trying when Nita Thompson took Jesse's side.

"He's right, Connie. If Jesse or, worse, you came out and made a statement only to have it be wrong, it would be politically disastrous."

"Very well," the mayor said, waving at the waitress to hurry with the second martini. "Very well. Shall we order?"

Jesse didn't feel much like eating. That excess energy he'd had earlier in the day had evaporated. All he wanted to do now was sleep, but that was neither on the agenda nor on the menu.

48

When Jesse strode into the station the next day at seven, Molly was at the front desk. He was surprised to see her.

"What are you doing here?"

"Running up my overtime," she said. "My chief's a sucker."

"You always this funny at this hour?"

Molly ignored him. "How was dinner with Her Highness?"

"All right."

"Care to expand on that?"

"No."

She shook her head at him. "After those effusive answers, I shouldn't give you this."

"Give me what?"

Molly handed him two sheets of paper. "Those are the names, addresses, and phone numbers of people who stayed at Maude Cain's over the years."

"You do good work, Officer Crane. Play your cards right and your chief might actually authorize some of that overtime he promised."

"I'll just remind him of how this place ran when Suit was on the desk and Gabe was rehabbing."

"All right, Crane. I surrender. Make us some appointments and get someone in to cover the desk here."

"Us?"

"You heard me, Molly. Us."

Molly smiled in spite of herself and grabbed the list back out of Jesse's hand.

Their third appointment was in Salem with a Mrs. Deanna Banquer. She lived in a beautifully maintained saltbox house, its redbrick chimney sticking up through the center of the roof. A low hedge surrounded her lot. A pea-gravel walkway, bordered on both sides by carefully trimmed boxwoods, led from the curb to the house. Mrs. Banquer threw open the front door when Jesse's Explorer pulled up. And when Molly and he got out of the SUV, she stepped out of the house and came to greet them. It had been Jesse's experience that very few people were this enthusiastic about speaking to the police. On those rare occasions when he ran into someone this eager and cooperative, the results, in terms of evidence or information, were often less than sparkling.

The first two visits hadn't gone well, either. It wasn't that the people they'd spoken to weren't cooperative; they just had nothing helpful to say. Their first stop was in Paradise with a man named Brad Mercer. Mr. Mercer was in his forties and had rented a room from Maude Cain for two months in the late nineties. He had inherited a house in the Swap from his uncle Jack. The house was in tired condition and Mercer had to stay off-premises until the work on the house was completed.

"She was a lovely woman, good cook, too."

But beyond that, Mercer had little to say. He paid her in cash by the week. His room was on the second floor and faced the cove. Nothing unusual had happened during his stay. He didn't recall much about any of the other lodgers, though he was sure there were others there at the time he rented there.

Their second stop was equally unproductive. Swan Harbor was a tony village just north of Paradise. Jim Born was fifteen years on the job in town after doing twenty as a Boston cop. While his wife sold their house in Boston, he'd stayed at the Cain house for a few weeks.

"It was way less expensive than anything available in Swan Harbor."

But when Molly asked him about his time in the Cain house, Born gave an unsatisfying yet completely understandable answer.

"You'll have to forgive me, Molly, but that was during Nine-Eleven. Mostly I stayed in my room and watched TV. I don't recall much about those weeks except watching the planes slam into the Trade Center."

"Hello, hello," said Banquer as she met them halfway down the walkway. "You must be Officer Crane, and you're Chief Stone."

They all smiled and shook hands. Deanna Banquer was about five-six, in her late fifties or early sixties, with short hair that was in the final stages of conversion from mostly red to mostly gray. She had stunning blue eyes and a disarming smile. Jesse thanked her for her time, then she led them into the low-ceilinged house. She showed them into the kitchen, poured them all lemonade, and then joined them at the table.

"So, Chief Stone, what is it about my time at Maude's house in Paradise I can help you with?"

"Jesse. Call us Jesse and Molly, okay?"

Banquer smiled that smile of hers. "Wonderful. And please call me Deanna."

"Molly tells me you two discussed Maude Cain's death. I know you've read about it in the paper and heard it on the news."

"Horrible. Horrible. She was such a lovely woman. Very kind and generous to a fault."

Molly asked, "Why were you renting a room from her?"

Deanna's smile turned suddenly shy. "I'm originally from Ohio and I was trying to establish state residency so I could finish up college at UMass. I had visited this area as a kid with my family during a driving vacation. So I figured I might as well live in Paradise while I established residency, and Maude's hardly cost anything."

Jesse asked, "This was when?"

"The seventies. July of '76 thru July of '77. I had a good job at a restaurant here in Salem. Funny," she said, her eyes getting a faraway look about them, "I never did finish school. I met my husband-to-be at the restaurant one day and . . . Sorry."

Surprisingly, they'd gotten more information from Deanna than they had from their earlier visits. She was very fond of her time in Paradise with Maude, and Maude had been fond of her.

"Maude's husband had died a few years earlier and they never had children. I missed my family terribly and so we spent a lot of time together. She would tell me about her family's history. She was very proud of what they had done for Paradise."

Jesse took out his phone and showed Deanna the ring. "Did Maude ever mention —"

Deanna lit up. "She loved that ring. She even let me try it on once. God, it was beautiful."

"So she didn't keep the ring a secret," Molly said. "Other lodgers knew about it?"

"No, I don't think so. She swore me to secrecy. She said I was the only person she had ever shown it to, certainly the only person she had ever let try it on."

Jesse asked, "Do you remember any of the other people staying there while you lived with her?"

Deanna's expression did an about-face, souring. "There was one asshole, Evan. He gave Maude a hard time. He was always high, drank a lot, but he seemed to have a lot of money. So whenever Maude asked him to leave, he would pay her off. As nice as her house was and as rich as her family had been, she was pretty broke. I didn't like that she let him stay, but I understood it. She needed the money. When he tried breaking into my room one night, she threw him out once and for all."

After that there wasn't much more for them to discuss. Deanna said that she and Maude had kept in touch for a while afterward, but once Deanna had a family of her own, their conversations grew less frequent.

"I hope you find the ring," she said to them as they were leaving. "She was a woman who didn't care about wealth, but she did love that ring."

49

Back at the station, Molly was digging into the oldest of the composition notebooks, looking for Evan. It wasn't much of a lead. It wasn't at all clear that it was a lead at all. For a woman like Deanna Banquer to refer to someone as an asshole and for him to stick out in her memory made him worth a little investigation. Unfortunately, the world, even in the mid-seventies, was full of people like this Evan character. But Jesse and Molly agreed that from this point forward they wouldn't be rushing around Massachusetts to do in-person interviews unless they first got more substance on the phone.

Molly seemed so preoccupied by Maude Cain's notebooks that Brian Lundquist thought she might not have noticed him come through the station door, but when he tried to scoot by her he was proven wrong.

"Where do you think you're going?" she

said, never looking up. "Just because you're a big-shot statie now doesn't mean you just get to walk into Jesse's office."

"Sorry, Molly. You looked busy."

"I am. Is it important?"

He waved a file at her.

"Come with me."

She knocked on Jesse's pebbled-glass door and stuck her head into his office.

"What?"

"Lundquist is here."

"Get anywhere with this Evan guy?" Jesse asked.

"Not yet."

"Okay, send him in."

Lundquist came in and sat across the desk from Jesse and waved the file at him as he had at Molly.

"Full array of photos and forensics. Your man Perkins is good. Our guys said he did a first-rate job with the scene. Our guys don't drop compliments easily."

"I'll let Peter know. How about the index card?"

Lundquist pulled out several enlargements of areas of the index card, came around to Jesse's side of the desk, and laid them out on the blotter.

"See here, Jesse, these dark brown patches? This is old cellophane tape residue.

There were still some traces of the actual tape on the card. The lab says the tape is at least forty years old. And here, these indentations in the card that the lab highlighted, what's that look like to you?"

"A key."

"A safety-deposit box key, to be precise," Lundquist said.

"These numbers are the number of the box."

"That's the presumption."

"But what bank?"

Lundquist frowned. "Good question. See this." He pointed to an enlargement of the top left corner of the index card found in King Curnutt's rear pocket. "It's been torn here. Our best guess is that's where the name of the bank was probably written. In the meantime, we've sent all this to the FBI lab in the hope they'll be able to match the shape of the key and the number to the bank."

Now it was Jesse frowning. "Don't hold your breath. It will take months before they get to this. And when they do, the best they'll be able to do is to come up with the manufacturer of the key and a list of banks that might have used that type of key and lock. We're talking forty years ago."

"At least forty years. Maybe more."

Jesse asked, "Can your guys create a key from this?"

"I don't see why not. You mind me asking what for? We don't even know that this has anything to do with the case."

"I think we do. Look, Curnutt's body didn't have ID, money, a cell phone, or car or house keys on it. Only this old index card. So he either had it on him or the killer planted it on him."

"You're right, Jesse. But —"

Jesse stood out of his chair. "Let's go."

"What is it?"

Jesse didn't answer directly. "C'mon" was all he said.

50

The yellow tape was the only thing that indicated this patch of woods had been the scene of a murder. The Subaru had been towed away and the body long since removed. The old toolshed door creaked in the wind like the surrounding trees.

"You guys have the car?" Jesse said.

Lundquist nodded. "Nothing in it that didn't belong to the owner except Curnutt's prints. Since the car was boosted from a supermarket parking lot near the New Hampshire border, we're concentrating our search for Humphrey Bolton up there."

"If he's been watching TV or reading the papers, he'll be gone."

"Bolton's not the swiftest guy in the world, Jesse."

"He's evaded capture so far."

"Good point."

Jesse looked at where the car had been yesterday. "I didn't like it yesterday and I like it even less today."

"What don't you like, exactly? I know you don't buy into the ring scenario," Lundquist said. "You think Curnutt and Bolton were too thick for a jewel heist, but everything about this fits the scenario of them ripping the ring off from the Cain woman's house and then one partner eliminating the other. The way I see it is that they knew about the ring or, if not specifically the ring, about the Cain jewelry they thought the old woman had in the house. All they find is the ring and that would have been okay. Would have been a nice payday, too, but then things go sideways. The woman dies and they have to rough up the MassEx guy.

"Now they've got a murder rap and assault with a deadly weapon hanging over their heads and the money for the ring won't get them what they thought it would. Now it's about survival and getting as far away as possible, maybe even getting out of the country. But the money they get from fencing the ring will get one of them a lot farther away than it will get both of them. I don't care how dumb Bolton is supposed to be, he can do simple subtraction."

Jesse shook his head. "I still don't like it, Brian. Why come back here when they were in spitting distance of Canada? If Bolton wanted to kill Curnutt, why not do it up by where they were? There are plenty of isolated areas in that part of the state to leave a body, places where no one would find it for weeks or months. Why come back to Paradise? Why call it in? Why take everything off Curnutt's body and leave or plant the index card? I'm telling you there's something else going on here that we don't see or can't see."

"You surprise me, Jesse. Healy always told me you were big on saying the police should follow the evidence, not their hunches."

"Yesterday, it was a hunch, but it's more than that today. I am looking at the evidence. I'm not cherry-picking the evidence that fits a particular scenario. I'm trying to look at the evidence that hangs together and the evidence that doesn't."

"Okay, say I buy that and I got it wrong, that this isn't about the ring. I don't know why Curnutt was killed here or who killed him, but killed here he was. Sawtooth Creek is, what, a hundred yards that way? Why not put a bullet or two into Curnutt's lungs and submerge him in the creek?"

Jesse thought about it for a second. He rubbed his right cheek with the back of the folded fingers of his right hand.

"All the questions have one answer, the

same answer."

"I can't wait to hear this. Don't tell me we're looking at some twisted serial-killer type or an impulse kill, because the evidence doesn't support that."

"Just the opposite, Brian. I think this was completely calculated. You said it yourself at Daisy's: The homemade sound suppressor is evidence of premeditation."

"But premeditation by who?"

"I don't think Curnutt and Bolton picked Maude Cain's house because they heard some story about jewelry when they were inside together. Someone pointed them at that house."

"To steal the jewelry?"

Jesse said, "If Curnutt turned up dead anywhere else, if that index card wasn't on the body, or if we didn't get that anonymous tip, I might accept it."

"But if it wasn't about the jewelry, then what? The Cain woman was broke. She was trying to sell her house so she could live out her last few years. What else could she have had that had any value?"

"Good questions," Jesse said. "I don't know the answers. I know someone wants media attention and Curnutt's murder here was supposed to help get it."

"And if he doesn't get the attention he

wants, what then, Jesse, another body?"

"I don't think so."

"You better hope not or I'll be working that case with the next Paradise chief of police."

Jesse knew Lundquist was right and there was nothing more to say for now. It was time to go.

51

Hump remembered something one of the guys inside had told him way back when he was doing juvie time. That the bigger the sandbox, the easier it was to lose yourself. Of course that was before Nine-Eleven, before most city-center blocks had cameras everywhere. And if the city didn't have a camera on every lamppost, then private businesses had them outside their buildings. Even damned taxis had dashboard cameras. Despite that, he knew he was safer far away from New Hampshire and Paradise, safer from the cops and from the guy who had killed King. He supposed he could have easily made it to New York City, the biggest sandbox of them all, but he didn't know anybody there, didn't have anybody he could trust or with the right kind of connections.

But he knew Boston. He'd spent time here as a kid and for a few years between bids.

He felt comfortable in Boston and knew all sorts of people in town, people who might give him a room until things cooled down or who could hook him up if and when he decided to fence the dragonfly ring. He'd been inside when that marathon-bombing thing happened, but he knew the town was different now, that there were eyes all over the place that hadn't been there before. Still, if he had to keep looking over his shoulder, he felt more relaxed doing it in a place he was familiar with, a place full of people who didn't look anybody in the eye or care about anybody else's business.

So far, he felt good about his choice. He hadn't gotten a second look since getting into town. He'd already found a place to hunker down for a night or two or until he could make contact with someone who could find a better spot for him. Now he had to make a call. He hadn't wanted to make the call until he was in a safer place. That's what he told himself. The truth was he didn't want to make the call because he didn't want to face the fact that King had fucked him. He guessed he should have figured it out because of the extra two grand King left behind with the note. Knowing that, he should have been happy King got what was coming to him. The thing about it was that it just made him feel more sad and stupid than betrayed.

He felt pretty stupid to begin with, that he could have let King play him the way he had. The worst part of it was that King had so little respect for Hump that he hadn't even bothered covering his tracks. King had left intact the notepad where he'd scribbled down the phone number. Hump kept shaking his head whenever he thought about King's lack of respect for him. Sure, King'd ripped off the sheet with the phone number on it, but didn't bother with the sheets beneath it. *Did he really think I was so dumb I wouldn't know how to shade in the next sheet on the notepad with the side of the pencil lead?* The answer was painfully obvious. He was shaking his head as he walked into Dennis's, a dreary local bar in Southie.

Hump knew the place had an old-fashioned phone booth in the back by the bathrooms. What else he knew about Dennis's was that Mickey Coyle hung out there. They weren't friends or nothing. Coyle was the kind of person who didn't need to make friends inside because he was protected by Gino Fish's money. Coyle was heavily connected and that counted for a lot, especially in the position Hump was in. If he couldn't squeeze more money out of the guy who'd hired him and King, he was going to have to sell the ring. Mickey Coyle was the type of guy to know people who might take the ring off his hands.

The back of the bar was beautifully mirrored, the way they used to do it. The bar itself was vintage but beat up, and the stools looked pretty wobbly. There were a few guys at the bar, minding their own business. Dennis's was the kind of place where people minded their own business and drank shots with tall boys back. There wasn't a blender, an olive, or an orange slice in sight. Nobody turned or looked directly at Hump. You didn't look people in the face in Dennis's. Instead they all rolled their eyes up from their drinks or papers to see what the bar mirror told them about the big guy walking into the place.

"Phone booth still in the back?" Hump asked the barman.

"Ain't moved since I seen it last. Drink?"

"Harpoon tap. I'll be back in a minute."

Hump found the phone booth where he remembered it. It smelled of stale beer and ancient cigarette smoke preserved inside the sticky wall grime like insects trapped inside amber. He pulled quarters out of his pocket, sat down on the rounded ledge of a seat, and closed the booth door. He dropped the coins in the slot and punched in the number. It rang and rang and rang and rang. He put the phone back in its cradle.

Hump's beer was on a coaster on the bar by a stool far away from the others. He sat down, took a sip, and waved the barman over.

"What I owe ya?"

"Three bucks."

Hump put a twenty on the bar. When the bartender turned to walk away, Hump stopped him.

"Mickey Coyle still come in here?"

"Who?" The bartender was a bloated guy in his thirties with shaggy gray hair and a prison stare.

"Mickey Coyle. Works for Gino Fish."

The bartender gave Hump a strange look and laughed at him.

"I say something funny?"

"Not funny, just ignorant."

Hump's skin burned with anger and it took everything he had not to crack the beer glass against the side of the barman's fat face. Instead, he finished his beer in a sip and said. "You got a pencil?"

The barman reached over by the register and gave him a pen. "Best I can do."

Hump ripped the sheet of notepaper in half. He wrote something down and handed it and the pen to the bartender.

"When Mickey comes in, give him that. Keep the change." Hump was moving to the door.

"Who?" the barman asked again without any heart, because the door was already closing.

52

When he left the station for the night, someone was waiting for him by his Explorer. Jesse thought the guy looked vaguely familiar, a face he'd seen in a sea of other faces. But he'd be damned if he could remember which sea and the name that belonged to this guy's face.

"Can I help you?"

"Maybe. Maybe we can help each other, Chief."

Then it clicked. *Reporter.*

"*Boston Globe,* right?"

"Very good. Ed Selko."

Selko was a short, desiccated man whose breath smelled of cigarettes. His breath also smelled of something else, something that Jesse's breath often smelled of: scotch whiskey. The reporter was fifty going on sixty and had that ruffled, careless look that newspaper people could afford to have. Selko was never going have to stand in front of a camera doing a remote.

Jesse gave Selko his blank stare and silence to fill up with chatter. When all Selko gave in response was silence of his own, it was clear to Jesse that the newspaperman understood silence in the way a detective understands it. TV and radio reporters didn't have the luxury of silence. Dead air was their enemy. Not so for newspaper people.

"Can I buy you a drink, Chief?"

Jesse snorted. "I'm not that easy, Selko."

"Come on, Stone, gimme a break. A drink will grease the skids . . . for me, anyway."

"You talk, but you don't say anything. What do we have to discuss?"

"A frayed old index card."

"I'm listening."

"Drink first."

They sat alone in the banquet room at the Lobster Claw, a second glass of Lagavulin in front of Selko and a beer in Jesse's hand. Jesse was happy to let Selko get a few single malts in him while he nursed his beer. As much as Jesse loved scotch, single malts didn't hold much appeal for him, especially the godawful smoky ones like Lagavulin. The nose of the scotch stank like a campfire after a rainstorm.

"You've got expensive taste in scotch," Jesse said.

"The other half of my diet is cigarettes, so I can afford it. How's your pal Johnnie Walker these days?"

"We're not talking about me, Selko."

The reporter first took a sip, then slugged the rest down. "You know, Chief, when I said we should have a drink, an empty banquet room wasn't what I had in mind."

"Privacy is what I had in mind. You mentioned an index card."

"You know, the one you found on Curnutt's body. The one you didn't tell the press about," Selko said, staring at Jesse's face, looking for any reaction. "You're good, Stone. You get about as worked up as an Easter Island totem. I've always admired that about you. How you don't give anything away."

"You'll make me blush." Jesse was getting impatient. "The index card."

Selko fished out his cell phone, tapped, scrolled, and turned the screen to Jesse. It was a photo of what looked to be the index card Jesse had pulled out of Curnutt's pocket.

"It's definitely an index card," Jesse said.

"Someone faxed that to me this afternoon."

Jesse continued to play it close to the vest. "Which proves what, exactly?"

"I'm not sure. The note that came with it suggested I ask you about it."

"Okay, you've asked."

"It's curious, Chief, no?"

"What is?"

"Your department just found the body of a murdered man in a Paradise nature preserve and the murdered man was a suspect in the murder of Maude Cain."

Jesse pointed at the image on the cell. "You can buy an index card like that in any office-supply store in the country."

"Let's stop playing games here, okay, Stone? I'm a drunk, but a good reporter. You know how that is. Remember I mentioned that the person who sent me the note suggested I ask you about the index card?"

"How could I forget? Let's see this note."

Selko shook his head. "Nope. I'm not showing you mine until you show me yours. But I can tell you this: You found the index card in Curnutt's left rear pocket."

Jesse said, "What do you want?"

"To do my job. I want a story."

"What if I've got no story to give you? All you've got is an image of an index card and some tale about a note. It would take some mighty impressive hoop jumping to make a story out of that."

Selko screwed up his mouth. "The police

chief doth protest too much. I was hoping you'd be straight with me, Stone."

"You think calling me a liar is going to improve your chances for a story?"

"I'm not calling you a liar," Selko said, sliding a folded sheet of white paper across the table. "He is."

Jesse unfolded the paper and read it. When he was done, he stood up and tugged Selko by the arm. "C'mon, we're going."

"Where to?"

"The station."

53

Ed Selko wasn't pleased about being "asked" to go down to the station with Jesse, but he hadn't been foolish enough to bark about it too loudly. Even with two drinks in him, the reporter hadn't lost sight of the fact that getting a story was the point, nor had he lost sight of the fact that the story would be a better one with Stone on board. At the paper, pure speculation sprinkled with some interesting facts did not a story make. Still, he had his limits.

"Look, Stone," Selko said, no longer able to contain his frustration. "I came down here voluntarily. I've answered all of your questions, several times, but that's now officially over. Unless there's more of a give-and-take between us, I'm calling my paper and you'll be the story."

Jesse had a decision to make. He could just let the reporter walk without saying another word. Selko might be annoyed at that. Might even get his editor to give him a few inches in the next edition detailing the faxed photo, note, and his treatment at the hands of the Paradise PD. Jesse could live with the slings and arrows that came his way. That didn't worry him. People had written much worse about Jesse than anything Selko might print. No, it was the rest of the story that was the problem. The media was a copycat business. Once Selko intimated that the police had been less than forthcoming about the circumstances surrounding Curnutt's murder, the town would be crawling with media people looking to one-up Selko.

"No promises," Jesse said. "Ask your questions and we'll see if there's a deal to be made here."

Selko made some noises about how the press, on behalf of the public, had a right to know and that the state had no right to withhold information that was in the public interest. Jesse had heard it all before. It was what media types always said just before making a deal.

Jesse walked to the other end of his office and opened the door.

"Listen, Selko, you can walk out of here with no story and your principles intact anytime you want or we can make a deal."

"What did you have in mind?"

"I will give you some details about the Curnutt homicide that you can make a story out of and then when we get close, you get the exclusive."

"And in return?"

Jesse cleared his throat. "Not a word of speculation about the meaning of the signature at the bottom of the note."

Selko didn't jump at the offer. "Come on, Stone. We both know what it means."

"Speculation."

"Bull! Face it, Stone, the note telling me where the index card was establishes his bona fides that he either killed Curnutt himself or learned about it from the man who did. We now both know what this story is really about, but I can pretend otherwise. Even with the little I've got now, I can make a hell of a story out of this. Look, it's always better to have police cooperation, and I get why you withheld info about the index card, but now that you've got that note . . . Either way, I have a story and you have a major media shit storm on your hands."

"Don't you get it, Selko, that's what the killer wants? You interested in abetting murderers?"

"I get it, but unless you haven't noticed, Chief, the business I'm in is dying by the inch. If I don't use this, my editor will kill me. I lose this job, I've got no safety net."

"Good point. One day, Selko. Give me one more day before you go to press with the bigger story. I'll give you enough for tomorrow's story, details about Curnutt's murder that no one else has. For now, leave out any mention of the index card and the signature at the bottom of the note."

Selko took out a voice recorder, a pad, and a pen. "What didn't you share with the press about Curnutt's murder?"

"The killer used a homemade sound suppressor. Fragments of it were found in the victim's wounds. The weapon was a .22-caliber handgun. You can see a video online of the exact type of suppressor and handgun used."

"Was the guy who killed Curnutt a pro or an amateur, you know, some guy who watched that video you mentioned?"

"We don't know that."

"Guess."

Jesse shook his head. "Speculation is what you do, not what I do."

"That's a start, but you'll have to do better than that, Stone."

Jesse considered disclosing the information about the stolen dragonfly ring, but realized he'd probably lose a shot at finding

Hump Bolton if he did. Instead he turned to the photos in the murder book and put it in front of Selko.

"The killer shot Curnutt at very close range: one to the head and one to the heart."

"Contact wounds?"

"There were powder burns, but they weren't contact wounds."

Selko nodded, smiling. "Okay, Chief, that'll work for now."

Five minutes later, Jesse was driving Selko back to his car. The reporter was talking to him, but Jesse was barely listening. There was something about the fax to Selko that Jesse didn't like, but he was damned if he could figure out exactly what it was.

"One day, Stone," Selko said. "But I don't see what one day buys you. Either way this thing is going to blow up."

"One day," Jesse repeated, returning to the present. "What does it buy me? Time to prepare for the explosion."

54

Jesse watched Selko drive his dinged and dented old Camry away, the car's rear bumper held on by duct tape and a prayer. They say people's dogs are a reflection of their owners. Jesse didn't know if Selko had a dog, but it seemed to him that the reporter's car was a pretty accurate reflection of its owner: beat up, ruffled, but persistent. Jesse thought about heading straight home, but that was no longer a viable option. Selko was right, no matter what, this was about to turn into a mess and he had what remained of the night plus twenty-four hours before the crap hit the fan. After that Paradise would become a circus and a zoo all rolled into one.

Nita Thompson lived in a condo development at the edge of the Swap, a place Jesse had thought about moving to if he could ever sell his house. The development was tastefully done, the architecture blending in perfectly with the older houses surrounding it. Getting this development built had been one of the mayor's pet projects. She understood that as Bostonians continued to move into Paradise and commute, that there would be a need to expand available housing and develop the Swap, while maintaining the town's quaint seaside appeal.

He'd thought about calling Nita to give her the news or at least to let her know he was coming, but decided against it. He wanted to catch her off guard. He wanted to be able to read her reactions without giving her time to prepare. Maybe that wasn't it at all. If he was being honest with himself, he had to admit he was more than a little curious about her, about how her attitude toward him had seemed to shift before his eyes.

"Jesse!" she said, real surprise in her voice. "What are you doing here?"

She was dressed in a faded Harvard T-shirt, running shorts, and black tennis socks. Her long, shapely legs were lightly tanned and looked lovely freed of the business suit slacks and skirts she always wore. Her shimmery, dark brown hair, which was usually pulled tightly to her scalp and done in a small bun atop her head or tied back in a neat ponytail, fell around her angular face to just above her shoulders. She was makeup-less and looked about ready for bed.

"There's something I need to discuss with you," he said.

"That's what phones are for."

She wasn't smiling, but Jesse couldn't decide whether that was because she just didn't want him there or because there was someone else already at her apartment.

"Am I interrupting?" he asked.

"Just my attempt to get some sleep."

"Sorry, but it's something we need to discuss face-to-face."

"Couldn't it wait until morning?"

"If it could have, I wouldn't be here."

"Come on in," she said, frowning.

The apartment looked like an IKEA showroom and lacked a sense of home. In spite of himself, Jesse felt sad for Nita. Even his crappy minor-league apartments had more personality than this place. There was a lack of permanence to the atmosphere: a place where someone lived, but not anyone in particular.

"Scotch?" she asked. "I'm having one. Dewar's okay? It's all I've got."

"Sure. Rocks and soda, if that's okay?"

Less than a minute later, Jesse had his drink and Nita had hers. They were seated across from each other, Nita on a red leather chair and Jesse on a gray fabric couch. They raised their glasses to each other and sipped.

"So, what's the current emergency?"

Jesse explained the deal he'd made with Selko. About the photo of the index card and the note.

"We knew it would come out eventually. You can explain the rest away, can't you?"

"Uh-huh. I can always say it was a way to weed through the people who confess to any crime and to ensure we had the right suspect when we caught him."

"That'll play. You may take some hits, but I think I can even get the mayor to defend you on this."

"I'm not worried about taking hits in the press. Cops are everybody's favorite targets. But the index card where Curnutt's body was found, that's the least of it."

Thompson made a face, her eyes suddenly wary. "You never struck me as a man who enjoyed talking in riddles, Jesse. Why start now?"

He took a copy of the note Selko had shown him and handed it to Nita.

"So," she said when she was done.

"Did you see how the note was signed?"

"Yes, I see the note is signed 'The

Hangman.' So what? Is that supposed to mean something to me?"

"Do you believe in coincidences?" Jesse asked, not waiting for an answer. "I don't like coincidences."

"More riddles. Look, Jesse, it's not that I don't appreciate your company, but it's late. I'm beat. If I'm missing something, just tell me."

"Terry Jester."

"I know, I know," Nita said, her voice thick with impatience. "They're having a big birthday bash for him here next month. I'm the one who told the mayor she should make the most out of it."

"You don't know about *The Hangman's Sonnet*?"

"The only sonnet I'm familiar with begins, 'Shall I compare thee to a summer's day.' "

"*The Hangman's Sonnet* was a Terry Jester record."

"Record!" She laughed at him. "Next thing you know, you'll be telling me about dial phones and cassette tapes. Jeez, my parents were kids when Terry Jester was a star."

Jesse shook his empty glass at Nita. "Pour us another. I've got a story to tell you."

55

Jesse repeated for Nita Thompson what Roscoe Niles had told him about the missing master tape for *The Hangman's Sonnet* and the fallout that ensued. As she listened, she sipped her scotch, keeping her handsome face expressionless. She remained calm and unconvinced.

She shrugged. "So this guy signed the note 'The Hangman.' So what? You may not believe in coincidences, but that doesn't mean they don't happen. Maybe you're wrong about the killing and this guy really is a psycho looking for as much attention as possible by signing the note that way. There's been a lot of stuff in the papers about Terry Jester recently."

"C'mon, Nita. Everything that's been going on around here, from what happened in Maude Cain's house to Curnutt's murder, is about that missing master tape. It wasn't the dragonfly ring they were looking for in

Maude's house. It was all about that key to that safety-deposit box and what was in the box. My guess is the master tape was in the box. The Hangman, whoever he really is, must have it."

"You can't be sure that's what this is all about," she said, finishing her drink in a single swallow. "If it is about that, why not just come out and say it?"

"Because he's building interest or he's trying to create buzz by leaking out little bits of information at a time. That's why Curnutt was killed back in Paradise, why the killer called it in to us, why he leaked the info to this Selko guy at *The Globe*. He's trying to create as much attention as he can."

"For what purpose, Jesse?"

"My friend Roscoe Niles says the missing tape would be worth several million dollars to a collector if it ever resurfaced. Think about what it would be worth if there was a bidding war. Once the press gets hold of this, that's exactly what will happen."

"If you're right, and I'm still unconvinced, it's going to be a zoo," she said. "Not only are we going to get the regular media, we're going to get the music and entertainment crowd, the bloggers, the groupies . . . It's going to be a nightmare."

"Maybe we can buy ourselves a little more time."

"How?" she asked. "You said you only bought us a day with Selko."

"How much pull do you have further up the political food chain?"

"Some. Before I went out on my own, I used to work for the consultant to the governor and one of our senators. Why do you ask?"

"As bad as newspapers want to increase their circulation, they don't like being used, especially by murderers. You have the governor and that senator call the publisher and put on some pressure, you never know. Happened in L.A. all the time."

"Did it help?"

"Sometimes. The stories always made it into the papers eventually, but the extra time usually gave us the cushion we needed to get the suspect before word leaked out."

"I'll make some calls." She clinked her glass against his now empty glass. "Let me freshen that for you."

He waved her offer off in spite of himself.

Nita said, "Suit yourself. I can't believe I ever underestimated you."

"You say that a lot."

She twisted up her mouth. "I'm not usually wrong about people, but I was about

314

you. Still, Jesse, even if we buy an extra few days, what does that give us except time?"

"Whoever this Hangman is, he didn't go through all this trouble to acquire the tape —"

Nita interrupted. "If that's what this is really about."

"If that's what this is about, The Hangman didn't go through all this because he's a Terry Jester fan. Murder is usually about one of three things: money, rage, or sex. Given that the two victims were a ninety-one-year-old woman who died of a heart attack and a low-life thief executed with two clean shots, we can eliminate sex and rage. That leaves —"

"Money."

"Whoever this guy is, he wants to use the papers to drive up the market value of the tape. The extra time will frustrate him, force his hand. Maybe he'll get sloppy and make a mistake. Look, he's already gotten impatient twice. First he called in the murder, then he sent the index-card photo and note to Selko."

"Or maybe he'll release the story to other outlets."

"Could be. But I'm also wondering why of all the possible reporters in the world, this guy sent the stuff to Selko. The extra time will give me a chance to go down to Boston and do some digging."

"About Selko?"

"About him and some other stuff. We can also alert Stan White about the possibility that the *Hangman's Sonnet* tape might have been found. He could be useful. Can I get a glass of water?"

Nita smiled a nasty smile at him.

"What's that smile about?" Jesse wanted to know.

"I offered you another drink, Jesse," she said, grabbing the Dewar's bottle. "You don't have to pretend with me. I know all about your drinking. It's not exactly a secret."

His face went cold. "No, thank you, and forget the water. I'm going. Let's meet in the mayor's office tomorrow at eight."

Nita looked almost hurt but recovered quickly. "Seven," she said. "Mayor Walker will want to get as far out in front of this as she can. I'll make some calls right now."

Jesse stood, putting his glass down on the coffee table.

She walked Jesse to the door, but when they got there, Nita stood in his way. "Do you really think all of this, the break-in and the murders, is about a stupid recording tape?"

"No."

Her face reddened. "But you just —"

"The tape is only a thing. You said it yourself just before. It's about money."

She liked that answer better.

"You don't have to go, Jesse. Like I was saying the other night, it would be nice to have a conversation with someone about something other than poll numbers and politics."

"Some other time," he said.

She thought about protesting, but she knew that once Jesse Stone had made up his mind, there was no profit in arguing with him. She opened the door, stepped out of his way, and watched him disappear around the corner of the hall.

56

By midafternoon, Jesse had been through two meetings and was on the outskirts of Boston. The first hadn't been exactly what he anticipated it would be. He'd strode into the mayor's office at seven sharp, expecting that the only people in attendance would be the mayor, Nita Thompson, and himself. He'd already called Lundquist and filled him in. Jesse was surprised and more than a little pissed off to see that Stan White, Bella Lawton, and Roger Bascom were there as well.

Someone had once told Jesse that there was no such thing as a secret if more than one person knew it. People always had someone in their lives they felt they could trust with anything. Problem was, that person also had one person in his or her life he or she trusted with anything. By the time people got done trusting all those other people, whatever had begun as one person's secret was being broadcast over the Internet in thirty-five languages. The same was true of police operations: The fewer people involved, the better the chances of success. The way Jesse saw it, they already had a steep hill to climb and the slope had just gotten more severe.

Jesse didn't show his anger to anyone but Nita Thompson, who shrugged and shook her head as if to say, *It wasn't my idea.* He waved her over to a corner of the office while the rest of them looked at the morning papers.

"Are you kidding me? Why in the hell are they here?"

Nita raised her palms in surrender. "Don't look at me, but didn't you say Stan White might be helpful if your theory about the tape is right?"

"I said he might be useful. Useful and helpful, two different things. I was going to approach him with a hypothetical about the value of the tape. But forget him for now. There's a publicist with him. She's the last thing we need. And Bascom? He's a square badge who's got nothing to do with a police matter."

"They're uninvited guests courtesy of Stan White."

"Of course they are. This big birthday he's

throwing Jester is going over like a lead balloon. Bella confessed to me they're having trouble getting C-list celebrities to come. Once this gets out, they'll be turning people away."

Nita tilted her head, confused. "Bella, is it? You two on a first-name basis? When did you glean this bit of intelligence?"

The other day when she was sunbathing nude and I got to see that she was even more of a knockout with her clothes off.

He ignored the question. "What about the governor and the senator? Do we have more time?"

"We've bought ourselves an extra day, maybe two, but that's it," she said. "Remember, politicians are beholden to the media these days as much as if not more than the media is beholden to politicians. No one is going to the mat for a small-town mayor, especially with elections coming up next year. At least Selko kept his word. Today's story focuses only on the details of Curnutt's murder: the homemade silencer, the caliber of the weapon, like that."

Jesse was still pissed about Bella Lawton and Bascom's presence, but there was nothing he could do about it now.

"Chief, Nita, please join us," Mayor Walker said, calling them over to her desk.

After a quick round of handshakes and hot air from the mayor, she turned the floor over to Jesse. Stan White wasn't the kind of man interested in Robert's Rules of Order.

"Do you think this guy," White said before Jesse opened his mouth, "this Hangman character, really has the tape?"

Jesse answered White's question with one of his own. "If he does, how much would it be worth?"

"Millions," he said, parroting Roscoe Niles's answer to the same question. "Five, maybe six million. Maybe more. Who knows? It's one of the last few great mysteries of Baby Boomer rock, along with whether or not the Beatles intentionally fueled the Paul-is-dead rumor and what really happened to Bobby Fuller. The difference is that this one really might get solved."

Both Nita Thompson and Bella Lawton looked at Stan White as if he had just sprouted a second head.

"Bobby Fuller?" Bella said, almost unaware the words had actually come out of her mouth. "Who's Bobby Fuller?"

The mayor sang. "I fought the law and the law won . . ."

"I thought that was a Green Day song," Nita said.

Stan White threw his hands up. "Please!

The song was written by Sonny Curtis, who was in the Crickets, but the Bobby Fuller Four made it a hit in the mid-sixties."

"Thanks for the lesson in rock history, Stan," Jesse said. "But here's the deal. You have a few days at most to prepare for the media blitz that's bound to come if this guy can prove he really does have the tape. The tape isn't my concern. My job is to bring this guy in to see if he was the person who hired Curnutt and Bolton to break into Maude Cain's house, and to find out if he was the person who murdered Curnutt."

Nita was still unconvinced. "Aren't we getting ahead of ourselves? With all due respect, what if Jesse is wrong about this? We're operating on the basis of a big *if* here."

But the others in the room acted as if they hadn't heard her or as if they had fully bought into Jesse's theory.

"No," Stan White said, a hint of desperation in his voice. "Jesse's right. He's got to be."

The mayor asked. "If you are right, wouldn't it be safe to assume that the man with the tape and the man you should be focusing on is Humphrey Bolton?"

"Assumptions are never safe, Your Honor. Especially not in police work."

57

Getting together at Daisy's was usually something Molly and Jesse enjoyed, but Molly looked worn-out from all the overtime she'd been putting in. At least the more difficult of the two meetings, though there were no unexpected guests. She picked at her eggs as Jesse explained the situation to her. Not even the smell of freshly ground coffee or the sweetly sulphurous aroma of the frying onions and peppers on the griddle lifted her spirits.

"Two people dead, another in the hospital . . . All this over a stupid record album?" she said, staring at her food.

Before Jesse could answer, Daisy came by to refill their cups. "You look like you lost your best friend, there, Molly Crane."

"Just lost sleep," Jesse answered for her.

Daisy wagged her finger at him. "Well, stop working her so hard, Jesse. You two need a refill, just wave."

When Daisy moved on to the next table, Molly repeated her question about the missing tape.

"I do, Molly. It's got to be. Nothing else makes much sense."

"I hate how this makes Paradise look."

Jesse nodded. "I do, too, but if Stan White and Roscoe Niles are right about how much the missing tape is worth, no one will really be focused on the murders or on Paradise. The tape and the money will be what everyone is talking about. And that may even help us catch this guy. It's what he'll be thinking about, too."

"I guess." Molly, like Nita Thompson, seemed less than sold. "But if it's about that, why kill Curnutt? Why not let him just disappear?"

"This Hangman guy, whether he was the one to actually kill Curnutt or not, is trying to get as much attention as he can and he doesn't seem to care what he has to do to get it."

"What's he going to do with the media attention? I don't see the point."

"The Hangman, if he's really got the tape, is whetting bidders' appetites and driving up the price."

"What do you mean, 'if he has the tape'?"

"So far, he hasn't proved a thing. He

hasn't even really claimed to have the tape, not yet, but he will. He's going to have to prove he has it, or why go through all of this? There's already a trail of bodies. If he didn't have the tape, he'd get as far away from the press and the cops as possible instead of waving at us and calling attention to himself."

"And he thinks he's going to get away with this?"

"Seems so. This isn't being done on the spur of the moment, Molly. It was planned out, and my guess is that if Maude Cain hadn't died, the whole world would already know about it. Once she died, it complicated everything. It upped the stakes for Curnutt and Bolton because it went from B&E and assault to felony murder. They — Curnutt, at least — probably tried to blackmail the man who hired him and got whacked for his troubles. The killer figured that since he had to get rid of Curnutt, he might as well make good use of his body."

Molly didn't like it. "That's twisted."

"And practical."

"You think it might be Bolton behind it?"

"I don't think so. There's a reason his nickname is Hump."

"Doesn't mean he's too stupid to kill."

"True, but I spoke to Lundquist this

morning. He tells me he's checked with prison officials and that Curnutt and Bolton were close. That if one was going to screw the other, it would be Curnutt. No, Molly, the guy we're dealing with is smart. Smarter than Hump Bolton, at least. Let's hope he thinks he's a lot smarter than he actually is."

"Another criminal mastermind. I know your opinion on the subject."

"Overconfidence on the bad guy's part never hurts us."

"Never, Jesse?" Molly asked, immediately regretting it.

Jesse stood, threw some money on the table, and walked away. When he was almost to the door, he turned back to his officer and old friend.

"Almost never, Molly. Almost never."

58

Jesse pulled his Explorer into the faceless office park that was home to the studios of WBMB-FM. As confident as he was about what was going on in Paradise, he realized he had climbed out onto a ledge based on supposition and very few facts. There was little doubt that Mayor Walker and Nita Thompson, in spite of her recent friendly overtures, would happily watch him slip off that ledge. Although Roscoe had said the value of the master tape would be in the millions even before Stan White had an inkling *The Hangman's Sonnet* might reappear, Jesse needed to double-check the little he did have to go on. There was something about White he just didn't trust and the man was a little too self-interested for Jesse's taste. After all, he was Terry Jester's manager and had a vested interest in making this bash on Stiles Island into much more than a birthday party. The plan had been for Roscoe to be waiting outside the studio and for Jesse to take him out for a few drinks. Problem was, Niles was nowhere in sight. That wasn't like Niles, especially when free drinks were on the line.

"Roscoe Niles," Jesse said, enunciating carefully so that his phone dialed the right number.

"Stone?"

"Where are you? I'm downstairs."

"I think you better park your car and come in. Bring an evidence bag and gloves with you?"

"What the —"

"Just do it, Jesse."

Ten minutes later, Jesse was standing at the reception desk at WBMB-FM.

"I'll call back and tell him you're here," said the girl at the desk.

She looked about fifteen years old but was probably a college kid. Then Jesse remembered the last conversation he'd had with Niles and how Roscoe claimed the owners of WBMB-FM were in the process of selling the station.

Niles appeared out of the shadows of the hallway, his big belly straining the worn fabric of his ancient Emerson, Lake, and Palmer T-shirt. Still, Jesse was impressed by how gracefully the fat man moved. He wasn't exactly catlike, but he was athletic for a man his age and size.

"Come on back to my office."

Jesse followed Niles down the hallway, a pair of latex gloves and an evidence bag in hand. They passed the studios and went into Roscoe's cubbyhole of an office. Jesse was surprised at the sight of it. The last time he'd been in this office, its walls were covered in framed vintage posters, a guitar signed by Stevie Ray Vaughan, photos of a thinner, younger Roscoe Niles in his Marine uniform. The shelves of his bookcases full of records, CDs, knickknacks from a hundred concerts and appearances. But now the walls were bare, the shelves empty. Niles laughed, seeing the expression on Jesse's face.

"I'm outta here next month," he said.

"You were right? They sold?"

"I'm the Teacher, Jesse, man. The Teacher always knows best."

"I have an acquaintance in town who's going to be pretty upset you won't be on the air anymore."

Niles laughed again, joylessly. "Yeah, your friend and about fifteen other people."

Jesse got lost in his own head for a second. What *was* Vinnie Morris to him?

"Yo, Jesse!" Roscoe Niles snapped his fingers.

"Yeah, sorry. So what's all this about? Why do I need gloves and an evidence bag?"

"For this."

Niles pulled an eight-by-twelve-inch brown envelope out of his top drawer and slid it across the desktop to Jesse. By then Jesse was already slipping into the gloves. As he was putting the gloves on, he noticed there was a computer-generated white label on the envelope. Printed on the label in black ink were Roscoe Niles's name and the station's address.

"What's in it?"

Roscoe Niles smiled a crooked smile, one Jesse had trouble reading. There was something feral about it, something angry in it, too. Jesse guessed he understood the anger. Roscoe Niles had been a fixture on FM radio for decades and was now being shown the door. No one was going to give someone Roscoe's age a job, not in this environment. Roscoe was a fellow alcoholic, and alcoholics didn't deal very well with big changes in their lives, though big changes, negative ones in particular, opened the self-pity spigot and nothing gave an alcoholic carte blanche like a healthy dose of self-pity. Jesse was well familiar with the mechanics of how that worked.

"Hey, man, you mind if I have one while you do that?" Niles asked, pulling two glasses and a bottle of Johnnie Walker Red Label out of his bottom drawer. "Want one?"

"No, you go ahead." Jesse repeated his question. "What's in the envelope?"

"A myth realized," Niles said, pouring himself his usual half-glass of scotch.

"Uh-huh. C'mon, Roscoe."

"I'm not yanking your chain, Jesse. I swear. You'll see."

Jesse flipped the envelope over, undid the two-pronged clasp, lifted up the edge of the flap with his pinkie, and reached his right thumb and index finger inside.

"Careful, man. It's pretty old and fragile, though it's in plastic."

Jesse felt the corner of the plastic and carefully pulled it out of the envelope. What *it* was was a very yellowed, almost brown sheet of unlined paper in a thick, clear plastic folder. There were fifteen handwritten lines on the paper. The handwriting was a beautiful, flowing cursive. The line at the top of the page read: *The Hangman's Sonnet.*

THE HANGMAN'S SONNET

By my own hand I have murdered love
And by so doing have thus murdered me.
Neither Devil below nor God above
Led me into my somber destiny.

My fair viper Jane May played well her
  part
For what she gave as love was a fiction.
Ice made nest where should have beaten
  her heart.
In lieu of her soul, a cold affliction.

So the rope and gallows are sturdy built
Sandbags dangling to counter my dead
  weight.
But I am troubled not by bloody guilt
Nor relive I Jane's agony or fate.

In death's black-lined womb I seek her
  grace.
The mirror has revealed my hangman's
  face.

59

Jesse read it and reread it. He wasn't much for poetry. He wasn't even sure he knew what distinguished a sonnet from any other kind of poem, but there was something about the verse in front of him that hit a raw nerve. So many times in his career he'd heard the confessions of the guilty, of men who had brutally murdered their wives, girlfriends, or lovers. Men who inevitably blamed it on their victims. Still, he wasn't sure what to make of the poem or his re-action. He'd worry about that later. For now, he slid the envelope and the poem into the evidence bag.

"There it is," Niles said, gunning down his scotch. "The genuine article. The actual 'Hangman's' fuckin' 'Sonnet.' I never quite believed the myth about the poem. I guess I'm going to have to readjust my chronic cynicism."

"What's the myth?"

Niles shrugged, poured himself another. "Story goes that Terry Jester took a motorcycle trip out west after he went into his funk. He was in some trading post on an Indian rez in Wyoming and he came across this poem stuck between the pages of a horse soldier's diary. The diary was in a different hand, so Jester knew it hadn't been written by the soldier. Apparently, he went nuts over it and spent the rest of his time out west writing a song cycle inspired by the poem, imagining who wrote it, thinking about this Jane May woman, and contemplating how the poet killed her and why. Like I said, I always thought it was a crock, some story dreamed up by Stan White to market the album. I mean, he never released the text of the poem. All anyone ever knew was that it was written by a condemned man forgiving his executioner. Turns out that it's way more complex than that."

"What is it you don't like about Stan White?"

"Ah, man, where to begin? We were pals once, but . . . I'd rather not relive the bad old days, not when I've got the unemployment line staring me in the face." Roscoe took a big gulp of scotch. "Sure you don't want one?"

Jesse refused. His next questions were the

kinds cops were supposed to ask, not questions about myths or music. He asked about who had delivered the envelope. *Somebody said a messenger dropped it at the reception desk.* What did the messenger look like? *The girl wasn't at the desk and the guy who saw him barely noticed. The girl found it there when she got back from lunch.* How many people had handled the envelope? *The messenger, the girl, and me.*

Niles leaned across the desk and looked Jesse in the eye. "Jesse, we've been friends a few years now. What the hell's going on?"

"I'll answer that, but we need to talk about something else first."

"Shoot."

"What if I were to tell you that I think the missing master tape is about to reappear?"

"Holy shit, man!" Roscoe stood up out of his chair, banging his knee against his desk. "Ow!" He bent over and rubbed his knee. "Are you making conversation, Jesse, or are you telling me that's what this is about?"

Jesse didn't answer him directly. "Last time I was here I asked you how much it would be worth and you said millions. That was then, two friends shooting the breeze. Now I'm asking for real. How much?"

Niles stopped rubbing his knee, rubbing his fleshy, gray-stubbled cheek instead.

"Five million. Six, maybe. Ten. Twenty. More. Depends."

"That much?"

"Every time some putz finds an acetate or reel-to-reel of a Beatles song or performance, it goes for big money."

"Jester isn't the Beatles."

"No, but the shroud of mystery surrounding Jester, the secretive recording of this album, the disappearance of the tape almost makes it better. Plus it's Baby Boomer music. Baby Boomers hate new stuff, but they will flock to buy anything from the old days. They spend millions on Dylan box sets, Elvis box sets, even Monkees box sets, for chrissakes! Material from the old days sells like mad. It would be like some yahoo discovering an unknown van Gogh in his basement. There'd be a bidding war for it, no doubt. iTunes might snap it up for the exclusive rights or the legacy record labels might flex their tired old muscles. A private collector with billions might want it for his or her own. And you know what happens when there's only one of a thing and more than one person wants it."

"You know a reporter named Ed Selko?"

"Asshole at *The Globe*? Yeah, man, I know him. Started back in the day at *Rolling Stone* as an investigative reporter. Guy makes me look sober and you like a nun."

"That explains it," Jesse said to himself, but loud enough for Niles to hear.

"Explains what?"

"Never mind. And to answer your question, yes, I think the master tape is about to resurface."

"I'll drink to that," Niles said, pouring himself a glass.

"You'll drink to anything."

"But this isn't just anything, man. This is history. The music world has something to celebrate."

"Not yet, Roscoe."

Niles put his glass back down on his desk. "What's that supposed to mean?"

"Means we have to keep this under wraps for now. There's been two murders committed in connection with this, and that's what I've got to focus on."

Niles held his right thumb and forefinger an inch apart. "Man, I came this close to reading that damned sonnet on the air. Instead, I played a set of Jester tunes every hour. You can't keep this thing quiet forever and, truth be told, if the new owners were keeping me on, I probably would've read it on-air. As it is, I didn't want to give those fuckheads the satisfaction."

"Don't worry, Roscoe, it won't be too

much longer before the world knows," Jesse said, removing the gloves from his hands. "It's already taking on a life of its own."

After confirming with the girl at the front desk and the people in the office that no one had gotten a good look at the messenger, Jesse headed to his next stop in Boston.

60

For the second time in a week, Jesse found himself in the parking lot of the bowling alley out of which Vinnie Morris ran his operation. Of course Vinnie's name didn't appear on the deed to the building or the corporation papers. His name didn't appear on any of the buildings or businesses that he owned. It had been the same with Gino Fish. Any smart man knee-deep in organized crime made sure never to leave a paper trail. Vinnie's favorite four-letter word was *cash.* It's why he'd lasted as long as he had. There were other reasons, too, like doing the occasional favor for the cops. That was the reason for Jesse's visit. This time, he'd called ahead. So when Jesse asked for Vinnie at the front desk, he didn't get the usual I'm-too-stupid-to-breathe routine from the counterman.

"He's waiting for you at the bar," the dull-eyed guy said, nodding toward the bar.

He hadn't lied. Vinnie Morris was sitting at the bar, swirling a glass of ice cubes around with a splash of some amber alcohol or other.

"Stone."

"Vinnie. What are you playing with?"

"Some flavored bourbon crap my liquor guy dropped off a sample of. Horrible stuff, but he tells me the kids like it. You want to try some?" Jesse shook his head at Morris. "I didn't think so. Tony," he said to the barman, "two Black Labels, rocks."

Jesse thought about turning it down, but he didn't think about it too long. It had been a hard day that wasn't yet over. If this turned out to be the last stop of the night, which he hoped it wouldn't be, he still had the drive back to Paradise to deal with. Vinnie had hinted to him over the phone that he might have some information for him, but like with everything else, Vinnie had been careful not to say too much over the phone.

"Cheers," Vinnie said, raising his glass.

Jesse just nodded and drank. Sometimes scotch went down better than it did at other times. This was one of those times. It was magic, the way the chilled liquid burned at the back of his throat, how it warmed his whole body on the way down, and how it seemed to warm his face only when it reached his belly. It would have been so easy for him to have another and another and to lose himself, but no, that was his plight. That's what no one else saw, not Molly or Tamara, not Suit, not anyone. Maybe only Dix knew. And what he knew was that because of the way Jesse was built, because of his self-containment, he couldn't lose himself. That on the occasions he'd tried diving deep down into the bottle, like he had the other night, it never worked, and that the relief was only temporary and came at too high a price.

"So," Jesse said, after the initial warmth had receded. "You mentioned you had something for me."

"I said I might."

"That's what you said. You win."

"This Bolton strunz you're looking for."

"Uh-huh."

"I may have a line on him. Remember where you and me had our talk after Gino killed — after Gino died?"

"Dennis's?"

"That place, right."

"What about it?"

"Bolton walked in there the other day and left an address for one of my guys, a guy he did time with. My guy was out of town for the day and by the time he checked the address, Bolton had already split. He ain't the brightest mutt in the world, but he's smart enough to change his bed every night."

"You think he's still in town?" Jesse asked, finishing his drink.

"Sure. He reached out once. He'll reach out again. When he does, you'll hear about it."

"Thanks for the info and for the drink."

Vinnie laughed like a hyena laughed stalking prey. "Always glad to help the cops."

"I got some bad news for you. WBMB-FM was sold and the Teacher will be no more."

"Too bad. I love that drunk bastard. He brings me back to when I was a kid."

"I have trouble picturing you as a kid."

"Me too, Stone. That's why I'll miss Roscoe Niles."

"Remember when we talked about the missing Terry Jester tape?"

"Sure. What about it?"

"You mentioned a PI who worked the case. You got a name?"

Vinnie laughed again. "Spenser. Know him?"

"We met once. Wouldn't say I know him."

"His office is on the corner of Berkeley and Boylston. Third floor. Need directions?"

"Thanks. I'll manage."

"Any particular reason you want to talk to him, Stone? Might help you pay back the favor."

"You're a smart man, Vinnie. Why do you think I want to talk to Spenser?"

Morris showed his white teeth to Jesse in a Cheshire Cat grin. Jesse wasn't sure how Morris could possibly profit from knowledge of the tape's reemergence, but Vinnie was clearly pleased. Mob guys, as Jesse was aware, were good at figuring angles that people on the straight couldn't conceive of. That's what Jesse was thinking about as he shook Morris's hand good-bye.

61

Jesse wasn't sure the PI would be in but thought stopping by his office was worth a shot. He might be able to get the same information from the man over the phone. The thing was, he always thought it was better to see a person's face and body language. The phone robbed you of that. After he rapped on Spenser's office door, Jesse heard a vaguely familiar voice telling him to come in.

Spenser was at his desk, leaning back in his chair, his head turned to look out through the bowed window at nighttime Boston below. The office smelled of fresh-brewed coffee and of something else: dog. The source of the coffee aroma was obvious enough. A Mr. Coffee machine atop some metal filing cabinets burbled away, but there was no dog.

"How you doing, Stone?" Spenser asked without turning to face him.

"Vinnie Morris give you a heads-up?"

"Either that or I'm going to take my mind-reading act on the road. Look at it down there. You think you know this city, but it's never the same place two days in a row. How's Paradise?"

"Got two open murder cases. Other than that, it's heaven."

"Sunny always said you had a strange sense of humor."

"Most people don't credit me with having one at all."

Spenser turned his attention away from the street. He stood up and came around the desk, right hand extended.

"You hear from Sunny lately?" Jesse asked, shaking Spenser's hand.

"I was going to ask you the same question. She had it bad for you, Stone."

"I had it bad for her, too. Sometimes that's not enough."

"Vinnie told me about what happened to your fiancée. Sorry to hear it."

"Thanks."

Jesse studied Spenser's face to see if he meant it and that it wasn't just a thing the PI thought he should say. One look into Spenser's eyes and Jesse knew he'd meant it. Spenser looked a little older than he had the first time they'd met, his hair a touch grayer. Jesse imagined the PI was thinking the same thing of him. Older or not, Spenser was an imposing man. His arms were thick and muscular, his grip like a metal press. And he moved his six-foot-two two hundred and twenty pounds like he was still in the ring. One look at his boxer's nose and the scar tissue around his eyes would be warning enough for most people.

"Coffee, Bushmills, water, or any combination thereof?" Spenser said, walking over to the coffee machine and pouring himself a cup.

"Coffee with a little Irish."

"Have a seat."

A minute later Spenser was back behind his desk, Jesse across from him, both holding coffee mugs.

Jesse raised his mug. *"Sláinte."*

Spenser decided it was time to skip the rest of the small talk and move on.

"Vinnie also tells me you're interested in one of my old cases."

"The Hangman's Sonnet," Jesse said as if that explained it all. Apparently, it did.

Spenser laughed. "It was an insurance job, sort of."

"Sort of?"

"There had been lawsuits and settlements decades before over the missing tape, but it stuck in the craw of the original insurance investigator, a guy I crossed paths with over the years, Joe Didio. He was retiring and that missing tape was the one case that ate at him and kept him up at night."

"There's an old homicide from when I was in L.A. that haunts me. So what about the case?"

"We all have them. Look, I'm happy to help, but why's a man with two open murder cases in a seaside village north of here sitting in front of me discussing my old case, one that wasn't right to begin with? And what's with that envelope in the evidence bag. You going to the post office after this?"

Jesse put the evidence bag on the desk and tossed Spenser a pair of latex gloves. "Be gentle."

"You sound like my first girlfriend," he said, sliding the plastic sheet containing the poem out of the envelope. He took some time reading it. "I'm surprised it exists. It's not terrible, but I'll stick with Shakespeare. So is the tape going to finally surface?"

"That's my best guess," Jesse said. "It explains the two open cases in Paradise."

"Somebody's going to have a big payday."

"Seems to be the prevailing opinion. What did you mean when you said the case wasn't right?"

"You know how when a case ages, people talk because there's not as much at stake anymore. On this, the statute of limitations had been expired more than fifteen years earlier, but I couldn't find a thing. Only a few people connected to the case would even talk to me. The ones who did were on the periphery of things. Jester and his manager wouldn't return my calls, wouldn't answer the door when I knocked, and even tried to have me roughed up when I persisted."

"How'd that work out?"

"Not so well for the tough guy. He had no defense for my uppercut. Broke his jaw. The owner of the recording studio gave me five minutes but had nothing to say and was still fuming over the whole incident. The A-and-R man from the record label had long since given up the music business for car sales. All he said was that the label had taken a big hit and had gotten a lot of people fired. The only person who really spoke to me was the recording engineer who did the sessions. A nasty piece of work, that one. Guy gave drug abuse a bad name. Him, I couldn't get to shut up. All he did was go on and on about what prima donnas all the musicians were at the sessions and how he hated the business. Sour grapes."

"Did he mention any of the musicians by name?"

Spenser nodded, sipped from his mug. "But when I tried to contact them, they either ignored my inquiries or denied any involvement at all. Joni Mitchell's rep even went so far as to send me her tour itinerary to prove she couldn't have been at the sessions."

Jesse drank some, too. "Do you remember this engineer's name?"

"Not off the top of my head. I might have it in my notes, but those notes aren't here. Sorry."

"What did you make of it in the end?"

"The smoke surrounding the missing tape was made by a smoke machine and not a fire," Spenser said. "If you get my meaning. There was a lot of hype, but nothing to hold on to. If this album was all it was cracked up to be, why has everyone run away from it? If people were proud of it, you'd think all these Rock and Roll Hall of Famers would be telling stories about how cool the sessions were and how honored they were to be a part of it. Seems to me just the opposite is true."

After a few minutes of them discussing the open murders in Paradise and Hump Bolton's whereabouts, Jesse collected the sonnet and shook Spenser's hand for a second time.

"You hear from Sunny, let me know," Spenser said. "I'll do the same."

"Thanks for the help. You remember that engineer's name, please give me a call."

"I'll find it."

When Jesse was down on the street, he looked back up to where Spenser's office was and wondered if he could live that kind of life after he retired. If he didn't solve the two murders, he thought he might find out sooner than later.

62

Jesse felt spent as he drove back from Boston, his mind almost blank. He hadn't thought of Diana, as he usually did when he made the drive, nor had he thought about Vinnie Morris. He hadn't given a thought to Hump Bolton, the dragonfly ring, Kirk Curnutt, Maude Cain, Mayor Walker, or Nita Thompson. He wasn't even thinking about the sonnet in the envelope on the seat next to him. The one thing that kept going through his mind was a single word Spenser had said: *hype.*

Everyone else, from Stan White to Roscoe Niles to Vinnie Morris, had been so damned positive about the surfacing of the missing master tape, but not Spenser. Sure, he thought somebody was going to make a big payday out of it, though he was the only one who seemed skeptical of all the mythology surrounding the album. Jesse wasn't sure the PI's skepticism meant anything or would have any effect on the murder cases. Still, he couldn't get the word *hype* out of his head.

As he turned toward home, past the forlorn FOR SALE sign at the edge of the road, Jesse noticed a car parked near the front of his house. As he got closer, he saw that it was Tamara Elkin's Jeep and that the ME seemed to be asleep in the driver's seat. Even when Jesse's headlights shone through her side window, she didn't stir. Jesse's heart pounded in his chest in spite of his attempts at being rational. *Calm down. She's fine. She's just sleeping. Calm down. If you had your way, you'd be asleep, too. She's just here to talk to you. Calm down.* It was a waste of time. What had happened with Diana all came flooding back in.

He slammed on his brakes and jumped out of his Explorer, unholstering his nine-millimeter as he approached Tamara's Wrangler. He checked the vehicle for bullet holes or any other signs of violence. Finding none, he tapped the muzzle of his weapon against the driver's-side window. Tamara stirred immediately and the sleepy look of confusion on her face was quickly replaced by a smile, but the smile was just as quickly replaced by something else. Maybe because he was so tired himself, Jesse couldn't decipher the full meaning of Tamara's expression. Whatever her look's deeper meaning, Jesse could tell it wasn't good.

She rolled down her window. "Hi, Jesse. Sorry if I scared you."

"Have you been crying? Your mascara is —"

"I'll be in in a minute."

He knew better than to argue. "I know we're not supposed to be drinking together, but you look like you could use a —"

She didn't let him finish. "Make it a double, one cube."

Jesse left the door opened behind him, kicked off his shoes, put the evidence bag containing the envelope down on the kitchen table, and headed straight to the bar. He waved a finger of hello at Ozzie Smith, then poured her drink. He hesitated, but also made one for himself, light on Black Label and heavy on soda. He made Tamara's as she prescribed, a lot of scotch and more scotch with a single lonely ice cube.

When Tamara came in, it was obvious to Jesse that she'd fixed her makeup in the car. The streaks of mascara were gone from her cheeks and her fresh coat of lipstick shone in the light, but the makeup could do nothing to hide her red-rimmed eyes. He thought about hugging her, but he knew enough to do this her way and handed her the drink instead. She didn't even make a weak attempt at a toast or raise her glass except to drink. And drink she did. When she was done, Jesse took the glass from her.

"Another?"

"Less scotch, more ice, but yeah, another."

After polishing off half of her second Black Label, Tamara said, "Jesse, there's something . . . We need to talk."

He took a small swallow of his drink, put the glass down, and sat on his leather sofa.

"Okay, let's talk."

"First," she said, "I need a hug. I need to be held a little."

He pulled his right arm back, waving for her to come to him with his left hand. She sat down next to him and placed her head in his lap. Jesse ran his fingers through her impossible tangle of brown curls. It was very intimate, but there was nothing sexual about it.

"I had a date when I was a kid," he said, breaking the silence. "Was going pretty well, I thought. But when we were in her living room alone staring at each other, I reached out and stroked her hair. That did it. She made a face at me and she complained she wasn't a golden retriever and didn't feel like being petted."

Tamara laughed. It was a kind of shrill, manic laugh, not her usual deep laugh.

"What is it?" he asked when she calmed down. "What's wrong?"

"I got offered a job with the Travis County Medical Examiner's Office. Travis County. That's Austin, Texas."

"When would you have to leave? Are you going to take it?"

She sat up, stared him in the eyes. "Do you want me to — I mean, do you think I should? I'd start after Labor Day. It means I'd have to give notice now and leave next month."

"Is it a step up?"

"Of course it is. You know why I took the job here, because of the mess in New York."

"Uh-huh."

"Uh-huh! Is that all you're going to say?"

"Uh-huh."

She punched him in the arm. "Damn you, Jesse Stone."

He smiled, then asked, "Why would you take it?"

"The pay is higher. The taxes are lower. The weather's better. It'd be more of a challenge. My folks are still down there and they're not getting any younger."

"Sounds to me like you've made a pretty

airtight case for taking the job."

She sat up, kissed him softly on the cheek, paused. "That's why I'm here, stupid."

"How's that?"

"To let you talk me out of it," she said. "Or to make me hesitate a little."

"Your decision, Doc."

"At least tell me you'll miss me."

"You know I will. I miss you already."

"That's better," she said, resting her head on his shoulder. "Tell me more."

63

Tamara was gone by the time he woke up. Soon she would be gone for good. Another woman out of his life forever. He didn't want to think about that.

It had all been a desperate evening, sad, but with some laughs, too. They hadn't known each other all that long, yet they'd been through a lot together. In spite of their protestations about friendship and no commitments, they'd fallen a little bit in love with each other. How could they not? They were both such loners by nature and temperament, so willing to accept the limitations they each imposed on the relationship, there was an inevitability to love. Yet neither one of them would make the first move toward the bedroom. The time for that, if there had ever been one, had passed. Their love was built on friendship. It was an easy kind of love, short on expectations and long on comfort.

In the shower, Jesse's thoughts turned away from Tamara's pending departure to the events of the previous day. He couldn't get the sonnet out of his head. *In death's black-lined womb I seek her grace. The mirror has revealed my hangman's face.* And with the sonnet in play, it probably wouldn't be long before word of the missing tape would become public. Once that happened, there would be no controlling what followed. There was no way to get ahead of, around, or over what was headed his way. Maybe, he thought, the best thing to do was to run straight for it.

Jesse had lathered up half his face when the doorbell rang. His cell was on the vanity to his right. He checked it to make sure he hadn't missed calls from the station while he was in the shower. The last thing he needed was for Molly and Alisha to show up at his door again. No calls. He wiped the shaving cream off his face, threw on his old Dodgers shorts, and headed down the stairs. *Probably Tamara,* he thought, reaching for the doorknob. Although he was confident she was going to take the job in Austin, she hadn't said as much. She probably wanted to come over and get that on the record or give him another chance to talk her out of it. He hadn't done a very good job of discouraging her last night.

There was a woman standing on the other side of the door, but it wasn't Tamara Elkin. Bella Lawton smiled her electric smile at Jesse, and while she had on more clothing than she'd worn the other day by the pool, she was no less attractive. She was dressed in a sheer midriff-baring blouse that left almost nothing for Jesse's imagination to work with. She wore tight white shorts that were similarly stingy and open-toed shoes with chunky heels. Chunky or not, the heels somehow managed to exaggerate the perfect shape and flawless tan of her legs. And even from where he stood, Jesse could smell the raw scent of Bella's perfume, all crushed herbs with undertones of patchouli and citrus.

"Aren't you going to invite me in, Chief — Jesse?"

"Come in," he said, and stood back to let her pass.

She purposefully brushed lightly against him as she came into the house.

"I was about to shave," he said, not reacting to her touch. "What can I do for you, Bella?"

She smiled at him in a way that made her answer pretty clear. Then added, "Too bad you already showered."

Jesse wasn't in the mood for innuendo. "Why are you here?"

"I got tired of waiting for you to call me, so I took the initiative. That's how I've gotten to where I'm at, Jesse . . . initiative."

"Watch out for that. Initiative cuts both ways. It may get you far, but initiative almost got one of my cops killed a few years back."

"Don't you like me?"

"Well enough, but I don't really know you."

She laughed a coy little laugh. "I think that's the point of my visit, Jesse," she said, stepping very close to him and brushing her hand across his chest. "Letting you get to know me."

He stepped back and away from her and headed into the kitchen.

He called to her. "I'm putting up some coffee. You want some?"

She trailed after him, abandoning innuendo and nuance. "I want some, but not coffee."

"Sorry, not interested," he said, though it wasn't completely true. Any straight man with a pulse would have been interested in Bella, but he was more interested in something else: what she was doing there. Why had she come knocking today and not yesterday or tomorrow? Jesse understood Tamara. He even understood Nita Thompson's loneliness and why she had reached out to him. She was a loner, too. But Bella was different. Her being here felt like part of a calculation.

"Coffee's all I've got to offer."

"Too bad for you."

"I don't doubt it, but I'm probably about twice your age and you don't strike me as someone starved for male attention."

"Young men are fools." She waved her red-tipped fingers dismissively. "And they're too hungry."

"Watch that, Bella. I was young once and you won't be forever."

"Exactly." There was that smile again.

"How do you like your coffee?"

"Come on, Jesse, I'm going to be in and out of town for at least the next month. We could have some fun."

"Not going to happen."

She came around the counter, leaned against him, and put her lips to his ear. "Going once . . . going twice . . ."

He stepped back again. "Great perfume. The cream's in the fridge. Sugar's over there."

She shook her head. "You had your chance. Maybe if you're nice, you can have another."

"Very generous."

"You'd be amazed at how generous I can be."

"Probably. And Bella," he said, "I'll be in the mayor's office in about an hour. Why don't you meet me there? Bring Stan and Bascom with you."

That got her attention. "Now I'm curious. What's going on?"

"See you in an hour."

64

Jesse didn't know what to make of it, the feeling that he was being watched. He'd checked his mirrors many times on his way into town. He'd done all the tricks: made unexpected stops, pulled off the road, changed his route, doubled back, but he didn't see anyone or anything that was out of place. In the end he attributed it to his coming to terms with Tamara's news and to that little scene Bella Lawton had played out in his kitchen. He was still trying to make sense of that when he strode into Mayor Walker's office.

At least Bella had heeded his suggestion about bringing Stan White and Bascom along for the meeting. None of them looked very pleased about being summoned to a meeting, and Stan White let everyone know about it.

"Damn it, Stone, what the hell kinda town is this? Yesterday you seemed pissed that

Bella, Roger, and I were at the meeting. Today it's practically a command performance. What's with that?"

Bella Lawton hung back, almost as if trying to blend into the wainscoting. Jesse guessed she might have been a little bit embarrassed by her showing up at his house and coming on as strong as she had. Or maybe that wasn't it at all. Strangely, it was Bella who would probably be most pleased by what he was about to say, but it was Stan White's reaction Jesse was most interested in.

"Yesterday, a package was delivered by messenger to Roscoe Niles at WBMB-FM," Jesse said. "No one got a good look at the messenger."

Bella Lawton was puzzled. "Roscoe Niles. Who's he?"

"He's a fat old drunk, a DJ whose best days were behind him by 1980," Stan White answered. "He's a real prick."

Jesse shook his head. "He loves you, too. But he told me you were once friends."

White began to speak, but the mayor interrupted.

"I'm sure this is all very fascinating . . . or not. Someone please tell me why we're all here."

Jesse removed several sheets of paper from

a brown folder and handed them out. He scanned everyone for their reaction, but focused most intently on White.

Bascom grumbled, not even bothering to look at the sheet. "What's this?"

There was stunned silence from Mayor Walker and Nita Thompson. Bella Lawton tried hard to hide her smile but couldn't contain it. Stan White didn't even try to contain his smile. Still, his reaction seemed far too muted for Jesse's liking.

"Is this authentic?" Jesse asked White.

White didn't answer, not directly. "Where is it, the original?"

"I gave it to the state police for analysis before I came here," Jesse said. "Does this look like the original?"

"It does," White said. "But the original is on a sheet of old brown paper."

"What does it mean, Stan, if what was delivered to Roscoe Niles's station is the genuine article?"

"What does it mean?" White threw up his hands. "It means that whoever had the poem also has the tape. We were told by the police never to divulge that to the public. But both things were stolen at the same time. Terry, God bless him, always kept this poem in the studio for inspiration during the recording sessions. And one day, poof, both went missing."

Nita asked, "Jesse, why do you think the poem was sent to Roscoe Niles?"

"Because whoever has the tape is frustrated by the lack of coverage he's received. I suppose he hoped Roscoe Niles would read the poem on the air and blow this whole thing wide open. Let's be clear, it's going to come out. He's got the tape and he wants to auction it off to the highest bidder."

Bascom didn't like it. "The guy's a murderer."

"Probably," Jesse said. "But we'd have to catch him and then we'd have to tie the murders to the tape and him to the murders. Sounds simple enough, but all we've got at the moment is speculation and circumstantial evidence. We're going to have to play this thing out or we'll lose him."

"Chief, you can't be serious," Mayor Walker said.

"Deadly serious. Right now, he's holding fifty-one of the fifty-two cards in the deck. The only card we have to play is that he seems to want to do this with a big splash of publicity to create a bidding war for the tape. If we play it tough and refuse to negotiate, he'll take the tape off-shore and sell it to a foreign buyer who lives in a country less concerned about intellectual property rights than we are. He may get a smaller deal that way, but he'll have his money and disappear, Stan and Terry Jester will be screwed again, and we'll have two unresolved homicides."

"Jesse's right, Mayor Walker," Stan said. "In places like China, they don't care too much about copyrights."

Bascom nodded in agreement.

"If we play it out," Jesse said, "he may get cocky and overconfident. That breeds sloppiness, and, remember, at some point the tape and the money will have to change hands. That may be our one chance."

Mayor Walker asked everyone but Jesse and Nita to leave.

"You're taking an awfully big risk here, Jesse," Nita said after the other three had gone. "The problem is, the biggest risk isn't yours to take."

Walker waved the copy of the sonnet at Jesse. "It's my neck, pardon the expression, you'll be putting in the noose if this goes wrong. If this man doesn't get sloppy and gets away with it, I'll look like a fool for letting it happen. And firing your ass won't placate anyone but me."

"And if we don't play it out, we'll have two open murder cases. What do I tell my cops and the people of Paradise about that? That your career is more important than catching the bad guy? Should I tell them justice is a political equation?" Jesse said, pulling a book off a shelf behind the mayor's desk and placing it on her desk. "My job is to do right by the people of this town, not by your career."

She didn't bother looking at the book. "What's this?"

"It's a dictionary, Connie. Look up the words *public* and *servant*. We're supposed to serve the citizens of Paradise, not the other way around. You want to fire me, fire me now. Or maybe I'll resign and lay it all at your doorstep."

Mayor Walker stepped close to Jesse. "You wouldn't!"

"He would, Your Honor," Nita said, stepping between them. "Don't underestimate him."

Jesse turned so that they couldn't see his smile. "Let me know your decision, Connie. Until I hear otherwise, I'll be doing my job."

65

Jesse stopped at the donut shop and then went straight to the station. He'd hoped to catch up with Stan White and Bella Lawton after leaving the mayor's office. He'd missed them and decided it would be better if he spoke to them separately.

Molly had a grin on her face when he came through the station door. Jesse barely noticed. He was preoccupied with Stan White's reaction to the news about the sonnet. Sure, Jester's manager had smiled a big smile when he saw the copy of the poem, but Jesse had expected much more. After all, White and Jester stood to make millions once the tape was recovered and the legalities were sorted out.

Molly didn't wait for Jesse to ask. "I think I've got something."

"A summer cold?"

"You're an ass."

"Sorry. I've got a lot on my mind." He

held the box open to her. "Donut?"

"I shouldn't."

"Why do women always say that?"

"Because women are judged differently than men."

"How many times have I told you that you would have been a great cop anywhere you chose?"

"That's not what I mean and you know it," she said, looking up at him. "Suit can put on twenty pounds and you wouldn't see him any differently. You can't say that would be true of me. Diana used to talk to me about not being taken seriously at the Bureau because she was beautiful. Women always have to walk a fine line between looking good enough and not looking too good." When she saw Jesse's grim face, she realized what she'd said. "Oh, Jesse, I'm sorry. I didn't mean to bring up —"

He reached out, putting his free hand on her shoulder. "It's okay to talk about her, Molly. I like thinking about her sometimes. And you're right, women are judged differently and it's not fair."

"Then what's wrong?"

He decided against telling her about Tamara's job offer. It wasn't his place to make it public knowledge and it was his job to sort through his own feelings.

"I just told the mayor to fire me or to let me resign."

"One day, Jesse, you'll go to that well once too often and a mayor will call your bluff."

"And then you'll wear the crown."

"Stop saying that."

"You said you had something for me?"

"I'll be in your office in a minute," she said, reaching into the donut box.

He pulled the box away. "You shouldn't."

"Jesse Stone, when you're the voice of my conscience, I'll shoot myself. Now put that box back here." She grabbed a jelly donut.

A few minutes later, their roles were reversed. Molly was standing in front of Jesse's desk, holding the composition notebooks from Maude Cain's house in one hand and a file in the other.

"Remember we met with Deanna Banquer and she described that nasty lodger —"

"Evan. Any luck?"

"Well, I looked through every page in these notebooks, Jesse, and there's not a single mention of anyone named Evan. And the name didn't ring a bell for anyone I spoke with on the phone."

"I know you, Crane. You didn't come in here to tell me you failed."

"Evan wasn't in the books because Maude

Cain didn't consider him a lodger, at least not a lodger like the other people who stayed in her house."

"Why not?"

"Because he was her nephew." She put the file in front of Jesse. "The day Maude's body was discovered you told me to start searching for next of kin. Well, after the ME positively identified her, I dropped that search, but I got this back from the municipal clerk's office in Blue Ridge, Vermont. That's the town where Maude Cain's older sister, Mercy Updike, lived."

"Certificate of Live Birth," Jesse said. "Evan Cain Updike. May twenty-sixth, 1946. I'm not sure this gets us anywhere, but it's something. See if you can find him."

"Gee, Poirot, I never would've thought of that on my own."

"Wiseass. Get out of my office." She left.

Jesse stood, stretching some of the weariness out of his muscles, staring out his office window. He would head over to Stiles Island in a little while, but first he wanted to have a chat with Roscoe Niles. The night before, Spenser had mentioned the guy who had worked as the engineer for *The Hangman's Sonnet* recording sessions. If anyone might know the man's name, it would be Roscoe Niles. Niles had an encyclopedic knowledge of those sorts of facts. He could tell you who played tambourine or triangle on obscure tracks. Jesse would ask Stan White the same question in a little while, but he didn't trust White to begin with and trusted him even less after his reaction in the mayor's office. Unfortunately, his calls to Roscoe's house went unanswered. Jesse was in the process of leaving a voicemail message when Molly burst back into his office.

"Jesse, you better get over to the nature preserve," she said.

"Why?"

"I just got a call on the station number. Said we'd find something in the old toolshed."

"Same anonymous guy as before?"

"The number was blocked like before, but I couldn't tell for sure. I sent Gabe ahead to secure the area."

"Good. Did the caller say what we'd find?"

"Only that we'd find something in the shed."

Jesse smiled. Whoever they were dealing with was getting impatient. Maybe too impatient for his own good.

66

Gabe Weathers was leaning against the front fender of his cruiser when Jesse pulled up.

"Did you approach the shed?"

"No, Jesse. The tape is still up from when the body was found over there, so I just stayed here to make sure no runners or hikers approached the shed. I haven't seen a soul since I arrived."

"Okay, you sit tight," Jesse said, putting on gloves. "Get Peter down here, just in case I find something in there."

"Think it's another body?"

"If it is, you'll be calling Molly Chief Crane."

Gabe laughed. When he saw that Jesse was serious, he stopped.

But for the sounds of chirping birds, small animals rustling the leaf litter, and the barking of angry squirrels, there was a strange stillness in the air. Jesse didn't like it, but he hadn't liked much of anything lately. From the morning of Suit's wedding, when he hid his shaky hands as he listened to Bascom, White, and Bella go on about Terry Jester, to that moment in the woods, everything had seemed just a little off. He thought back to earlier in the day, to how Bella Lawton had just shown up at his door to offer herself up to him for the asking and he recalled how on his drive into town he'd had the sense he was being watched. He felt that way now. He ducked under the tape and felt the earth give under his weight.

"Did it rain last night?" he asked, turning back to Gabe.

"Sprinkled on and off for about a few hours, but nothing to speak of."

"And you're sure you haven't seen any-one?"

"Not unless you count a doe and her fawn."

"You're a funny man, Gabe."

"My wife doesn't think so. By the way, Peter's en route."

Jesse stayed close to the tape as he approached the shed. As he walked, he looked at the ground near the shed. He noted the deer tracks but didn't see fresh shoeprints anywhere. That didn't necessarily mean there wasn't something in the shed. The call to Molly might have come in only fifteen minutes ago, but what was left in the shed might've been left there before it rained. He stood by the shed, looked it over thoroughly before opening the door. He wasn't exactly sure what he was looking for, but whatever it was, he didn't find it. He pulled the door back.

Nothing. Well, nothing but what had been there the day they found Curnutt's body. Just spiderwebs and the handle to an old rake or shovel that had probably been there, untouched, for years.

"Anything, Jesse?" Gabe called to him.

"Not a thing. Call Peter and tell him not to bother. False alarm."

Weathers, ducked his head into his cruiser and did as he was told.

"Okay, Jesse. Peter's gone back on patrol."

Jesse came away from the shed and stood about dead center of the tape perimeter. He was facing away from Weathers, toward Sawtooth Creek. "Gabe," he said, not turning around. "Were you a ballplayer as a kid?"

"I was a shooting guard on my high-school basketball team." His voice was full of pride.

"Any good?"

"I could shoot the lights out, but I wasn't great at creating shots for myself off the dribble."

"How did you feel when the other team controlled the tempo?"

"I hated it."

"Me too, Gabe. I've never liked it when other people dictated the pace of things or when a guy on the other team deked me into making a stupid move."

"What's this about, Jesse?"

"It's about me being tired of the other team controlling the tempo and trying to distract me."

"Whatever you say."

Jesse turned to face his man. "Okay, Gabe, you can get back to work."

When Gabe was gone, Jesse spun around. Unable to shake the feeling that he was being watched, he stared into the woods between him and the creek but saw nothing. He made a slow sweep with his eyes, swiveling his head, looking for something, anything to lock onto. Then, to his left, in the thickest part of the woods, he thought he caught sight of something, a shape moving among the trees. Then there was no movement but for the leaves and limbs swaying in the breeze. He kept looking, waiting for the shape to emerge from the backdrop. There it was again, movement in the trees not caused by the wind. Jesse still couldn't make out the shape, its silhouette broken up by the sway of the leaves and shadows. Things got very still, unnaturally still. That's when Jesse noticed a glint, the sun reflecting off something near where he had last seen the shape.

His reflexes took over and Jesse dove to his left. Behind him something slammed into the side of the shed, tiny splinters flying off into space. The sound of the rifle shot echoed through the woods. Another shot, this one much lower, cut another hole in the side of the shed, the echo seeming to almost overwhelm the report of the first shot. Jesse combat-crawled away from the shed as quickly as he could manage, his right shoulder barking at him as he went. He found cover behind some trees, stayed flat on his belly, waiting for more shots to follow. They never came.

After a few minutes, his nine-millimeter in hand, Jesse looked around to where he had seen the shape against the trees and reflection in the leaves. There was nothing to see. The only shapes visible were ones that belonged to nature. Still, Jesse kept low as he worked his way to his Explorer. *At least I'm not imagining things,* he thought as he drove back into town. Someone had been watching.

67

What had just happened in the preserve didn't make any sense to Jesse. He was about to call an old friend to discuss it when the sound of a ringing phone came over the speakers in his car and Roscoe Niles's name flashed onto the dashboard screen.

"I've been trying to call."

"Yeah, Jesse, what?" Roscoe's voice was almost comically thick with drink.

"Rough evening?"

"At my age, with my vices, they're all rough. Some are just rougher than others."

"Why didn't you pick up before?"

Niles was surprised. "You called? I was out of it, man. Johnnie Red and I spent a lot of time together last night. What can I do you for?"

"Two things. Are you on the air today?"

"I'm always on the air. Well . . . until I get the official word about my last day. Why?"

"Can you do me a favor?"

"Depends. What do you need?"

"I might call you later and ask you to read the sonnet on the air. And if I do, read it as many times as you want. Play wall-to-wall Terry Jester if you feel like it and imply that the missing tape may soon resurface."

"You sure about this, Jesse. Yesterday you told me —"

"Yesterday was yesterday. Things have changed."

"Like what?"

"My mood."

Niles's laugh was phlegmy, and laughing set him off on a coughing jag. "What the hell, they can only fire me once, right? I'll be glad to do it, man."

"Where are you, Roscoe? It sounds like you're outside."

"Oh . . . I had to . . . step out to smoke, man. What's the other thing, Jesse?"

"Do you know who engineered *The Hangman's Sonnet* sessions?"

There was a long pause and then he said, "Sorry, pal, but like everything else about those sessions, the names of the people who worked in the studio are shrouded in secrecy."

"But there are rumors, like the rumors about the musicians."

"Not really, Jesse. The musicians matter

to the public. No one gives a shit about who worked the board. Why do you ask?"

"Someone mentioned him to me but didn't recall his name," Jesse said, unwilling to go into the details of his conversation with Spenser.

"Sorry, man. I wish I could be more helpful. Listen, are you sure about the poem?"

"No, but do it anyway."

Jesse clicked off and called Healy.

"Jesse! How the hell are you?"

"Someone just tried to kill me."

"That's not funny, Jesse. Don't even joke like that."

"I wasn't joking."

"What do you need?"

Jesse asked, "Can you meet me at the Rusty Scupper in the Swap in a half-hour?"

"Only if you say 'please.' "

"Please."

68

Healy was nursing a Jameson at a booth at the back of the Scupper. Jesse couldn't help but smile at the sight of his old friend. Jesse shared a bond with Healy that he shared with very few other men. They'd both been minor-league baseball players. Healy was a drinker, too. They'd shared many a late-night whiskey together in Jesse's office — some celebratory, some not. As the former head of the state Homicide Bureau, Healy understood murder intimately, the way Jesse understood it. But there was one thing that tied them together in a way nothing else could: Healy had been there when Diana was killed and had looked the other way when Jesse did what he'd had to do.

"Let me get you a Black Label," Healy said as Jesse slid in across from him.

"Nothing for me."

"I don't know, Jesse. Getting shot at would give me a powerful thirst."

"It gives me a knot in my belly."

"Any idea who it was?" Healy asked, sipping his Irish.

Jesse answered with his own question. "You been keeping up with what's been going on around here?"

"You mean about the break-in at the Cain place and the body you found out in the woods?"

"It's more complicated than that."

Healy laughed. "Usually is."

Jesse laid it out for him, every detail of the case including the index card, the missing dragonfly ring, the master tape, and the appearance of the sonnet.

"So you think it was this Hangman character who took shots at you?"

Jesse shook his head. "I don't. Everything the guy's done until today made sense. There seemed to be a purpose behind all the moves he made. Everything from calling in the location of Curnutt's body, to faxing the photo of the index card and note to Selko, to having the sonnet delivered to Roscoe Niles all made sense. They were all done to whet people's interest, to get a buzz going, and to create a seller's market. But what does killing me get him?"

"Well, maybe he figures he'll stop you

from blocking the press from going big with it."

"Maybe, but it wouldn't be worth it because he'd be killing a cop. That's not like having an old woman die on you or killing an ex-con who caused the old woman's death."

"You're right," Healy said. "Kill a cop and screws up the deal."

"Exactly. You can't have that tape associated with the murder of a cop. That's going to cut out any legitimate bidders for the tape if it resurfaces. That's just dumb and this guy isn't dumb."

"So what does that tell you?"

"That there's more than one person involved."

"Could be, but also could be one person and for some reason he's trying to distract or confuse you. Maybe he's trying to create chaos or he wants you looking left when you should be looking right."

"That's too bad for him, because the only two people who are ever going to know about the shooting are sitting right here."

"You're not going to make a report?"

Jesse shook his head. "I don't think he shot at me to create chaos or distract me. It felt personal."

"Strangulation is personal. Sticking a

potato peeler in your jugular, that's personal, Jesse. A rifle with a scope . . . I'm not so certain."

"I know, but that's how this felt."

Healy finished his drink. Jesse waved at the barman, pointed at his friend's empty glass, and said, "Another."

The barman was less than thrilled at playing waitress, but brought the second drink over to the table. Jesse paid for it and gave him a five-dollar tip.

"So why the powwow, Jesse? You can't miss me that much. I saw you at the wedding last Saturday. Besides, I'm not telling you anything you don't already know."

"I need you to do something for me."

"I'm going to regret this, but ask away."

When Jesse was done explaining himself to Healy, they shook hands. Jesse stood as they did.

"I'm headed to the Wickham place now. You can get started tomorrow. You sure this won't interfere with your golf game?"

Healy laughed. "Even though I was a pitcher, I used to be a fair hitter. I could hit the curve pretty well, but I can't hit a damn ball that's sitting still on a tee. Anyway, it will get me out of my wife's hair. Let me tell you, Jesse, nothing tests a marriage like retirement."

"Tomorrow, then."

With Healy in the fold, Jesse decided he was going to push back. He called Roscoe Niles and told him to read the sonnet on-air. His next call was to Molly.

"Call the mayor's office for me and warn her the shit's about to hit the fan."

"Did someone leak it?"

"Uh-huh."

"Do you know who?"

"Me."

"Why?"

"Because it was time for us to stop playing defense and take control of the situation."

Molly was skeptical. "But how can we take control of things?"

"My field training officer told me that opportunities to control a situation may not be obvious, but they're always there. It's all about the choices you make."

"Choices?"

"Even a man with a gun to his head has a choice, Molly. It may not be a great choice, but as long as there's any room for a choice, the man with the gun doesn't have total control."

Jesse didn't bother to explain. Molly was smart enough to work it out for herself.

"If you need me, I'm going over to Stiles to have a talk with White and Bella Lawton."

"I bet you are," Molly said, wriggling her eyebrows.

"Later."

As Jesse drove out of the Swap, a Paradise firetruck went screaming by him, siren blaring and light bar whirling. Jesse had a strict rule about his cops using their lights and sirens within village limits, but he guessed it was a little bit different for the fire department. He was curious about where the firetruck was headed, but not too curious. He figured he already had enough on his plate.

69

This time, Jesse came through the gate of the estate and entered the house through the front door. Stan White came to the door, cell phone wedged between his cheek and neck. He was nodding as if the person on the other end of the line could see him agreeing with what was being said.

"You shouldn't have done it anyway, friend or not," White said into the phone. "Listen, I've got to go. The police are here. For what, I don't know. Okay, yeah, we'll speak later."

After he put the phone back in his pocket, White offered his hand to Jesse. Jesse took it, gave it a shake that wasn't exactly warm and friendly, nor was it icy and belligerent. It was a shake to signal he was here on business. White understood.

"You look like a man on a mission, huh?"

"Uh-huh."

"Let's go into the kitchen to talk. I need

some coffee."

Jesse followed White into the enormous country kitchen of the Wickham house. He sat at the island while White fussed with the coffee machine.

"Look at this thing, Chief. It's more complicated than the Saturn Five rocket. It grinds the beans, brews the coffee, steams the milk. I don't know, I miss the days when coffee came in a can, you threw a few scoops in a basket, added some water to the pot, and you percolated the shit out of it. I'm getting old, Stone."

Jesse, who'd didn't have much use for White, thought this was the first human moment they'd shared. It was the first time White let his guard down and stopped being Terry Jester's blustery manager and promoter. And White wasn't done showing his human face.

"The music business, too. It used to be a glorious thing. Now it's like a bad-paying hobby. Kids don't think you should have to pay for anything anymore. They've been raised in a Walmart and Amazon economy where everything can be shopped down to prices so low no one can make a living. Art for them is free. With file sharing and piracy . . . I'm glad I'm almost out of it." White got a faraway look in his faded blue eyes. "The business used to be exciting, so full of characters. We used to create product you could hold in your hands. Now what do you have? You have atoms rearranged on a hard drive. Where's the album cover, the liner notes? It's all gone down the crapper." He came back into the moment as he finished steaming his milk and pouring it into his espresso. "So, what can I do for you?"

"This morning, when I showed you the sonnet, you didn't react the way I would have expected you to react."

"What, you wanted me to kick up my heels? I'm old, Chief. Yeah, so even if the tape reappears, and we work through all the legal hassles, and we get the rights back, and we make some money, so what? What then? Is a beautiful babe like Bella gonna crawl into my bed? I've been around the world two or three times. What can the world show me that it hasn't shown me before? What kind of car can I buy that I didn't drive already? You see what I mean?" White shrugged and leaned across the island. "Please don't share this, but Terry is ill. He's not really there anymore, hasn't been for years. All that stuff I said about him singing at the party, it was hype. I don't even know if he'll be aware of what's going on at the party, but I wanted to give him a grand send-off. One he deserves."

"Sorry to hear it."

"You didn't come here to listen to my sentimental ramblings. So what is it I can do for you?"

"The engineer on the *Hangman's Sonnet* sessions. What was his name?"

White laughed, took a sip of his coffee, and shook his head. "That idiot! But you're wrong, Stone. It's not him with the tape. Couldn't be. He was the prime suspect when the poem and the tape disappeared. They searched his house, his car, his locker at the studio. Nothing. I even paid a whole series of PIs to follow him for the next year. Paid girls to, you know, get close to him. Again, nothing. Of course he refused to take a lie-detector test. Claimed they were bullshit and infringed on his rights. We couldn't force him, and even if he took one and failed it, it wasn't admissible in court. And let's face it, if he had it, he could have sold it long before this or sold it back to me or a record company years ago."

"All good points, but why don't you let me do the police work? What was his —" At that precise moment, Jesse's cell buzzed in his pocket. "Excuse me, Stan. I've got to take this."

"Sure, Chief, go ahead."

"Jesse Stone," he said, walking out of the kitchen into the great room.

"Spenser here. I've got that name for you. The engineer was named Evan Updike. I hope that helps."

"More than you know. Thanks."

"Anytime."

When Jesse reentered the kitchen, White was gone, his half-empty cup of coffee cooling on the white marble countertop. Jesse no longer needed him, but that didn't mean he wouldn't pursue the conversation further. He called Molly.

"We have a suspect," he said. "Guess who the engineer was on the *Hangman's Sonnet* sessions."

"Casey Jones."

"Wrong kind of engineer, Molly. It was Evan Updike."

"Who lived in his aunt Maude's house just around the time the master tape went missing."

"Dig up photos of him and any info you can get. Put a call into the Yarmouth PD. I'm sure the cops who worked the case are retired by now, but see if you can't get some names and addresses. And don't put word out yet. What did the mayor say when you told her the bad news?"

"She wasn't happy, but I think she was resigned that it would leak eventually."

"Okay. Thanks."

Jesse set out to find Bella Lawton.

70

Bella was again sunbathing by the pool. She had on less clothing than she did during her unexpected visit to his house, but more than she'd had on the last time he'd been here. She was wearing a shimmery silver bikini that tempted Jesse to ask why she even bothered with a bathing suit.

Bella used her right hand as a visor, placing it above her sunglasses. "Jesse." She sounded pleased and gave him a full-on smile. "Have you reconsidered?"

He sat on the edge of the lounge chair beside hers. "No, sorry. I came to talk to Stan. I'm surprised to see you out here. Don't you ever work? I thought you'd be burning up the phones."

She laughed. It was the laugh of a teenage girl caught by her mom doing something in her room they both knew she shouldn't be doing, not in her room, maybe not anywhere. Bella sat up, the smile vanishing.

"Can I tell you something, Jesse?"

"Uh-huh."

"My PR firm, the one I gave you that fancy card for . . . It's kind of an exaggeration. I mean, I've done some promo work, but not this kind of thing. This Jester thing is way above my paygrade. I was a club promoter in Boston. Do you know what that is, a club promoter?"

He nodded. "Bar and club owners hire you to get people through their front doors."

"Right. I was good at it, too. People usually have trouble saying no to me. Well, most people."

"I'm sure that's true."

"That's how Stan found me. He came to me and offered to set me up in my own business, to make it legitimate. He got me incorporated, got me an accountant and everything. Bought me cards, showed me the ropes. He's really smart about promo stuff and he knows a million people."

"But why you? Why did he choose you? No offense, Bella, but there are hundreds of firms he could have gone to who have the same contacts, better contacts than he does."

Without a hint of embarrassment, she said, "Because I came cheap and I'm beautiful. Stan's an old man, but he's not dead.

He likes having me on his arm. He likes the respect in other men's eyes when they see me with him. He gets off thinking about what those other men think when they see me with him."

Remembering Diana's struggles at the FBI and his conversation with Molly, he asked, "You're okay with that?"

"People use each other all the time, Jesse. I'm young, but I learned that lesson a long time ago. When I hear someone say they were used, I always want to call bullshit on that. Nothing is ever one-sided. And so, sure, Stan is using me, but I'm learning things. I'm meeting people. I'm collecting contact information, making connections, networking. When this Terry Jester gig is done, I'll collect my fees and be on my way. Stan can look at the photos of me standing beside him, put them up in his office, and dream his dreams. What's wrong with that?"

"I'm a cop, not a judge, Bella."

"I like you, Jesse, even though you hurt my feelings this morning. You're less full of shit than most men. But I can tell you disapprove."

"I know a little something about trading on beauty."

"I just bet you do. What about it?"

"It's got a limited shelf life and it gets you

just so far."

She sat up, faced Jesse, her expression going steely before his eyes. "Thanks for the advice, but let me worry about that. I've got all sorts of charms, some less obvious than others. The offer stands. Just say the word."

He ignored that. "But why aren't you working the phones to get people to come to the party? It's a pretty solid assumption that whoever has the tape is going to approach Stan once word gets out, and I feel pretty confident word is about to come out."

She laughed again, only this time it was a laugh as cold as her expression. "Stan's already been working the phones."

"Has he?"

"I think it's safe to say that when it goes wide, he'll already have offers in place for new bidders to compete against. I told you, Jesse," she said, leaning back down on her chaise, "I'm learning a lot from Stan. Why aren't I working the phones? Because when word about *The Hangman's Sonnet* gets out, all the A-listers who couldn't even be bothered to return my calls and emails will be begging to get a second chance to attend the birthday party. I won't have to call them. They'll be calling me."

"You have learned a lot," he said. "Let me ask you one more question before I go."

"Anything."

"How much has Stan paid you so far?"

Unlike with her previous snappy answers, Bella hesitated. Her lip twitched almost imperceptibly.

"He's paid for my wardrobe, put me up here, given me spending money. The payoff's a percentage on the back end," she said, her voice louder, too loud.

"Thanks, Bella."

He turned and went back into the house.

71

Molly had called him before he'd even made it out the front gate of the Wickham estate with the name of the retired cop who had led the investigation into the missing *Hangman's Sonnet* master tape.

"His name's James Flint and he lives on Mayflower Way in Swan Harbor."

Tamara Elkin lived in Swan Harbor, but in a different part of town. Three-eleven Mayflower Way was a brick colonial only a few blocks from the Atlantic in an older part of town than Tamara's condo. All the houses on the street were fronted by hand-built stone walls and surrounded by big old oaks and maples. Jesse parked in front and walked up the entrance. The front door swung open even before he was halfway to the small granite stoop. A tall but bent man, his hair a wiry steel gray, stepped out and called to Jesse.

"Chief Stone, walk around back. I'll meet

you out there."

Flint retreated back inside as Jesse veered to his right and made his way around back. There was a small cedar deck butted up against the house. There was a picnic-style table on the deck, on the table a pitcher of iced tea and two glasses. As Jesse was sitting down, Flint came out the back door, carrying a thick, dark brown accordion file in his left arm.

"Chief," Flint said, shaking Jesse's hand. "I'm Jimmy Flint."

"Please call me Jesse."

"Yeah, I s'pose it's better than us calling each other Flint and Stone." Flint poured out the iced tea.

"Means we can skip the Fred-and-Barney jokes."

The left corner of Flint's lips turned up in what passed as a smile. "Officer Crane tells me there's a break in the case," he said, thumping the accordion file down on the table.

"See for yourself." Jesse unfolded a copy of the sonnet and slid it over to the old cop.

Flint shook his head. "I'll tell you what, Jesse. There were many times I didn't believe the damned poem existed."

"But there it is."

"That it is."

"I've held the original in my hand, but what made you say that, about not believing the poem existed?"

"Look, Jesse, the Yarmouth PD isn't exactly the FBI or the Boston PD, and I suppose it was even less of a force back in the mid-seventies when I worked the case, but Jester wouldn't even talk to us. It was all Stan White, the manager. White said there were no copies of the poem because Jester wouldn't let copies be made, so we had nothing to go on there. And no one other than White and Jester had seen it."

Jesse asked about the tape.

"Yeah, we had the box the tape was stored in. Here!" Flint reached into the file and produced several faded color photos of an empty plastic box. "The prints on the box were Jester's, White's, and Evan Updike's."

"The engineer. That's who I'm interested in," Jesse said.

"What an asshole. I liked him for it. We all did."

"But?"

"But there was no hard evidence against him. All of their prints were all over the damned studio. No one saw him take it. We executed warrants on his room and on his car. We even kept him under surveillance until he left Cape Cod. We knew exactly what we were looking for, too."

Flint pulled out another faded photo. This one was black-and-white. It was a shot of Terry Jester, a much younger Stan White, and a man Jesse assumed was Evan Updike, holding a reel of tape toward the camera. The top side of the reel faced the camera. On one of the wide metal spokes of the reel was a piece of masking tape and on the masking tape was written THE HANGMAN'S SONNET MASTER in black marker. White and Updike were smiling, but Jester's expression was flat and distant.

"That Updike there?"

"Yup," Flint said. "A nasty piece of work, that one. Must've been a hell of an engineer for people to put up with the bastard."

"Seems he had that effect on everyone. I never met the man and I don't like him."

"So, Jesse, do you really think this is it? Is the tape going to resurface after all these years?"

Jesse explained the details, about where Curnutt's body had been found, about Updike being Maude Cain's nephew, about how he'd rented a room from her in the period of time after the tape went missing, and about Roscoe Niles receiving the original poem at the station.

"I'd appreciate a call if and when the

tape's recovered. This damned case has kept me up nights on and off for forty years. Be nice to know for sure before I kick."

"It's a promise," Jesse said, shaking Flint's hand.

Flint pushed the accordion file toward Jesse. "Here, take this. Been nothing but a damned albatross to me all these years. Hope it ain't one for you, son."

Jesse hoped so, too.

72

Hump knew it was late when he cracked his lids open, but he was still tired and fell back into that nether space between waking and sleep. Trapped inside since he'd come to Boston, moving only at night from place to place, he'd had very little option but to eat and watch TV in the shithole apartments of the men who'd been willing to put him up for the night. Overeating made him lazy and fat and he found that all he wanted to do was to escape into sleep. That morning it was especially bad because he was stressed and up against it.

He was running out of time and options. He was already taking stupid chances by staying with the last two guys he'd asked to put him up for a night. He had iffy relationships with both of them. Two days ago it was someone he knew as a kid but not exactly a friend and not a person he had a whole lot of faith in. Still, it had worked out. He'd thrown the guy two hundred bucks and asked him to forget he'd ever been there. Yesterday he'd taken a much bigger risk, staying at Milo Byrnes's dump. Milo was a full-on tweaker, the kind of guy who'd steal anything from anyone and worry about consequences and the swag's worth afterward. That's how he'd ended up inside with Hump and King in the first place.

Hump was quickly falling out of the in-between world and back into sleep, his body relaxing as he fell. Somewhere in his head he thought he was at the beginning of an unpleasant dream. It was a dream of noises and odors, of a squeaking door hinge, creaking floorboards, the gentle rustling of fabric against fabric. It stank of old sweat and smoke. It didn't take long for Hump to decipher that the stench and the noises were coming not from dreamland but from Milo Byrnes rifling through his stuff.

If Hump had been fully awake, there'd be no contest between a skinny, decayed weasel like Milo Byrnes and himself. Hump had been horrified at the sight of Byrnes when he'd come through his apartment door the night before. The guy's skin was a sickly yellow, his teeth were rotting out of his head, and he looked like a walking skeleton.

Hump opened his eyes just enough to get a sense of what was happening, but he was facing a wall, his back to Byrnes. Hump had his nine in bed with him and his cash was in a bag taped to the inside of his left thigh. The ring, though, was in one of his bundled-up socks. He couldn't let a skel like Byrnes get to it.

Hump rolled around, tossing the moth-eaten sheet off him, raising the nine-millimeter toward Byrnes.

"What the fuck, Milo, you piece of —"

But he couldn't finish the sentence because Byrnes had come armed, too, and plunged a serrated kitchen knife into Hump's belly. Hump reached out with his left hand, grabbing onto Byrnes's sweat-soaked T-shirt that hung off the tweaker like a tent. He pulled Byrnes close to him, put the muzzle of the gun into the flat of the bony man's abdomen, and fired. He fired again. Again. The third bullet went right through the bag of bones and skin and into the wall of the closet-sized bedroom. Some of the noise was swallowed up by Byrnes's now-lifeless body. Hump tossed the almost weightless dead man aside like an old foam pillow.

Ears ringing, light-headed, he stood. When he did, he collapsed back onto the bed. He noticed his shirt was slowly turning red, soaking with blood, and that the kitchen knife was still stuck in his belly. He laughed at his situation, wincing in pain as he did. The knife was going to have to come out, and when it did, it was going to hurt like a bastard. That wasn't the worst of it. He knew that when he pulled it out, the serrated edge would do more damage and the bleeding would get much worse.

Hump forced himself to get up again, tossing the gun down on the bed. He found his way into the filthy bathroom, going through the cabinets for anything that might work as an antiseptic, for gauze or cotton, anything he could use to stanch the wound, and tape to hold the makeshift bandage to the wound. What he found in the bathroom was some cotton wadding and toilet paper. Nothing else. In Byrnes's room, he found a syringe Milo had readied for himself and a pint bottle of cheap vodka with a few swallows left inside.

Hump took a swig of vodka, tied off his left biceps with the piece of rubber tubing Milo had meant to use for himself, poured a stream of vodka onto the syringe, and then stuck the needle into a bulging vein at the bend of his left arm. The jolt was immediate, intense. Hump's whole body clenched, his eyes widened, the noise on the street below turned into the buzzing of a million mosquito wings. In a single motion he tore his shirt off as if it were made of tissue paper. Strangely, what had frightened him so only a few seconds before — the thought of yanking the knife out of his gut — now seemed like something he couldn't wait to try. Without hesitating, he grabbed the knife's handle, took a few deep breaths, and pulled.

He collapsed to his knees, the weirdest thought going through his head. *Is this what getting hit by lightning feels like?* Lightning always frightened him. As bad as the pain was, it almost felt like it was happening to someone else. When he managed to get to his feet, Hump realized he was still holding the knife. He laughed at it, dropped it. He noticed the blood now pouring out of him and onto his pants. He poured the remainder of the vodka onto the wound, lightning striking a second time. Then he wadded up the cotton and shoved it into the mouth of the wound. He covered the cotton with sheets of toilet paper and pressed his hand hard against it. He found Milo's meth stash and pocketed it.

Hump went back into his room, rigged strapping out of some torn shirts, changed the bandage, and used the strapping to hold the new bandage to the wound. He got into different jeans, threw on a shirt and, in spite of the heat, a sweatshirt over that. He wiped off the bloody gun on the bedsheet, tucked it at the small of his back, and grabbed the Baggie of meth out of his old jeans. He thought about taking his duffel bag with him but decided not to try it. He had to travel light and move fast. Instead he collected the pair of socks in which he'd hidden the dragonfly ring. He had no choice now. He had to get to Dennis's Place and find Mickey Coyle.

73

Jesse didn't make a habit of driving over to
the county morgue unless it was business.
When he and Tamara were building their
friendship, he avoided seeing her at work.
He had spent too many hours at morgues
and hospitals, spent too many hours with
the dead and the dying. It was different at
the murder scene. The bodies there were
somehow less human when they were part
of the crime scene, but when they were laid
out naked on stainless-steel tables or slid
out of a refrigerator, you could really get a
sense of the violence and of what had been
taken from them.

"Spend too much time with the dead,
Stone, and you get dead inside," his first
detective partner said to him as they
watched the autopsy of a fifteen-year-old
girl. "Never become so familiar with it that
you don't see it."

Those days in L.A. now seemed like they

happened a long time ago and to someone else. Jesse hadn't understood what his partner meant back then. He understood it now.

He'd sat outside in the parking lot for an hour going through Flint's old accordion file. Jesse couldn't find anything the Yarmouth PD had done that he wouldn't have done or something they should have done that they didn't do. What was pretty clear through all of it was that no one, from Stan White to the guy who owned the recording studio, was very anxious to discuss the recording sessions or who had participated.

Given the status of the musicians Roscoe Niles had listed for him, the ones rumored to have been part of the recording of *The Hangman's Sonnet,* it was unlikely any of them would have taken the tape. But they certainly would have been people Jesse would have interviewed. It wasn't as if the Yarmouth PD hadn't tried. It was impossible to know what someone might have seen or overheard. One of the musicians might have knowledge about the theft that they weren't even aware of. Yet White refused to release the names of the musicians involved, saying that they had only participated in the recording of the album under the promise of strict confidentiality and that he would never break his word to them. In Flint's interview notes, there was a quote from White:

"Look, if it was up to me, I would co-operate with you and give you the names. But if I give you even one of their names, I can have the crap sued out of me and Terry. These musicians, they may all seem like drug-addled hippies to you, but believe me, they are anything but. They are sharks, and sharks with managers, lawyers, and agents. Besides, all the musicians were gone before the tape went missing."

In the file was a blank copy of the confidentiality agreement. Jesse was no lawyer, but the agreement did seem ironclad. There were also many, many photographs in the file. Photos of the studio, of the box in which the tape had been stored, of Evan Updike and Stan White, of Terry Jester. Jesse had seen Jester's face before, but the shots of Jester on his album covers were vastly different from the shots in the file. On his album covers, Jester usually wore a knowing smirk as if he was winking at the person looking at the album cover. *You and me, we know the truth.* The photos in the file depicted a man buried deep within his own head or of someone losing it, if not lost. Now what Stan White had confided to him earlier about Jester's state of mind made more sense.

Jesse's cell started buzzing like mad, but he didn't answer the calls. They were from Nita, from the mayor, from Stan White, from Bella. He looked at his watch. Roscoe Niles had been on the air for an hour. Jesse wondered how many times he had read *The Hangman's Sonnet* on the air by now. He turned on the radio, and with a Terry Jester song playing in the background, Roscoe was reading the poem. And by the time tomorrow morning's *Globe* hit the streets, the story would explode. Jesse hoped his career wouldn't explode with it. He shut off the radio and got out of the Explorer.

Tamara tried to hide her smile when he walked into her office. It was futile. She lit up, but her expression quickly turned to sadness.

"See that?" she said. "Leaving you is going to be tough. You're the best goddamned friend I've ever had."

"The friendship's not going to stop when you leave."

"I'm not so sure. Out of sight, out of mind."

"The price you're paying for fame, fortune, and the dead of Texas."

She laughed that loud, goofy laugh of hers.

"You can always make me feel better, Jesse Stone."

"That's what I had in mind."

"What?"

"Making you feel better. Tonight's about the last sane time we're going to have in Paradise for a while. Dinner?"

"Fine. I'm in."

"Deal," he said. "But let's make it late. I've got to meet with Lundquist and then I'm going to have to do a lot of hand-holding for the next few hours after that."

"Why?"

Without confessing his part in it, Jesse told her that word had leaked out about the poem and that it would be only a matter of time before the tape was offered up for bidding.

"Do you really think so, after all this time?"

He said, "I'm not much of a gambler, but if I could find someone to take my action, I'd put every dime I had on it. It's the only thing that makes any sense."

On his ride back to Paradise, he listened to Roscoe Niles play side one of Terry Jester's second album, *God's Middle Name.*

74

He brought the accordion folder into the station with him.

Molly said, "Lundquist is in there waiting for you."

"Good."

"I found a few addresses on Evan Updike, but nothing current. Nothing even remotely current. Can't find any recent photos of him, either. He's got no social-media presence or phones listed under his name."

"Death certificate?"

"Gee, Jesse, I wish I was smart like you. First thing I thought of when I couldn't find anything on the guy later than 1985. No luck there, either."

"He was a major drug abuser. Who knows, maybe he found God, got straight, and changed his name or joined a cult."

"Maybe. What's that file about?"

"From your buddy Jim Flint of the Yarmouth PD. It's his case file."

"Thick."

"Uh-huh. Thorough, too," Jesse said. "When Lundquist leaves, give him everything you've got on Updike. We'll let the staties put the word out about him. We have to remember we're trying to close two homicides. The tape is secondary and maybe our way to the killer."

"Weren't Bolton and Curnutt responsible for Maude Cain's death?"

"Probably, but we don't have Bolton, and that still leaves Curnutt's homicide to deal with."

"You think it's Evan Updike behind the missing tape?"

"Flint liked him for it and he seems the most likely suspect. I think Stan White thinks so, too, though he says different. Until we can do better, Updike's it. Can you do me a favor, Molly? I need you to make a few calls for me. It's not strictly police business, but it'll mean a lot to me."

"Sure," she said, making a face. "Tell me what you need."

Lundquist was holding Jesse's old baseball mitt in his hands. He didn't have it on. He was too respectful a person for that. It was more like he was inspecting it, revering it, wondering whether the object itself could reveal anything about the man who owned it.

"Did you play ball?" Jesse asked, walking around his desk, laying the file down.

"A little. All hit. No field. And the curveball was as mysterious to me as the Second Coming."

Jesse laughed. "If it wasn't for the curveball, Brian, the major leagues would be much more crowded."

"Could you hit the curve?"

"Uh-huh."

"How?"

"Part of it was being blessed with great eyesight. Sometimes I could pick up the rotation on the ball and knew it was a curve. And I was observant. If you watched a pitcher enough, you could see him tipping off his pitches. Sometimes it was how he held his glove when it was a curve. Sometimes his arm angle changed when he threw a curve. But as I moved up in class, pitchers were more polished, many had pitched in the bigs and had corrected their tells. So in Triple-A it was a matter of working the count, getting the pitcher in a spot where you had a pretty good sense of what pitch he would throw in a given situation and where he would throw it. There are a lot of people with the physical gifts to play baseball, but it's the mental aspects of things that separate the good from the great."

"Jeez, Jesse, why didn't you go into coaching?" Lundquist asked, placing the ball back in the glove and the glove back on Jesse's desk. "You sound like you would've made a great manager."

Jesse shook his head. "Last thing on earth I would have done. It would have been like an author who could no longer get published working in a bookstore. Too frustrating and not enough money in it. No, when my shoulder got wrecked, that was the end of baseball for me forever."

"Why am I here, Jesse?"

"Because I'm going to need you to back me up when the tape is finally offered up."

"What do you need?"

"I'm not sure, but I suspect the DA is going to object when the tape is offered to the highest bidder and money is to be exchanged. But I think it's going to be our only chance to clear the books of the two open homicides."

"Risky."

"Very, but the only lead I've got is on a guy the Yarmouth PD cleared years ago. Molly will give you all the details when you leave. Everything else is a dead end. The forensics have gotten us nowhere. Hump

Bolton has gone to ground. If we balk at the exchange, then Curnutt's killer will be gone with the wind."

"Do you really care about who killed a mutt like Curnutt?"

"I care about any open homicide in my town, no matter who the victim was."

"Fair enough. Okay, Jesse, I'll back you with the DA. I hope you're right."

"Me too."

75

It wasn't the Gray Gull. It wasn't the Lobster Claw. It wasn't Daisy's, nor was it any one of thirty other restaurants in the area. Instead, Jesse took Tamara to a chain restaurant out near the highway. It was one of those places with laminated menus, table tents, and annoyingly bubbly servers who told you their names in breathless voices and went on about their all-day two-fers. When she saw the place in the distance, Tamara leaned over and hugged Jesse, hard.

"I love you, Jesse Stone. You are one of a kind."

Two years earlier this had been the place in which they'd shared their first meal out together. It hadn't been a date, but it was where they'd first shared dark truths with each other about their pasts and established the trust that bound them together as friends. They hadn't been back since.

"My treat," he said, pulling into a yellow-lined parking spot. "You can even have the shrimp-and-steak fajita combo if you'd like."

"A big spender, my goodness."

When the hostess saw Jesse's PPD hat, she winked at him.

"Your table is ready, Chief Stone," she said, walking them to the booth they'd sat in two years earlier.

Tamara stopped in her tracks about five feet short of the booth when she noticed the bouquet of yellow roses and the bottle of champagne on the table. She punched Jesse's left biceps.

"You son of a —" She stopped herself as silent tears rolled down her cheeks. "Damn you, Jesse."

"I didn't want you to think I wouldn't miss you or that I wasn't proud of you."

"I'm not leaving yet," she said, choking slightly on her words.

"I know that. C'mon, let's eat."

"Yellow roses," Tamara said, sliding into the booth, clutching her bouquet.

"Only appropriate, given that you're moving back down to Texas."

"What's the champagne for?"

"For us to drink on a mutually agreed-upon date," he said.

"We'll see about that."

They both ordered Black Labels.

421

"Are you sure it's okay for us to drink scotch together?" Jesse asked. "You've been on the warpath about that lately."

"One drink and this one time, it's okay."

The server was dismayed. "I'm sorry, folks, but that's not part of the two-fers."

Jesse assured her that it was fine and to just bring the drinks. When the server left, Jesse and Tamara laughed, if a bit sadly, remembering that they'd gotten the same speech about the scotch the first time they'd been here.

"So how'd it go with Mayor Walker and Nita Thompson?"

The server brought their drinks and took their order: an omelet for Jesse and the fajita combo for Tamara.

Jesse raised his glass. "To your success."

"To the best friend I've ever had . . . and, dare I say it, the sexiest one, too."

"I'll drink to that."

After they drank, Tamara repeated the question. "How'd they react?"

"They were resigned to it coming out eventually and they were glad to have had some warning about it. We discussed how we'd handle the press conference, what we would confirm or deny, stuff like that. They were pretty calm about it."

"Yeah, I'll just bet they were. I'll also bet

you offered to give the mayor political cover."

"You're too smart for your own good, Doc."

"And why would you do that, let her hide behind you?"

"Let's just say it was more of a trade than me being benevolent."

"Still, Jesse, why?"

"If I'm going to find out what's really going on here, I need her to back me up. If that means keeping her head off the chopping block by putting mine on it, so be it."

"But —"

"No buts. It's the right thing to do. There've been two murders in my town, an old woman's house was destroyed, and a man was nearly beaten to death. I can't let that stand. The mayor can afford to worry about covering her ass. I can't."

Tamara was about to say something when the food came. As the server was squeezing lime on Tamara's fajitas and creating a choking cloud of smoke, Jesse's phone buzzed. When he saw who the caller was, he stood up from the table and picked up.

"Stone?"

"Vinnie. What's up?"

"That Bolton guy you're looking for, he's at a back booth at Dennis's, waiting for my guy, Mickey Coyle."

"Thanks, Vinnie. I owe you."

"I know you do. You better get down here pronto, Stone."

"Why's that?"

"The bartender says Bolton looks like he's in pretty bad shape."

When Jesse got back to the booth, he threw three twenties on the table and said, "Hey, Doc, how would you like to take a drive down to Boston with me? If not, I'll get someone to drive you home."

She slid out of the booth, grabbing her flowers and the champagne. "I wasn't that hungry anyway."

76

Jesse pulled to the curb down the block from the bar. Before they got out of the car, he grabbed Tamara's forearm and stared her in the eyes.

"You hang back outside, okay? This guy's probably armed, and if he's hurt . . ."

"I'll be all right, Jesse."

"Please, Doc, no heroics. I can't lose anybody else."

She stroked his cheek. "I promise, Jesse. I won't come into the bar until you send for me."

Jesse took off his hat and his cop shirt and pulled his white tee over his beltline. He unclipped his hip holster, removed his weapon, and fished his softball warmup jacket out of the rear seat. He wrapped his hand around the nine-millimeter's grip and threw the jacket over his gun hand.

"Shouldn't you call the BPD for backup?"

Tamara asked as they walked toward Dennis's.

"They'll come sirens blaring and it might create a hostage situation."

Jesse spotted him the second he came through the bar door. As Morris had said, Hump Bolton was sitting alone at a back booth, facing the front door.

"Where's the head?" he asked the barman.

The barman pointed to the right of where Bolton was seated. "Through there."

As Jesse walked back, he counted three other people in the place besides Bolton, the bartender, and himself. Two were up front at the bar and one was at the far end of the bar about ten feet from Bolton. The other thing Jesse noticed as he got closer to the rear booth was that Bolton looked bad-off. His skin was grayish and his face was covered in sweat. His eyes were glassy, his pupils black pinpricks, and he was bent over slightly. Both of Bolton's arms were below table level, and it seemed to Jesse as if the man was clutching his abdomen. But he walked right past Bolton and toward the bathroom and the old phone booth. While back there, he racked the slide on his nine and counted to thirty.

When he came back through the doors, he stopped next to Bolton's booth. "Mickey

Coyle sent me. You Hump?"

Bolton straightened up in his seat, wincing in pain at the effort, looking at Jesse. There was a strange blankness in the big man's expression, but Bolton didn't say anything.

Jesse pushed him. "Look, you got something for me to look at or not?"

Bolton still didn't say anything. As Jesse waited him out, he saw that below table level, Bolton's sweatshirt was soaked through with blood. His pants were wet with it, too.

"Sit," Bolton said finally.

Jesse sat across from him, resting his gun hand on his thigh, making sure the barrel was pointed directly at Bolton's midsection. "So, Bolton, what you got? Let's see."

"Coyle didn't send you or . . . maybe he did. He always was a scumbag. You a cop?" Bolton asked. "What you got under the jacket, a .38 or a nine-millimeter?"

Jesse didn't figure it was worth arguing. "A nine, and it's pointed right at your gut."

Bolton laughed, his body twisting in pain. "Find another target, cop. I already got a nice hole in me there."

"Shot?"

"Stabbed. Son-of-a-bitch tweaker I stayed with last night stuck a kitchen knife in my belly. I think he clipped my liver. I don't think he got a liver no more, not after what I done to him."

"I've got a doctor outside. You slide out of the booth, let me pat you down, and I'll get her in here to look at you."

Bolton ignored him. "You Boston PD?"

"Paradise police chief, Jesse Stone."

"Chief, huh?" He laughed, his body clenching in pain again. "I'm moving up in the world. Listen, Stone, we didn't mean to kill the old woman, I swear on my mother. She just . . . you know."

"I know. Who hired you?"

Hump shrugged. "King made all of them arrangements."

"What were you looking for in the house?"

"A key or a piece of paper with numbers on it, stuff like that."

"Curnutt found it. Did you know he found it?"

"No, he fucked me with that."

"You think the guy who hired you guys killed King?"

"Maybe. I don't know. Just because it figures don't make it so."

"Let me get the doctor in here for you."

"Nah, I'm done. The only reason I'm even still breathing is because I've been tooting on some crank every few minutes."

Jesse asked, "You still have the ring?"

"In the balled-up socks in my sweatshirt," Bolton said, his words slurred, his eyes fluttering. "It's a beautiful thing. You seen it?"

"Uh-huh. Pictures of it."

"Maybe you should get that doctor in here. I don't think —"

But before Hump Bolton could finish, he slumped over in the booth and fell onto the floor. Jesse quickly stepped around to Bolton, dragged him away from the booth, and laid him on his back. Jesse patted Bolton down, pulled the gun out of his waistband, and pushed it along the floor behind him.

Jesse held up his shield. "Police. Call nine-one-one and get an ambulance and backup here. You." He pointed to one of the guys sitting at the bar. "Go outside. There's a woman doctor out there. Get her in here. Now!"

The guy jumped off his barstool and ran through the door. But by the time Tamara made it inside, it was too late. Hump Bolton was dead. Jesse didn't need the medical examiner now standing over his shoulder to tell him so. He knew death when he saw it.

77

Tamara had tried her best to get Bolton's heart started again. When the ambulance got there, the EMTs took over, but it was all wasted effort.

"I've got no clue how he was even talking to you, Jesse," Tamara said between giving statements to the Boston cops. "He was suffering from profound blood loss and that was a nasty wound." She shook her head. "I usually get them when they're already dead and their stories are already written. Sometimes I forget how powerful and stubborn the mind can be. It can make the human body ignore the fact that it should have stopped functioning."

"You should have been a philosopher, Doc."

Before she could answer, a man who introduced himself as Detective Hanrahan interrupted.

"Chief Stone," he said. "We need to talk."

Hanrahan was a few inches shorter and about ten years younger than Jesse, but his blue eyes were weary. They sat down across from each other at a front booth.

"Boston's not your patch, Chief. What were you doing here?"

"Bolton was a suspect in a homicide and an assault in Paradise. His partner was —"

"Yeah, yeah, I read the papers. Still don't explain what you were doing here."

"I got a tip from a CI."

Hanrahan laughed a sneering laugh. "A confidential informant, huh? This is one of Vinnie Morris's joints. Nothing happens here without him knowing about it."

"You'd know better than me."

"Why didn't you alert the BPD?"

Jesse answered with a cocktail of lies and the truth. "Because I heard Bolton wanted to give himself up, but that he'd only surrender to me. I was afraid that if I did anything else, it might create a hostage situation."

Hanrahan liked that answer about as much as he would a cancer diagnosis, but he couldn't argue with it except to say, "You should have let us know before you went in. You always travel with an ME?"

"Friend. We were having dinner together when I got the call."

They went round and round like that for another fifteen minutes, Jesse going over the details of the statement he'd given to the uniforms.

"Last thing, Chief. You take anything off the body?"

"Just his weapon. I felt something along his left thigh, but it was soft and I didn't think it was a gun or a knife."

"Six-grand-plus cash in a plastic bag taped there."

"Probably his share of the money for the job in Paradise. Also said the missing ring from the Cain house was in a balled-up sock in his sweatshirt pocket."

"Yeah, it's there."

Jesse asked, "Did you find a cell phone on him?"

"No. Why?"

"Might have evidence on it pertaining to my cases."

"Ain't that a shame?"

"You want to bust my chops, Hanrahan? Fine. But before he died, Bolton pretty much admitted to killing the guy who gutted him. Said it was the guy he stayed with last night. Find that body and close the case. Might even make you look good with the brass."

"I'll take it under advisement. Bolton tell

you anything else about him, this guy you say he offed?"

"He was a tweaker and, if I had to guess, he probably did time with Bolton or Curnutt along the way."

"Jeez, Chief, you almost sound like you know what you're doing."

"LAPD Robbery-Homicide for ten years."

Hanrahan was confused. "And you gave that up for the thrills and challenges of Paradise?"

"It gave up on me, not the other way around."

The detective seemed to understand. "Okay, Chief. Thanks. You two can go. I know where to find you if I have to."

As Jesse and Tamara made it back to the Explorer, he realized that although one of the two open homicides in Paradise was now closed and that the dragonfly ring was as good as recovered, the night's excitement was only the beginning.

78

It wasn't the media circus they had anticipated it would be. It was much worse. The
streets around the police station and town
hall were choked with satellite trucks. News
organizations from CNN to the BBC to
TMZ to PBS had set up temporary outposts
in Paradise. Although Jesse had played a big
part in unleashing the beast, even he was
surprised by its appetite. He'd worked in
L.A. and understood that people had a
fascination with lost treasures, rumors, and
celebrity, but Terry Jester wasn't King Tut,
nor was *The Hangman's Sonnet* master tape
the Dead Sea Scrolls. Yet just the possibility
that the tape might resurface after forty
years had created a feeding frenzy.

What surprised Jesse even more was the
media's apathy toward human life. No one
at the press conference seemed to care
about the fact that Hump Bolton had bled
to death in a Southie bar or where King

Curnutt's body had been discovered. No one was interested in the fact that Maude Cain's murder and Rudy Walsh's assault were now closed cases. Maude Cain, Curnutt, Bolton, and Rudy Walsh had been reduced to sideshow status at the circus. They mattered only as adjuncts, as bit players in the drama of the tape. The press were far more interested in Jesse's mention of the dragonfly ring and its pending return to the Cain Museum than they were in the lives and deaths Jesse described to the assembled crowd.

"No one ever lost a bet underestimating human decency," Nita Thompson had said to Jesse at one point in the proceedings. "Believe me, I know. I work with politicians."

Mayor Walker was nowhere in sight, of course. That was part of the deal Jesse had made with her. For her backing, allowing him to handle things his way, Jesse had agreed to be out front and to take the flak. But the mayor had sent Nita Thompson along to keep an eye on him and to protect her interests.

There were several questions about Evan Updike. Oh, the press was very interested in him, and that was great with Jesse.

"I don't mind telling you that Mr. Updike

seems to have vanished. The last best photo we have of him is from the mid-eighties. Here are some images we do have of him." Photos, both black-and-white and color, appeared on a screen off to Jesse's left. "These photos are downloadable off our website. Any help we receive from the public about his whereabouts is appreciated."

After Updike's images went up, there was finally some interest in Maude Cain, Curnutt, and Bolton. But most of the questions were hypotheticals. *Why did Updike choose to do this now? When do you think the tape will finally resurface? Who actually owns the tape? Will Terry Jester come out of seclusion if the tape reappears?*

When the press conference was finally winding down, cell phones began ringing, trilling, and buzzing. Even the reporter asking the question stopped midsentence to check her phone. Jesse looked back at Nita Thompson, who shrugged. Jesse, not prone to overreaction, got a sick feeling in his gut remembering how all the cell phones in the room had gone off simultaneously in the immediate wake of the Boston Marathon bombing.

"Okay," he said. "Someone tell me what's going on."

Several of the correspondents turned their

phones around to face the lectern, but it was impossible for Jesse to make out what they were showing him. It was only when Ed Selko stepped up to the microphones and handed Jesse his phone that he finally understood. He felt a great sense of relief at what he was shown. There were no explosions, no bodies, no sirens, no panic. On Selko's screen was an image of a metal reel. On top of the metal reel was a crinkled piece of masking tape, and on the masking tape, written in very faded black marker, were with the words THE HANGMAN'S SONNET MASTER.

Jesse turned to Nita Thompson and said, "It won't be long now."

79

Whoever had the tape, whether it was Updike or not, had finally gotten exactly what he wanted: a worldwide audience. Jesse's comment to Nita Thompson was spot-on. That evening, about six hours after the press conference ended, Jesse heard from Roger Bascom.

"You better get over to the Wickham estate."

"Why?"

"He called."

Jesse didn't need further explanation. Before leaving for Stiles Island, he called Lundquist.

"We're going to need your people at the Wickham estate. The guy with the tape called. He'll call again, and when he does, we're going to need equipment the PPD doesn't have."

Lundquist said, "Understood," and hung up.

When Jesse got to the house, the electricity in the air was palpable. Stan White, chomping mercilessly on a cigar, was pacing back and forth in front of an end table on which sat a cordless phone in its dock. Bella Lawton, dressed in black slacks, a lightweight green sweater, and flats, was pacing a parallel course to White's but in the opposite direction. She had a cell phone stuck to her right ear and a predatory smile on her face. As she walked through a plume of White's cigar smoke, she waved it away with her left hand. Only Bascom, seated on the sofa, seemed disconcerted.

Bella pulled the phone away from her ear and pumped her fist. "Both Mick and Keith are in."

White stopped in his tracks, nodded his approval, and said, "Good. How about McCartney?"

"His people still haven't gotten back to me, but almost everyone else on the list who couldn't be bothered is now calling and apologizing."

"But what are they saying?" White asked.

"Yes."

White smiled and started pacing again. Bascom, looking relieved, noticed Jesse was there.

"Thanks for coming," Bascom said.

That finally got Bella and White's attention. Jesse didn't waste any time with niceties.

"When did he call?"

Bascom looked at his watch, but White answered. "Twenty-six — no, twenty-seven — minutes ago."

"Was it Updike?"

"Who knows?" White said, turning his palms up. "His voice was distorted, like in horror movies."

"What did he say?"

" 'What did he say?' " White repeated Jesse's question, his voice heavy with sarcasm. "What do you think he said? He said he had the tape and that he wanted enough money to choke a stud farm full of horses to give it up."

"Anything else?"

White blanched a little. "Yeah, that he would burn the tape if we didn't meet his demands or if we tried to pull a fast one."

"Did he say when he'd call again?"

"No," Bella said. "Only that he would call again soon."

Jesse kept at it. "Did he say anything about not involving the cops?"

Both White and Bella laughed at that.

Jesse was confused. "Did I say something funny?"

"Just ironic," Bella said. "He specifically asked for you. He said he'd heard about your reputation and that when the money and tape were to be exchanged, he wanted you to do it."

Jesse didn't like it. He hadn't liked much about this whole affair from day one. The request to involve him seemed particularly odd. Maybe not. He knew better than most that crime and criminals didn't follow a script, that it wasn't like on TV. Logic didn't always come into it. People did stupid things. Cops depended on people doing stupid, impulsive things. Still, he didn't like it, but he didn't have time to dwell on it.

"The call came in to this phone?" Jesse asked, pointing to the end table.

Bascom said, "It did. Remember, the Wickhams rent this place out every summer, so getting this number isn't like hacking the NSA."

"I guess not." Jesse turned back to White. "Did he prove to you he has the tape?"

"What do you mean?"

"I mean did he prove to you he actually has the tape as opposed to having a photograph of it."

"Yeah, yeah, yeah. He listed all the songs on the tape in order. He even played a little of the first track for me. The guy had the balls to say he thought the piano was a little out of tune on the second cut. Can you believe the onions on this guy? Believe me, Chief Stone, he has it."

Jesse rubbed his palm over his cheek. "Do you have the money he's asking for?"

White laughed again, puffs of earthy cigar smoke blowing in Jesse's direction. "Trump wouldn't have the money this guy wants. So no, I don't have it. But don't worry, give old Stan twenty-four hours and I'll get it."

"How?"

"Chief, you worry about catching the bad guys. Leave this to me. People have wanted to hear this album for forty years. Forty years ago most of them were teenage dreamers. Now some of them are rich. Very, very rich. And what, you don't think there's some music label or rock star out there who wants to get some publicity?"

But Jesse had already stopped listening to White, his mind busy piecing together the myriad things that were bugging him about the case.

80

The call came two days later. Although Jesse hadn't wanted word to get out that the tape was being offered for ransom, word had somehow gotten out. There was little mystery in that. Jesse had no doubt that Bella Lawton and/or Stan White had purposely let it slip. He who has the most to gain often has the loosest lips.

"This is the Hangman. Six million dollars in used, unmarked, untraceable bills," the distorted voice said over the speakers Lundquist's people had set up in an adjoining room. "One penny less and the tape burns. Any chemicals or other traces on the bills, the tape burns. When you raise the money, put a personal ad in the *Globe* that says 'I desperately want you back. — TJ.' I'll be in touch."

That was all he said. Through the use of cell towers, Lundquist's people traced the call to a rural area in western Massachusetts.

"It's probably a burner phone that's already been ditched or destroyed," Lundquist said. "In rural areas, we can be off by as far as twenty miles. He probably called from a car and if he's mobile, we're not going to catch him this way."

When Jesse talked to White, he was surprised to see Jester's manager looking so glum.

"What is it, Stan? Can you raise the six million?"

"It's not that. I have a big offer from one of the legacy record labels. They're willing to cover the ransom up to six mill, then pay Terry a generous advance and percentage."

"Then what's the problem?"

"You want to know what's the problem? The problem is me. The label wants independent verification of authenticity."

Lundquist was confused. "Why is that a problem?"

"It's a problem because the only people who can authenticate the tape are Stan, Updike, and Jester himself," Jesse said. "Jester and White are self-interested parties. Updike is the prime suspect."

Lundquist nodded. "I see your point. Let me get together with my people and see if we can't get a better handle on the caller."

Once Lundquist had left the room, White

444

said, "The tape's going to burn. None of the other offers are even close and it would take too long to piece together —"

"Wait a second," Jesse said, interrupting White. "I have an idea."

"What idea?"

"Not what, who. Roscoe Niles. He told me —"

It was White's turn to interrupt. "You know that fat, drunk bastard?"

"I do. He loves you, too, Stan."

"Screw him."

"You better rethink your attitude," Jesse said.

"Yeah, why's that?"

"Because I think he can authenticate the tape. He told me you played the tape for him just after it was recorded."

White clapped his hands together. "That's right. Oh my God! That's right. This was when he was still a big shot in New York radio and his word was gold. People used to line up to kiss his ring and get him to play their songs on the radio. Airplay on his show meant everything. I've heard rumors he was offered thousands to play songs. He was offered girls, cars, houses, trips around the world, but he never took a penny. The fucking guy wouldn't even let you buy him a drink. If he liked a song, he'd play it. If he didn't, it was dead. Sometimes you could get another jock on the station to give you a little airtime, but not Roscoe Niles."

"Did he dislike *The Hangman's Sonnet*? Is that why you two hate each other?"

"Nah, Chief. Roscoe loved the album. We fell out a few years later, after the master tape was stolen and Terry had flipped. It was during the New Wave era. His station had pretty much forsaken Terry Jester. I went to Roscoe and pleaded with him to get some of Terry's stuff back on the air. I asked for old times' sake. I mean, Roscoe had built some of his rep on Terry's back. I figured the least he could do was return the favor."

"He turned you down?"

"Better than that. He had me thrown out of the station by security, the drunk bastard."

Jesse asked, "You tried to bribe him, didn't you?"

"Not exactly."

"Exactly how was it?"

"He was having marital troubles at the time and maybe I had some unflattering photos of him with a woman about Bella's age."

"Blackmail. No wonder he had you thrown out. You sent his wife the photos?"

White waved his hands in disgust. "I'm not proud of what I did, but he owed Terry and he owed me and he pissed on us when we needed a little help."

"That's not the issue now," Jesse said. "If I can get him to do it, will the record company accept his word?"

"Mr. Honesty? With his rep? Sure."

Jesse grabbed his cell phone.

81

Roscoe Niles didn't make it easy on Jesse but caved in the end.

"For you, Jesse, and for Jenn and Diana. But make it clear to that prick I'm not doing it for him."

"I'm pretty sure he gets that, Roscoe."

The ad appeared in the paper the next day. But this time, when the Hangman called, he rang Stan White's cell phone, not the landline at the Wickham estate. Stan put it on speakerphone so they could all listen to the conversation.

"I have the money," White said, "but there's a problem."

"Bullshit!" The distorted voice crackled over the cell's speaker. "You're stalling. The tape's going to burn."

"No! No! Listen, it's not a stall. Don't burn it!" White pleaded his case, explaining about the record label's condition for payment.

There was a tense moment of hesitation. "Only Niles hears it. I sense the tape is being recorded or if the call is being traced, the tape burns. Give me his cell number."

Jesse gave White the number and White repeated it into the phone.

"Two hours from now, Niles gets into his car and drives straight to the Wrentham Village Outlets and parks in a spot as far away from the stores and other cars as possible. I'll know if he's being followed or watched. Remember, any tricks and the tape burns. I want the money, but money won't do me any good in prison. I'll call tonight."

At seven p.m., Roscoe Niles showed up at the Wickham estate. Jesse introduced Roscoe to Bella Lawton. Bella seemed unimpressed by her new acquaintance. Jesse had no trouble understanding because his friend was dressed in ragged jeans, red Chuck Taylors, and a Moody Blues T-shirt that featured the cover of *In Search of the Lost Chord*. The shirt was as stretched and faded as everything else in Roscoe's wardrobe.

"Nice outfit," Stan White said at the sight of his old nemesis.

"Screw you, Stan. Should I have worn a tux?"

White asked, "What happened? Did he

call? Did —"

Niles ignored the question, turning to Jesse. "I need a drink, man. Authentication is thirsty work."

Bella Lawton volunteered. "I'll get it."

"What the hell happened?" White asked, his face turning bright red.

"Relax, you old prick. As soon as I get my drink, I'll tell you."

Bella Lawton came back into the room, a rocks glass half full of scotch in her right hand. Conversation stopped the moment she reentered. She was dressed in a tight white dress and cream-colored heels. She really seemed to be turning it on, much like she had the morning she showed up at Jesse's door. But it was difficult to discern whether Roscoe Niles's eyes were bulging out at the sight of the scotch or at the woman delivering it. Both, Jesse decided. Niles gulped down the scotch.

"Well, what happened?" White asked again.

Niles smiled and shook the empty glass at Bella. She took the glass and said, "I'll be right back, Mr. Niles."

"What happened? You want to know what happened, man? I'll tell you what happened. Thirty years ago you ruined my marriage, you son of a bitch."

White wasn't having it. "I wasn't the one screwing some twenty-two-year-old chippie. That was you, you fat drunk. I did your wife a favor, freeing her from the likes of you."

Niles charged White, landing a glancing punch to White's jaw before Jesse could tackle him. Jesse was surprised at how powerful the old DJ was, but emotion and adrenaline counted for a lot.

"Calm down, Roscoe," Jesse said, putting his friend in an arm lock. "Are you all right, Stan?"

"Fine," White said, rubbing his jaw. "Fine. But the faster this schmuck tells me what happened, the sooner he can get out of here and we can get on with things."

"You going to behave if I let you up, Roscoe?"

"Yeah, yeah, man. I'm sorry. I've just been waiting thirty years to do that."

"Well, you did it. Now tell the man what he needs to know." Jesse released Niles.

The DJ got up in pieces, shaking the pain out of his arm as he stood.

Bella tried to deliver his second drink, but Jesse grabbed the glass. "Talk first, drink later."

"It's the real thing," Niles said. "And I'll be damned, it's fucking brilliant. He played me the whole tape, first song to last. Man, no wonder Terry Jester never rerecorded it. He would never have been able to recapture what's on that tape."

Jesse handed the scotch to Niles, who polished the drink off in a single gulp, some of the amber fluid dribbling down his chin.

"Will you tell that to the record execs?" White asked.

"I promised Jesse I would, so, yeah, I will. Have them call me."

Before Niles could finish his sentence, White was punching a number into his cell phone and handing the phone to Niles. When the DJ was done swearing the tape was the real deal, he said his good-byes and headed back to Boston.

82

It wasn't lost on Jesse that the last time he had done something like this, Suit wound up getting shot. Nor had he forgotten that the end result of what he'd done that fateful day eventually resulted in Diana's murder. But as he drove along a stretch of two-lane highway north and west of Paradise, the sun getting low in the sky, Jesse tried hard to push those thoughts out of his head and to keep all other demons at bay. He couldn't afford a lack of focus, not if he wanted a chance to recover the tape and to get Curnutt's killer.

It had all seemed to happen so quickly after Roscoe Niles had authenticated the tape. After that, the other hurdles were more easily cleared. In spite of the DA's objections, he gave his go-ahead to handle things Jesse's way. It helped that Lundquist had given his support and that Mayor Walker had kept her word, backing Jesse as well.

There was little chance she wouldn't. There was no downside for her. If he succeeded in capturing Curnutt's killer and recovering the tape, she would take partial credit for his success. If he failed, she had distanced herself enough that the fallout would all blow in Jesse's direction. Of course, what he hadn't shared with the mayor or anybody else involved was that he had hedged his bet. He was sticking his neck out a long way, just not quite as far as everyone assumed he was.

After the meeting at the DA's office, Nita Thompson pulled Jesse aside. "I hope you know what you're doing. This could blow up in your face."

"The day I start worrying more about covering my ass than doing the right thing, I'll quit."

"If you fail, Jesse, you won't have to quit. The mayor will do that for you."

"Uh-huh."

An entire day had passed since then. The record label had wired the money to a Boston bank and an armored car had carried it up to Paradise. It had taken a while to assemble six million dollars in varied denominations of used, nonconsecutive bills. Funny thing was that none of them, not Jesse or White or Lundquist, had anticipated just how big a pile six million dollars made.

"Good thing you've got an SUV, Jesse," Lundquist said. "That's not going to fit in anyone's carry-on bag."

Jesse had laughed at that but wondered if the blackmailer had bothered to calculate how he'd manage all that money. If not, Jesse thought, it might give him the opportunity he needed to grab the Hangman.

Lundquist and the DA had argued for Jesse to chemically mark the bills in spite of the Hangman's warnings and demands, but Jesse had rejected the idea.

"We're going to play this as much his way as we can. We're not going to mark the bills. We're not going to put a tracking device with the money. No one is going to follow me in a car."

These days, everyone walked around with a tracking device on his or her person. The Hangman would know that, and it was pretty much a given that Jesse would have to toss his cell phone somewhere along the route.

The Hangman's instructions had been simple. After emphasizing that he would burn the tape if any of his instructions weren't followed or if he sensed a trap was being set, he told Jesse to leave Paradise and travel back roads in a northwesterly direction toward the confluence of the Massachusetts, New Hampshire, and Vermont borders. Just south of Lowell he got the call he'd been expecting.

The Hangman directed him to a roadside gas station.

"Go into the men's room," the distorted voice said. "Drop your cell phone in the toilet. You'll find a new phone in a plastic bag in the toilet tank. And, Chief, if you have any tracking devices on you, planted in the money or your vehicle, this would be your chance to ditch them."

"There aren't any."

"Okay, then head back the way you came and keep the new phone close. I'll be calling you shortly."

The bathroom was like almost every other gas-station bathroom he'd been in. It stank of human waste and pine disinfectant. The mirror was cracked and duct-taped to the wall. He was glad he had brought gloves with him when he lifted up the top of the toilet and fished out the bagged phone floating inside. As Jesse left the bathroom, new phone in hand, he noticed the surveillance camera mounted on the edge of the building. It was aimed at the pumps, so he doubted it would have captured images of the person who had planted the phone in the toilet tank. But even as he got in his car and headed back toward Paradise, there was something about the camera that stuck in Jesse's head. It nagged at him until the ringing phone diverted his attention.

"Sorry to do this to you, Chief, but you're going to have to about-face and follow my directions. Do you understand?"

"I do."

"Good. When you get to where you're going, call the number taped to the back of the phone."

Jesse did as he was instructed, making a U-turn as soon as passing traffic allowed. And as he passed the gas station he'd pulled out of only a few minutes before, that nagging feeling about the surveillance camera came back to him.

83

It was full-blown night by the time Jesse got to where he was going, a hilly, densely wooded area just over the Vermont border. It wasn't lost on Jesse that Evan Updike, everyone's favorite suspect, was from Vermont. He pulled to the side of the road and called the number taped to the back of the cell phone.

"We're almost there, Chief," said the Hangman. "Don't screw it up now. Off to your right you should see an unpaved path that off-roaders use to access the trails up here. It's steep, but your vehicle should be able to handle it, no problem. Drive up along the path for about three hundred yards and stop where the road divides. When you get there, call me again." The phone went dead.

Bets hedged or not, Jesse was liking this less and less. It was dark, he was out of state, and the terrain was rugged. He took it slow up the unpaved road, the tires of his Explorer spitting out rocks as it climbed the hill. And just as the Hangman had said, there was a split in the woods where the road veered sharply to the left or continued climbing up the hill.

"Good," the Hangman said when Jesse called. "Listen carefully, Chief, because once I give you these instructions, you're going to toss the cell. Understood?"

"Uh-huh."

"Turn left. There's a big flat clearing there about a hundred yards ahead of you. Drive to the edge of the clearing. Shut off your headlights. Get out of your vehicle and walk about twenty paces to the lit flashlight on the ground. There'll be a package there with what you've come for. Use the flashlight to inspect it. When you're satisfied, put the flashlight and the package down, bring the money out of your vehicle, and place it next to the package. When you're done unloading the money, take the tape, toss the flashlight, turn around, and leave the way you came."

"How are you going to get the money out of here? You have any idea of how clumsy three duffel bags of money is?"

"You let me worry about that. Concern yourself with this: Vary your behavior in any way from these instructions and there will be consequences. Roll down your window and listen."

Almost before Jesse's window was down, there was a burst of automatic weapon fire.

"Do we understand each other, Chief? Let's both get what we want and get out of here."

"Understood."

"Good. Now toss the phone."

It was incredibly dark when he got out of his Explorer. The flashlight was on the ground where the Hangman said it would be. But for the swath of light the flashlight cut into the blackness, Jesse didn't think he would be able to make out the palm of his own hand held a foot in front of his face. He picked up the flashlight and the clear plastic package at his feet. Inside the package was a reel of professional recording tape with a shriveled strip of masking tape along one of its wide spokes. On the tape, written in now very faded black marker, were the words THE HANGMAN'S SONNET MASTER. It looked like pictures of the reel he had seen, but he had no idea whether he was holding a piece of history or a piece of fiction in his hand. Five minutes later, he had unloaded the money as instructed and had the tape next to him on the front passenger seat.

Jesse pressed the ignition button and turned the Explorer around. As he did, he caught sight of a van about fifty yards ahead of him and of a masked, shadowy figure of a man next to the van. There was something familiar about the man — his posture, his height, his build — that set alarm bells off in Jesse's head, but he remembered the burst of automatic weapon fire and didn't want to risk getting shot out here in the middle of nowhere.

Windows down, listening, Jesse proceeded slowly along the road back to the fork. He heard the sound of the van's engine coming to life. He stopped the Explorer at the fork in the trees, the sound of the van's engine now fading away. And then all he heard was the incessant chorus of crickets filling the void in the night. But when he turned back to head down to the paved road below, the night exploded.

The Explorer's two front tires blew, one after the other, then the back tires at once. Jesse was thrown into the door and the SUV almost slammed into a tree. With some slick handling, Jesse managed to avoid the tree. When he got out of the vehicle, he saw that someone had laid spike strips across the road. He'd used spike strips during his time in uniform in L.A. It was a non-lethal way of stopping a suspect's car during a chase. He was kneeling down to check out the damage to his tires when he realized he was screwed. As part of the ransom deal, he'd agreed to be unarmed. And even if he had been carrying, his nine-millimeter would have stood little chance against an M-4 or MP-5.

That was when the quiet of the night was shattered once again. Only this time it wasn't the sound of exploding tires or a burst of automatic weapon fire. It was one thunderous rifle shot. Then, a few seconds later, a second shot. This time the bullet slammed into a tree above Jesse's head. He had to get away from his Explorer in case the Hangman was doubling back his way. So he grabbed the old-style Maglite he kept in his Explorer. He ran as hard as he could away from the direction of the shot, darting in and out of the trees to make himself a difficult target.

Twenty minutes later, not having heard a shot, footsteps, or anything else but the crickets, Jesse wandered out from behind the fallen logs he'd hidden behind. He turned on the big flashlight and noticed what looked like a campfire burning near where he had left his Explorer. As he approached, Jesse realized the fuel for the campfire was the master tape of *The Hangman's Sonnet*. He used a stick to yank the metal reel out of the flames, but it was no good. What was left was charred metal and goo. It didn't make any sense, he thought, having the tape and the money only to destroy the tape. And then, suddenly, it made perfect sense.

Jesse left his SUV and headed up the hill to where he had unloaded the money. He found some spent shell casings and spotted the van's tire tracks in the dirt and grass. He followed them. They led west, in the opposite direction Jesse had used to get to the clearing. It was a long walk to the other side of the clearing. When he got there, Jesse found another unpaved trail. He pointed his flashlight down the trail. The body of the masked man was no more than a hundred feet down the hill.

Even as he slid down the slope, bracing himself with his left hand, Jesse got that same vibe he'd gotten earlier when his headlights caught the silhouette of the man in black. There was something familiar about him. When he reached the body — facedown in the dirt, arms and legs thrown out at unnatural angles — there was little doubt the man was dead. His body was still in that way only the dead can be: vacant and unbreathing. There was a large bloody hole through the man's right scapula. Jesse felt for the pulse he knew he wouldn't find and got the results he expected.

Now he had decisions to make. Procedure would have had him leave the body as he found it and go for the police. On his way here, Jesse had passed a small town several miles down the road and, if he was lucky, he might be able to flag a ride back there or get someone to call the police on their cell phone. Short of that, he could go back to where he had tossed the burner phone and try to find it in the woods. But if things worked as he hoped, as he had tried to ensure they would, cops would be showing up soon enough. As he heard the sound of distant sirens, Jesse broke the rules and lifted the mask off the dead man's face.

Roger Bascom didn't seem any more pleasant in death than he had in life.

84

"You Stone?" The first cop asked him.

Jesse held up his shield and said, "Jesse Stone, Paradise, Mass, chief of police."

"Yeah, we got a call from a retired captain from the Massachusetts State Police."

"Captain Healy."

"That's him."

"Healy said there was some shooting going on out here and that you might need some help."

Jesse pointed at Bascom's body.

"You do it?"

Jesse understood what the cop was asking. He shook his head. "No. I'm unarmed except for this." Jesse waved his Maglite. "Did you find a van on your way up here?"

The cop nodded, pointing over his back with his thumb. "Black cargo van on the road. Driver's-side window shattered."

"Find anything in it?"

"First I thought I better get up here to see

about you. Don't worry. There are units down there now checking it out." The cop was curious. "You know the vic?"

"Name is Roger Bascom. Listen, Officer . . . Miles," Jesse said, reading the cop's name off his chest tag. "Can I use your cell phone? I know it's not SOP, but it's urgent. I'll put it on speaker, so you can hear both sides of the conversation."

Miles hesitated but eventually handed his iPhone to Jesse.

"Who is this?" Healy, not recognizing the number, asked, his voice crackling over the speaker.

"It's me, Jesse. An Officer Miles let me use his phone. Thanks for having my back."

"What are friends for? Besides, I almost feel like a cop again. Who's the vic?"

"Bascom."

"Get out! Bascom, the head of security on Stiles Island?"

"Uh-huh."

"He never struck me as some criminal genius."

"He wasn't," Jesse said. "He was a pawn. Do you have the shooter in sight?"

"A few hundred yards ahead of me, yeah. He's tooling down the highway like he hasn't got a care in the world."

"He's got six million reasons to feel re-laxed."

"Not for long, but listen, Jesse . . ."

"What?"

"When I tell you who it is, you're not go-ing to like it."

"I know who it is," Jesse said.

"But how could you —"

"It clicked a few minutes ago. It has to do with surveillance cameras. I'll explain it to you later. For now, keep him in sight. You better call Lundquist and clue him in, but keep everyone else in the dark. Call Molly and tell her to have Peter Perkins search Bascom's apartment. Tell her to assign two units to the Wickham estate. Anyone com-ing or going from the estate except the mayor or Nita Thompson gets a tail."

"Got it. Anything else?"

"Nothing else for now."

Healy asked, "Did you get the tape?"

"It's destroyed."

"Damn!"

"Don't sweat it. I'll explain it to you later."

"Okay, Jesse."

"You know how I said Bascom was a pawn?"

"Yeah."

"He had company."

"Like who?"

"Me."

85

Jesse spent several hours recounting his story to the local and Vermont State Police. Only after Jesse assured them that he would arrest the killer within twenty-four hours did they arrange for him to get a ride back to Paradise. Once he was back at the station, he made calls to Nita Thompson and Stan White, who made a verbal show of feeling betrayed and distraught about the destruction of the tape. After that, Jesse made some other calls, all the pieces falling into place. He wished he could be happy about being right, but there were times, he thought, that wrong was better.

It was too late to worry about that now. At the moment, he stood outside the town house between Lundquist and Healy, waiting to be buzzed in. Healy was exhausted, having spent the entire night sitting on the suspect's house.

"The money?" Jesse asked.

Healy pointed at the garage door. "In there. The rifle, too. He came home, pulled into the garage, came out, locked the garage door behind him, and he's been inside ever since."

Jesse was beat, too. He'd caught a few minutes of shut-eye during the ride to Boston from Paradise with Lundquist. It was the only sleep he'd gotten since the night before. Lundquist was still upset at Jesse for not reporting the shooting incident in the nature preserve and for keeping him out of the loop when he brought Healy into a police matter.

"I had no choice, Brian. I had to use someone who had no official standing, someone I could trust who wasn't on anybody's radar screen. Nobody would be looking for Healy in their rearview mirrors."

Lundquist was unmoved.

"He'll get over it," Healy had said to Jesse when Lundquist was taking a call. "He's new in the job, so he's touchy. But he's good."

At a distance, the town house seemed a lovely brick affair with granite steps, black wrought-iron rails, boot scrapers, and converted gaslights. But up close it was more a reflection of its owner: weary and abused, something that looked better viewed through the lens of the past. The windows needed replacing. The bricks were in desperate need of repointing. Pieces of the fence were rusted and missing like rotted-out teeth in a once-glorious smile.

When the buzzer sounded, Jesse turned to the others and said, "I'm going in alone. It'll just be easier and I'll be able to trip him up. If I need you, you're certainly close enough."

Healy was uneasy. "This guy tried to kill you twice."

"If he wanted to kill me, I'd be dead. You saw the shot he made last night."

Lundquist shrugged. "You want him, he's yours . . . for now. He'll wind up in Vermont eventually."

Jesse stepped into the vestibule, the front door slamming shut behind him. The inside of Roscoe Niles's town house was even shabbier than the exterior. The wooden floors were warped and split in several spots, and whatever varnish or wax had once protected them was worn away to a dull memory. The furniture, which ten years earlier might have been called comfortable, was now frayed and scratched, the cushions flat and lifeless. The endless shelves of record albums, CDs, and tapes that had once lined the walls of his den were now as

471

empty as Old Mother Hubbard's cupboards, and his stereo equipment — tube amp, pre-amp, turntable, reel-to-reel, CD player, speakers — was gone.

There were rectangular ghosts on the walls of the hallways where framed posters and photos had hung, all signed to Roscoe Niles by megastars in the music industry. Jesse had always liked the photo of Roscoe holding David Bowie in his arms, big smiles on both their faces. The empty walls and shelves were eerily reminiscent of Niles's office at the radio station

As Jesse walked into the kitchen, he questioned himself as he had since last night when it all became clear to him. *Should I have seen it sooner?* He had never been a man given to second-guessing his decisions. That had changed a few years back after Suit had been shot. But if he was being honest with himself, he had to confess that since Diana's death, he'd spent a great many drunken hours doing nothing but questioning himself. It's what had made him vulnerable to manipulation. The only thing he had been sure of since Diana's murder was that he had been played for a fool by a man he considered a friend.

Niles was sitting at the kitchen table, head down, eyes distant, a freshly lit cigarette

472

between his lips. There was a full ashtray on the table, a coffee cup, and a half-empty bottle of Johnnie Walker Red Label before him. Niles was dressed in a ragged white terry-cloth bathrobe. His long steel-gray hair, which he usually kept rubber-banded in a ponytail, fell loosely around his bloated face. The steeliness of his hair and the cigarette's burning tip seemed to highlight the blooming gin blossoms on his nose. At the thump of Jesse's footsteps, the old DJ turned his head toward the kitchen entrance, the distance vanishing from his eyes.

"It's good to see you, man, but Christ, Jesse, you look like shit," Niles said, a smile slowly working its way across his lips.

"I've got an excuse. No sleep. What's yours?"

"I've got the same excuse." The DJ's rich voice was uncharacteristically brittle. "I don't sleep much at all these days. So why are you here? Did that asshole White get his tape back?"

"Never going to happen."

Niles acted confused. "The exchange hasn't happened? I mean, once I authenticated the tape I thought it would go fast after that."

"The exchange happened, all right," Jesse said.

Niles did his best to keep looking confused. "I'm slow on the uptake this morning, man. Am I missing something?"

"We'll get to that in a minute."

"Whatever you say. How much did the tape go for?"

Jesse didn't answer him directly. "Remember when you asked me why I was here?"

Roscoe Niles nodded.

"I'm here to arrest you."

"Arrest me?" Niles tried to act surprised but sounded defeated. "For what, man?"

"Murder, for starters," Jesse said, his voice calm.

Niles, hand shaking, poured scotch into his coffee cup and drank it down. Poured another. Drank it, too. "And who is it that I am supposed to have murdered?"

"Roger Bascom."

86

Roscoe Niles spent the next five minutes denying he knew Roger Bascom. Jesse let him, sitting silently across the table as the DJ swore up and down he'd never met the man. He figured Roscoe had to get it out of his system and he hoped Roscoe would say something to make this easier.

"Phone records don't lie," Jesse said. He was bluffing because it would take a little time before they got the LUDs, but Roscoe didn't know that. "And then there's this." Jesse tapped his cell phone screen, then handed it to the man across the table. "Scroll right to left. There's also dashboard-camera footage of you. Tells an interesting story."

Roscoe Niles's whole body sagged as he handed the phone back to Jesse.

"Pretty damning evidence, Roscoe: you getting out of your car with the gun case, you holding the rifle, you walking up into the woods . . . The man who took those photos is the retired head of the state Homicide Bureau," Jesse said. "So don't bullshit me. Understand?"

Niles nodded.

"Explain it to me."

"Nothing I say is going to change anything, is it?"

"Probably not legally, but it may help with the way I feel about you."

"That means a lot to me, man."

"Apparently not enough."

"I'm sorry, Jesse. You have to believe me. I really am, but I was desperate. You see what my place looks like. I'm tapped out and deep into the guys on the street. I haven't made any real money in years. There are so many mortgages on this dump that I'd have to live two hundred more years to pay them off. I sold everything I had in the world just to make my vig payments until this thing was over with."

"I figured you had to be desperate, but there are a lot of desperate people in the world who don't murder other people."

"Bascom needed killing." Niles lifted up the bottle, waved it at Jesse. "You want one?"

Jesse shook his head and watched his old friend fill his coffee mug with Red Label.

"To Diana." Niles lifted his coffee mug to drink.

Jesse slapped the mug out of Niles's hand. "Don't you speak her name in front of me again."

"Sorry, man."

"Why didn't you run, Roscoe? You had the money and you didn't know I had someone on you. With six mill, you could have been anywhere by now."

Niles laughed a coarse laugh like ripping fabric. "I wasn't going anywhere without Bella."

Jesse shook his head. "What was your cut going to be?"

"A mill."

Jesse said, "You undersold yourself."

"Story of my life. You have any idea of how much money, how many women I could have had when I was on the air in New York? But not me, no, sir, not Mr. Integrity."

"You're a saint."

There was that laugh again. "Ain't I, though?"

"Without you to authenticate the tape none of it would have worked. Why didn't you ask for a bigger cut?"

"At the time, a mill seemed like a fortune to me."

"But I bet Bella explained to you how it

could all be for the two of you. Kill Bascom and cut White out. White couldn't go to the cops."

The slump went out of Niles's body. "No, it was all my idea. Bella had nothing to do with it."

"Yeah," Jesse said, "I bet. Pure as the driven snow. Don't be an idiot, Roscoe. You know she was probably sleeping with Bascom, too."

Niles's face turned bright red and he seemed ready to pounce.

"Don't even think about it," Jesse said, placing his hand around the grip of his nine-millimeter. "You don't have a rifle in your hand now. It was you who shot at me in the woods the other day, but that wasn't part of the plan, was it? You followed Bella to my house that morning. You thought she was sleeping with me, too."

"Stop pushing me about Bella. You say another word about her and I'll ask for a lawyer."

"You're in no position to make threats, but okay, we'll leave her out of it for now."

Niles relaxed, the angry red bleaching out of his cheeks.

"It's all bullshit, isn't it, Roscoe? The poem, the tape, it's all smoke and mirrors. There never was a *Hangman's Sonnet* album. There was nothing on the tape. It was just a prop."

"The poem's real, man, but no, there was nothing on the tape. It wasn't a scam to begin with all those years ago. They meant to make the album, but Jester went over the edge before the project got started. Terry hasn't been functional since. The cost of his hospitalization has bankrupted them."

"What about royalties?" Jesse asked. "They play Jester's stuff on the radio all the time. He still sells."

"Stan has Jester's power of attorney. He sold the publishing rights about seven years ago when Jester's condition worsened and White needed the cash infusion to keep up Terry's level of care."

"Did you know there was no album before White approached you?"

Niles looked insulted, hurt. "Are you kidding me, man? No, I believed like the rest of the world. Everyone believed because we all want to believe in the Holy Grail or El Dorado or that the Walrus was Paul. Where would we be without myths, man? That's why it worked."

"Almost worked, Roscoe. Almost. So White came to you and . . ."

"And what choice did I have? I needed bread any way I could get it. But I wasn't in on this early. White came to me a few months ago because, as Mr. Integrity, I had credibility in the industry. He knew people who might be putting up big bucks would want more than his word alone that the tape was real."

"But it was you who suggested using me to vouch for you."

Niles couldn't look Jesse in the eye. "It was me. After Diana was killed I knew you'd . . . Anyway, I'm sorry."

"What if I didn't come to you to ask about Jester and *The Hangman's Sonnet*?"

"Who else would you go to?" Niles smirked. "If you didn't come on your own, White or Bella would've nudged you in my direction or I might've called to say hi and taken the conversation that way."

"So it was White, Bascom, you, and Bella. Is Evan Updike part of it?"

Niles was still determined to protect Bella. "It was White and Bascom. Bella wasn't part of it."

"If you only had as much respect for Diana's memory as for Bella, we wouldn't be here."

"I was desperate, man."

"So you say. What about Updike?"

"He was the straw man, the guy White wanted you to chase while we got out of

Dodge."

"So he had no part in this?"

Niles shrugged. "At first, yeah, I guess, when it went down in the seventies. I mean, he was the only other person who knew there was no real *Hangman's Sonnet* album, but I've never seen him and he was never mentioned as anything except as the fall guy. I can tell you this, though, Stan hates Updike's guts."

"You're going away for the rest of your life."

Niles dispensed with the coffee cup and took a slug straight from the bottle. "What life?"

87

Lundquist looked into the rearview and through the protective plexiglass at Roscoe Niles slumped against the backseat. He was passed out and snoring. Jesse had let him get dressed in something other than the ratty white bathrobe he'd been wearing, though the too-tight T-shirt, ripped jeans, and sneakers weren't much of an upgrade. He had also let Niles put his hair back into its usual ponytail.

"I don't get it," Lundquist said.

"What?"

"The thing old bikers and old rockers have with ponytails. Do they think it will distract people from noticing their receding hairlines and fat guts hanging over their beltlines?"

"It's about not letting go."

"Of what?"

"Their pasts."

"How did you get him to waive his right

to counsel and cooperate?"

"I explained that depending on the way we presented things to the DA, he could do hard time or very hard time."

"Yeah," Lundquist said, turning his gaze back to the road. "When you look at it that way, I guess it was an easy choice. But, Jesse, how did you know it was all bullshit?"

"I didn't know, not for sure, not until Roscoe admitted it to me. I knew something wasn't right, and then when I noticed the security cameras at the gas station they had me stop at, I realized how I was being played. Last night, after the Vermont cops dropped me back in Paradise, I got hold of the CCTV footage from where the WBMB studios are. The day the poem was allegedly delivered to Roscoe by messenger —"

"There was no messenger."

"Roscoe knew I would just take his word for it like I took his word for everything else."

"Good plan."

"Everybody involved was vouching for everyone else and all of it hinged on my vouching for Roscoe. Stan White's a sharp guy," Jesse said. "Except for greed and jealousy, it might've worked."

"But how? When the tape was played, there wouldn't be anything on it. Then they would all be exposed."

"That's the beauty of it, Brian. Even if they didn't manage to destroy the tape, all of their asses were covered because they set up a fall guy in Evan Updike. If there was nothing on the tape, it would be because Updike had fooled them and had kept the 'real' tape and the money. They could all point to the mysterious Evan Updike and say he was the Hangman. He was the recording engineer at the studio. The police believed he had stolen the tape in the first place. The safety-deposit box key was hidden in his aunt's rooming house. The exchange was made in Vermont, where he was born. We wouldn't be able to prove he didn't do it. Can't prove a negative.

"And even though killing Bascom probably wasn't part of the original plan — my guess is that was Bella's idea — Updike still worked as the fall guy because we would assume he and Bascom had been in it together and Updike double-crossed his partner. We would be chasing Updike and our own tails while White, Roscoe, and Bella Lawton were taking baths in ten-dollar bills."

"But was not seeing the messenger on the security footage enough to convince you it was a scam?"

"I also put in a call to Roscoe's ex. The

story he told me about their divorce was a lie. She divorced him because of his drinking, not because of photos she received in the mail. But White and Roscoe had to play up the feud between them so it would look like Roscoe would have no reason to help White out. It couldn't look like they were cozy or that Roscoe could somehow benefit. I should have seen it coming. Especially after someone took those shots at me in the woods."

That refreshed Lundquist's anger over Jesse not reporting the incident, but he asked why that should have alerted Jesse.

"Because when Roscoe would get really drunk, he would talk about his time in the Marines. 'I wasn't always a fat slug,' he'd say. 'I could move and I could shoot. They wanted to send me to sniper school, but I was a lover, not a killer.' "

Lundquist shrugged. "If they were all broke, how did they get the money to lease the Wickham place? I hear it costs twenty grand a month to rent."

"Wickham's a big Jester fan. He agreed to lower the fee and to let them pay after the party."

"Was there really going to be a party?"

"No. They were using it as a way to get stories in the paper about Jester's birthday and rekindle interest in —"

"The missing tape."

"Exactly."

"The thing is, Jesse, you've got Niles cold for Bascom's murder and stealing the ransom money, but not much else. You've got Niles's statement and a lot of speculation. You might be able to tie the others to the scam, but not to Bascom's or Curnutt's murders. Can you prove any of it?"

"I guess we're going to find out."

88

Lundquist dropped Jesse and Niles off at the station. One look at Molly and Jesse knew there was trouble, but first they had to deal with Roscoe Niles.

"Book him. Keep him isolated. No one knows he's here," he said. "When that's done, come into my office. I'm getting some coffee."

Fifteen minutes later, Molly came into Jesse's office with a file folder in her hand. Jesse was seated behind his desk, sipping coffee.

"What's wrong?"

Molly waved the file folder and placed it in front of Jesse.

"Forget it, Crane. I'm so tired I couldn't make sense of anything."

"We found a Walther P22 in Bascom's apartment and an oil filter box in the garbage that will probably match the homemade sound suppressor. The ballistics

match the slugs the ME dug out of Curnutt."

"Anything else?"

Molly shook her head. "Nothing you want
to hear. Peter also found a slip of paper with
a Vermont phone number on it."

"And when you called it?"

"No answer."

"Why am I not surprised? How about
Bascom's cell phone?"

"No."

"The Vermont cops didn't find one on his
body or in the van. We can subpoena those
records."

"There's this," Molly said, more upbeat.
"I did a quick background check on Bascom."

"And . . ."

"Guess who his employer was before he
hired on to be the security contractor for
Stiles Island."

"Crane!"

"The Massachusetts Department of Cor-
rections. His last assignment was on the
same block as —"

"Curnutt and Bolton. I know, Molly, don't
say it. I should have been a detective."

Lundquist's words echoed in Jesse's head.
So far all he could likely prove was that
Bascom had hired Curnutt and Bolton, that

he'd killed Curnutt, and that Niles had killed Bascom. Niles's statement was probably enough to implicate White but maybe not convict him. White could claim Niles was lying and point to Evan Updike. To save her own neck, Bella Lawton would back White up and probably walk away. Jesse had an idea about how he might change that, but he had something else to discuss with Molly.

"Take a seat."

She eyed him suspiciously but sat. "What's wrong, Jesse?"

"Listen, you know how I joke with you about you becoming chief, but —"

She cut him off. "Oh, no you don't. You're not quitting on me, Jesse Stone. I don't want the job."

"Depending on how this shakes out, you may not have a choice, but relax, I'm not quitting. I don't quit. When this is over, I'm taking some time off. I've got more than a decade's worth of vacation time and I'm going to use part of it."

"Going to travel?"

He thought about being coy but realized that if he owed anybody the truth, he owed it to Molly. "Rehab. I've given it a lot of thought over the last few days. If I hadn't been drinking so much since Diana's murder, I might've been able to see what's been going on here. I've fooled myself long enough that my drinking doesn't matter. It matters. You and Doc are right, it's selfish of me and my liver's not getting any younger."

"If you're waiting for me to talk you out of it, forget it. Under those circumstances, I can handle the job of chief until you get back."

"As far as anyone else knows, I'm going to Tucson to visit family."

She asked, "You going via Austin?"

"Doc told you she's leaving?"

"She's kind of great. I'll miss her."

"Me too, Crane. Okay, get out of here."

Jesse stood, stretching. He picked up his glove, turned to the window, and pounded the ball into the pocket. He had thinking to do.

89

"When you want the guy at the top, you start at the bottom of the totem pole and work your way up" is what Jesse's first detective partner had said to him. It was advice he heeded every time he'd built a case against someone up the food chain. And that was just what he meant to do now.

"You got it, Molly," he asked. "When you see me come to the glass and finger-comb my hair, you turn the speaker on in the breakroom. Make sure Roscoe Niles hears it loud and clear. And make sure he's shackled to the table. If she catches wind of this, she'll clam up."

"I heard you the first time, Jesse. We'll have Gabe and Peter in there with him. He's going to hear it."

"Her file?"

"On the table."

"I'll be in there," Jesse said, pointing at the interview room.

Jesse was seated, facing the mirrored glass, when Bella Lawton came into the room. She was dressed in tight white jeans, sandals, and a low-cut black top that accentuated her shape. She was perfectly made up, but there were cracks in her armor. Nobody, not even the most experienced criminals, enjoy a visit to the interview room. Jesse smiled, stood, and pulled out a chair for her. She sat as Jesse went back around the table and also sat.

"Frankly, Jesse, I would have preferred being summoned to a motel or your bedroom, but if this is your style . . . Isn't this where you interrogate people?"

"We prefer *interview* to *interrogate.*" Jesse opened the file in front of him on the table. "Bella Anne Ligari. You even photograph well in mugshots." He turned her Boston PD mugshot to face her.

She was unintimidated. "I was young and stupid and I needed money," she said. "None of my patrons left dissatisfied."

"Except for one," Jesse said. "The complaint says you stole his wallet, his Rolex, and his ring."

She laughed. "It was his wedding band. Can you believe it? The guy paid to have sex with an eighteen-year-old girl — he thought I was sixteen — and had the nerve to bitch about his wedding ring being lifted. Look, Jesse, people change. I changed. I've made a new life for myself, a better life."

"That's true. You've moved up a few rungs. Your website is beautifully done. I imagine your high-end clientele pay you well enough so that you don't need to pocket their jewelry anymore. But not quite enough to get you out of the trade completely."

She turned hard. "Okay, Jesse, what's this about?" She looked at her watch, made an impatient face. "Tick tock. Things to do."

"Like spend six million dollars?"

"I don't know what you're talking about."

Jesse left the room. When he came back in, he thumped a green duffel bag down on the table in front of her and laid a plastic-covered rifle and scope beside it. He opened the duffel and exposed the banded packs of bills.

"We've got two more duffels just like it in the evidence locker. Game over, Bella. You lose."

She tried denial. "I don't know what you're talking about, Jesse. I really don't. Stan told me the exchange was made and the tape was destroyed. What has any of this to do with me?"

He put his face very close to hers. "Don't

screw around with me, Bella. Just don't. Like I told that idiot ex-friend of mine, Roscoe Niles, there's hard time and there's really hard time. As hot as you are now, what do you think a ten- or twenty-year stretch in prison will do to your looks? At least you'll be popular inside, really popular. That much I can guarantee you."

"I want a —"

Jesse cut her off, walking up to the mirrored glass. "Don't say those words. You say the word *lawyer* and this stops being a negotiation." He finger-combed his hair.

"Negotiation?" She perked up. "Why didn't you say so? What do you want?"

"I have some pretty nasty suspicions about you, but I don't want you, Bella."

"Too bad," she said, standing and coming close to him. "I certainly want you. Even if it wasn't part of the deal, I would have wanted you, Jesse. You intrigue me. Men or women, they don't usually turn me down."

"What would Roscoe have said to that?"

She laughed a particularly cruel laugh. "That fat, limp old drunk? Talk about living in the past. He's lucky there are drugs for his condition. I thought I'd gotten past having to force myself to be with the likes of him. The Teacher! I taught him some things, all right."

"But you had the prospect of six million reasons to force yourself to be with him."

"I'm not saying another word until you put something on the table other than props I may or may not know anything about."

"By the way, Bella," Jesse said, "that fat, limp old drunk was ready to roll over on you for a cup of coffee, so don't give yourself too much credit." Jesse lied to get under her skin. It worked.

"What are you offering me?"

He explained that given her involvement in extortion, fraud, conspiracy, and other assorted crimes, there was no way she could avoid at least a little time in prison, but that depending on what she gave him, he could probably get her time limited to a few years in minimum security.

"You'd be out in eighteen months and we'd make sure you didn't get passed around. You say no to me, Bella, and I walk right out of here to Roscoe's cell and make him an offer. Going once. Going twice."

"Sold, damn it. Sold. What do you need from me?"

"The whole thing, from start to finish: details, names, dates." He pulled a legal pad out of the table drawer, pulled a pen out of his pocket, and placed them in front of her. "Everything, Bella. You leave anything out and it's no deal. I've already got Roscoe cold. Bascom's dead, but I want Stan White and Evan Updike."

She laughed that cruel laugh again.

Jesse asked, "I say something funny?"

"I can give you Stan, but Updike's going to be an issue."

"How's that?"

"He's dead. Stan killed him twenty years ago."

90

Bella's statement was like a detailed road-map of the entire conspiracy. She literally knew where the body was buried. In this case, Evan Updike's. Jesse put in a call to the New York State Police and gave them a location near Saratoga Springs where they might find the buried remains of a white male, approximately thirty-five years of age, and five feet eight inches tall. Three hours later Jesse got a call back. The trooper on the other end said, "He's there, Chief Stone, right where you said he'd be."

Bella only fudged one part of her statement, but Jesse expected that she would. People have a hard time implicating themselves in murder. According to her, it had been Roscoe's idea to kill Bascom and to keep the money. *"I attempted several times to talk him out of it and thought I had convinced him not to do it. Only after he went through with it and took the money did he call me to tell me what he had done. I told him I wanted nothing to do with him after that."* Jesse had read that section of her statement aloud to make certain Roscoe Niles got an earful.

Stan White was sitting alone by the pool, a bottle of vodka at his side and a .38 Smith & Wesson in his lap. When he heard Jesse's footsteps, he raised the .38 and pressed the muzzle into the bag of flesh that hung beneath his jaw.

"I've been expecting you, Jesse," White said.

"I can see that. Can we talk?"

"Sure, as long as you don't come any closer to me than right there, we can talk until the cows come home or until *The Hangman's Sonnet* comes out on iTunes." White laughed, but tears rolled down his cheeks. "They say you can't laugh and cry at the same time. Shows you what 'they' know, huh?"

"I've never been a big fan of 'they' myself."

"I knew it was going to shit when I couldn't get hold of anybody today. It's horrible to be alone in the world. That's why I did all this, to stop Terry from being alone. I could have just abandoned him to the state a long time ago, but I owed everything I

498

ever had to Terry. I couldn't abandon him."

"Tell me about it."

Stan laughed a joyless laugh. "We really meant to make the album. We really did, but Terry had a complete breakdown before we got started. Meanwhile, the label had already paid us an enormous advance. So I tried stringing it out until Terry got better, but he never got better." White grabbed the bottle with his free hand and took a slug. As he did, Jesse inched closer. "Where was I? Oh, so I thought up a scheme to keep the money."

"You created the myth of the album, leaked the names of the musicians who played on the recording, and then faked the theft of the master tape."

"Just like that, Jesse. Exactly. But I created two monsters: the myth itself and —"

"Evan Updike."

"That blackmailing little bastard. I needed someone who could give credibility to the myth other than me. He came cheap at first. Ten grand. That was nothing to me and Terry back then. But as the myth grew, Updike kept coming back for more and more, threatening to expose the truth. I couldn't afford that because the myth had taken on a life of its own. The myth became the engine behind Terry's sales. Every few years I would get the rumors going again and Terry's sales would spike."

"But you killed Updike."

"With my bare hands," White said, voice full of pride. "I strangled the life out of that weasel as soon as the lawsuits were settled. Otherwise, he would have kept soaking us. Terry's care cost so much money."

"But why this? Why now?" Jesse asked. "That's the one thing Roscoe and Bella couldn't tell me."

"Because I got word Terry's going to be dead in a few months. Leukemia." White's tears were flowing again. "I needed to finally cash out and use the myth one last time to do it."

"How'd you get Bascom on board?"

White laughed. "He was easy. He had gambling debts up the wazoo. He'd already blown most of his pension. And who can say no to Bella besides you? Bascom knew all the wrong people, which is what I needed. I planted the safety-deposit box key in the old lady's house a few months ago under the guise of a prospective buyer. It was my mother's key. She kept it like that, taped to an index card. Then I needed someone to discover the key and get the whole thing going. Bascom hired those two idiots. We didn't figure on the old lady dying. I'm sorry about that and the delivery guy."

"Too late for sorrow now, Stan. And killing Curnutt?"

White shrugged. "He became like another Updike. Once he figured out what was going on, he wanted a lot of money. We didn't have it. We had used almost every dime we had to set it all up, so what choice did we have? Besides, it gave us an opportunity to get the press involved. That was smart of you, Jesse, trying to force our hand by keeping the press starved for facts. We didn't count on you being so sharp. Roscoe said you were a drunk and lost after your fiancée's . . . you know."

"He was right, Stan."

"So where does this leave us, Jesse?" White took another big pull on the vodka bottle. Jesse edged a little closer. "I don't suppose there's any wiggle room for me here."

"Not an inch."

Jesse had hoped that might cause White to go for the vodka bottle again, but instead he went for the .38. Not even Ozzie Smith in his prime could have made up the distance between them and prevented Stan White from beating Terry Jester into the next life.

91

By the end of August, Paradise had fallen back into its usual late-summer rhythms. Suit was home with Elena. It still made Jesse smile remembering how Suit had asked if there was any excitement in town while he was gone.

"A little, Suit," Jesse had said. "Just a little."

The press was gone and were back at covering stories that mattered. True to his word, Jesse had given Ed Selko an exclusive. All the crime scene tape had been taken down from the Cain house and the nature preserve. The dragonfly ring had been returned to the museum and was on display with the remainder of the jewelry from the set. The Wickham estate had been rented for the fall to some painter Jesse had never heard of.

Jesse parked his Explorer, new tires et al., at the station, walked into his office, and tossed his keys onto his desk. The thing was, Molly was sitting behind the desk.

"Morning, Chief Crane," he said, saluting.

"That's Acting Chief Crane to you, Stone. I may hate you forever for this."

"I doubt it."

"Don't be so sure, Jesse. I'm about as comfortable in this chair as a man wearing sandpaper underwear."

"I'll be back in five or six weeks or so. Relax, Molly."

"I know. So how long you figure it'll take you and Tamara to get down to Austin?"

"A week. We're going to do a little sightseeing on the way. Then I'll spend a few days with her until she settles in."

"Are you sure about this, Jesse?"

"About rehab? No, but Dix says the place I'm going to is as good as any."

"I don't mean about will it work," she said, exasperated. "I mean are you sure you should go?"

"Uh-huh."

Molly changed subjects. "Do you think Bella Lawton will get prosecuted for Bascom's murder?"

"She deserves it. It's the right thing to do, but that's up to the DA. I told her all bets were off if she lied in the statement."

Molly shook her head. "That was brilliant the way you let Niles hear Bella's interview. He couldn't wait to give us a full statement implicating her after he heard that."

"Old trick."

"I hear you've got an offer on your house."

Jesse smiled. "It's all but sold. Closing should all be set up by the time I get back."

There was a knock on the office door.

Jesse opened his mouth to answer, but it was Molly who said, "Come in."

Nita Thompson came into the office looking unusually casual in jeans, a loose-fitting floral blouse, and sandals.

"Morning, Chief Crane," she said. "Can I borrow Jesse for a few minutes?"

"You can keep him for all I care." Both women laughed. Molly stood. "You two stay. I've got work to do."

When the door closed behind Molly, Nita said, "I wanted to say so long. I won't be here when you get back."

"No?"

"I'm movin' on up. I landed me a United States Senate candidate." Nita pantomimed hooking a fish and reeling it in.

"Congratulations."

"I also wanted to apologize for some of the things I said about you, Jesse. I'm sorry."

"It's forgotten."

She laughed. "I think I'm sorriest for me. If I'd been a little kinder, I think we could have been friends."

He winked. "Maybe."

She stepped close to him and kissed him on the cheek. "Good luck, Jesse Stone."

He watched her retreat, then went out front to wait for Tamara. Suit came out and stood next to him.

"You look like you lost some weight, Suit."

"Elena makes me eat right."

"Good. Now maybe we won't need a sundial anymore to time you running the bases."

Suit ignored the dig and brought up Roger Bascom. "I always thought the guy was a jerk, but I never thought he was a killer."

"Suit, people will do almost anything if they're hungry or needy enough."

"I guess."

Tamara pulled her Jeep up in front of them. "Hey, Suit."

"Hey, Doc. Good luck in Texas."

Suit loaded Jesse's duffel into the backseat and shook Jesse's hand good-bye. Jesse climbed into the bucket beside Tamara. He had a good idea of what Paradise would be like when he got back, but given that he was headed to rehab, he was much less certain about himself.

ACKNOWLEDGMENTS

I would like to thank The Estate of Robert B. Parker, Ivan Held, Chris Pepe, and David Hale Smith.

I would also like to express my appreciation to Richard Neer, Ming Liu Parson, Ace Atkins, Tom Schreck, and Ellen W. Schare for their help in the creation of this novel. Special thanks to Peter Spiegelman, who showed me the way out of the weeds on this one.

But I reserve my most heartfelt thanks for Rosanne, Kaitlin, and Dylan. They are the ones who made the hard sacrifices so I could follow my passion. Without their love and support, none of this would have any meaning.

ABOUT THE AUTHORS

Robert B. Parker was the author of seventy books, including the legendary Spenser detective series, the novels featuring Chief Jesse Stone, and the acclaimed Virgil Cole/ Everett Hitch westerns, as well as the Sunny Randall novels. Winner of the Mystery Writers of America Grand Master Award and long considered the undisputed dean of American crime fiction, he died in January 2010.

Reed Farrel Coleman, author of the *New York Times*–bestselling *Robert B. Parker's Debt to Pay*, has been called a "hard-boiled poet" by NPR's Maureen Corrigan and the "noir poet laureate" in *The Huffington Post*. He has published twenty-five previous novels, including nine books in the critically acclaimed Moe Prager series, and most recently *What You Break*, featuring Gus Murphy. A three-time winner of the Shamus

Award, he has also won the Anthony, Macavity, Barry, and Audie awards. Coleman lives with his family on Long Island.